MERMAID MAMBO

A Novel

Fawn Germer

NEWHOUSE BOOKS

Copyright © 2007 by Fawn Germer

All rights reserved.

Printed in the United States of America. All rights reserved. No part of this book may be reproduced in any form or by any electronic or mechanical means including information storage and retrieval systems without permission in writing from the publisher or author, except by a reviewer, who may quote brief passages in a review.

Edited by Christine LePorte

Cover design by Falcon Graphics
Book design by Teri Swift
Cover Art by Bill Dale

ISBN 978-1-4243-3177-2

For my friends, who have blessed me with one wild ride.

ACKNOWLEDGMENTS

Novels are scary things to writers like me, who have built careers in the nonfiction world. If your nonfiction stinks, it might be the subject. If your novel sucks, it's all your fault.

I've had so much fun writing because I got to be friends with the mermaids of Weeki Wachee—young and old. They've shown me that I may age, but I will never grow old. I will never forget the day mermaid Barbara Wynns (who originally swam from 1967 to 1969 and from 1972 to 1975) took me into the spring and showed me how to breathe like a mermaid. Note here, I have been a certified scuba diver since 1984, but I almost drowned. It was *hard*. Barbara has sprinkled my life with magic dust and hope. Mermaid Vicki Smith (who originally swam from 1957 to 1961) has inspired me to live large and wild. While we were tubing down the river, she pulled over to the side, climbed a tree, grabbed a rope, let out a yell, and swung through the air for a fantastic splash into the water. She was sixty-seven at the time.

I have to give a nod to Stephen King, who told me to have the confidence to chase this dream. And to Susan Morrill, who gave me the kick in the ass I needed to finish the book. Peter Ambraz gave me the title. Great thanks to my indefatigable editor, Christine LePorte. I also love Bill Dale, who drew the cover art. And the only reason I am able to live this dream of being a full-time author is this: Caroline Carney, my sister in life and agent.

What follows is a long list that I have found impossible to order because I love *all* of my friends so very, very much. There's Julie Hipp, my closest confidant and greatest source of light and adventure. And Pam "The Enforcer" Sarich, Keri Douglas, Liz Roberts, Jill Gould, Jeanne Elliott, Linda Brown, Marlene Levick, Carolyn Edmonson, George Edmonson, Trish Goldsmith, Cindy Shaw, Miriam Reed, Malea Guiriba, Jackie St. Joan, Connie Bouchard, Ora Sue McKinnon, Joyce Duarte, Kathy Bowers, Nancy Cummings, Jen Repo, Linda Lindsay, Rebecca Whitley, and Tina Proctor (my touchstone).

Thanks to "The Bookaneers," who gave me a deadline and the first critique that meant so much to me as a writer and a friend.

Among them: Kathleen Beatty, Beverly Burton, Melissa Brahm, Lois Daniels, Eileen Geer, Nan George, Brenda Hubbard, Marly McMillan, Cindy Michalik, Debbie Mueller, Renee Partain, and Betsy Schweitzer.

I owe so much to Lisa Pritchard, Carole Cole, Keri Douglas, Carol Folsom, Jill Gould, Pam Sarich, Linda Brown, Malea Guiriba, Jackie St. Joan, Lorna Bracewell, Jen Repo, Suzann Clark and the others who read this and gave me advice. My life is so full because of my friends. My Peeps in the Hood: Doug Swift (part Gladys Kravitz, part big brother), Teri Swift (his long-suffering wife), Chris Nightwine, Jill Waybright, Skip Remmert, and Renee Hardman. My advisors: Jonathan Alpert, John Collins, Kathy Gaye, Teresa Hoover, Lisa Rary, Liz Roberts, and Karen Waddell. The Scoobies (my writing group): Jayne Bray, Betsy Buffo, Gerry Gil, Lisa Pritchard, and Ron Rowe. My Good (and Fabulous) Men: Brian Campbell, Mike Finney, Michael Hendren, Joe Moran.

Friends: Sally Hudson, Teresa Lawrence, Lorraine Anderson, Tracy Torres, Dee Boehm, Keri Smith, Patricia Tucker, Meredith Tupper, Kathy Witt, and Helen and Jack Whitley. My sisters from NEW, led by Helayne Angelus and Joan Toth. My relatives: the Himelhoch, Hirsch, and Rubinstein families. My brother, Jim Germer.

I need to mention the rest of my mermaid friends. My other "Mermaids of Yesteryear" buddies: Crystal Robson, Bev Sutton, Susie Pennoyer, Billie Fuller, Lynn Colombo, Dottie Meares, Marianne "Mirt" Bennett, and Becky Young. I love all the current mermaids, especially because they have so closely bonded with the mermaids who came before them who are from other generations. The currents include: Abby Anderson, Marcy Terry, Amy Purnell, Megan Ryan, Carli Dofka, Crystal Videgar, Heather Flowers, Angela Schommer, Denise McGrath, Heather Miller, Nikki Wilkerson, Justen Durr, Karri Aviles, Stayce McConnell, Jeredan Bibler, Kimi Vincent, Cyndi Gay, Brian Donnelly and Heather Miller. Thanks to John Athanason for bringing all of them into my life.

Finally, I am thankful for so much in this life, but most of all, for being the daughter of Fred and Betty Germer. My mom was sixty-six when she was severely disabled by a stroke. She continues to bravely face one obstacle after another, and when I ask her why she wants to live, she always says, "Because I love my family." She is eighty now, doing her own mermaid mambo in a nursing home. Daddy's held our family together with his love and endless hope. He visits mom four times a day, the living definition of true devotion. Everyone tells me how lucky I am to be their daughter, but I've known that since I was a little girl. I am so blessed.

People always ask me who Ruby is modeled after. I got some of the inspiration from friends, but the more time I spend with her, the more I realize Ruby is who I want to be – in a few decades. We should all be so lucky as to frolic like her, so remember that and I'll see you on the Road to Weeki Wachee.

Chapter One

The appointment with the plastic surgeon was inevitable, and the only remaining question was when Joni would actually make the call, which she did on August 26 at 11:07 a.m., the day she finally decided to get dressed. When the nurse asked what she wanted to see Dr. Case about, Joni first said eyes, then she said chin, then lips, then she mumbled, "Everything. Cut it, peel it, suck it out, Botox it to death. Do something."

It's not funny. Forty-two should not look so spent.

One inch at a time, she cursed and squeezed herself into the one pair of pants that still fit. Size twenty, good God! How could she have let it happen—again? It's amazing that one can gain twenty pounds in sixteen days, but it can happen and Joni was proof. No wonder that son of a bitch dumped her.

And could the guy have humiliated her any worse? Consider his timing. Two days before the split, Oprah hugged Joni on television and proclaimed her the "Diva of Desire" for the bestselling romance novels she wrote under the pen name of "Desiree Damone." Diva of Desire, that's right. Forty-two years old, never married, never with a man for more than two years. Joni Herrschwitz, diva. Dumped, duped, devastated, depressed, deceived, discarded…worthless! Not that bald, fat, liver-spotted Doug was any great shakes, but he was the only serious prospect she'd had in a long damned time, and now there were no prospects and likely would never be any prospects. Damn him! Joni wished his dick would shrivel and fall off. He didn't deserve to have a penis, much less use it.

After he walked out, she shut herself in, limiting her outside contact to the grocery delivery people who made her pay a queen's premium for tending her depression. At first, she stayed home because she didn't want to miss Doug's call, but of course he never called. So then she stayed in because she couldn't bear to go out there, exposed. REJECT! FAILURE! UNLOVED! FAT! NAÏVE! STUPID! The voice in her head would not relent.

But on the seventeenth day of solitary confinement in her two-bedroom Upper West Side condo, Joni turned on the *E! True Hollywood Story*, and there was Tammy Faye Bakker.

"Tammy Faye is a survivor," Ann Curry said in an old *Today* show interview. "In the late 1980s, she endured the sex scandal between her now-former husband, televangelist Jim Bakker, and church secretary Jessica Hahn. Since then, she has battled colon cancer, drug addiction, and her share of public humiliation…"

Tight shot of Tammy Faye.

"You need to live for today," Tammy said. "Tomorrow might not come and yesterday is gone, there is nothing you can do about it."

Joni sat in front of the plasma screen, nodding.

As usual, Tammy Faye looked silly and sounded nuts, but Joni marveled at how the woman trudged onward while the whole world mocked her.

"Let's talk about how you've lived," coaxed Curry.

"It's all attitude. It's not the things in life that will destroy you. It's your attitude."

Joni nodded some more.

Tammy Faye then spent some time promoting her book, which explored the full gamut of coping skills that included everything from grief management to make-up application.

"Every woman ought to put on lipstick. That shows you care," Tammy Faye said, looking through the television to Joni. "It shows you care about yourself."

I don't care, Joni thought. But a tube of lipstick sat on the nightstand beside her bed, along with her diamond solitaire necklace and the diamond earrings she'd taken off sixteen nights ago when she came home from girls' night at the theater. That was the night Doug left her "just because," and it was the last time Joni cared.

Estée Lauder Rosa Rosa. Joni reached for the lipstick and pulled off the top. She glanced in the mirror on her dresser and it hit her how amazing it was that she could stay in bed beside that mirror for that many days without looking at herself, but she hadn't looked, not even once. The woman in the mirror was a miserable mess. Who the hell was it? Joni's brown hair was matted, her face bloated and colorless, her hazel eyes filled with dread.

Joni ran the Rosa Rosa across her lips and blew Tammy Faye a kiss for telling her to care again, even if Joni could barely care at all. Whatever. Thanks, Tammy Faye. Joni forced herself out of bed, showered, shaved her legs, washed and rewashed her hair, and then colored her roots. She manicured her nails and put white strips on her teeth. She felt a little of something she hadn't felt in a long time—herself. The Supremes came on the radio singing, *"Stop! In the name of love!"* and Joni sang with them as she danced into the kitchen for a pair of scissors and chopped inches from her hair until she'd given herself a rather punked out cut for a frumpy middle-aged woman.

She made her call to the plastic surgeon's office for the appointment, then stepped outside into a world that scared the hell out of her.

Fresh air felt good, even if it was only New York fresh. She hadn't been outdoors in forever—not once in nearly 400 hours— but the masses around her neither noticed nor cared about her re-emergence. They pushed by her like they push by everyone else. New York is forgiving like that. It doesn't give a damn how you look, just keep moving. So, she moved. She moved down Lex to Sixty-fourth, then over to the carousel in the park where children squealing with delight reminded her that not only had she never married, but she had also missed her chance to bring a child into the world.

Joni stood there watching the carousel spinning, listening to the Wurlitzer playing "My Blue Heaven," wishing the kids wouldn't squeal so much. Apparently they had nothing better to do with their time than screech and squeal. Delight. God, it had been a long time since Joni had squealed about anything. Life with Doug? Not great, but it beat being alone. It felt secure. Safe. What a joke!

"You're sure deep in thought."

A woman who had to be pushing eighty broke into Joni's space zone, violated it.

"Mmmm hmmm," Joni said, shuffling a few steps away from the old bluehair.

"Want to ride the carousel?"

Joni ignored her. New York nutcase, obviously.

"Miss? Would you like to ride the carousel? I love the carousel. Let's ride it." The lady seemed insulted at Joni's lack of response.

"No, thank you. I am just out for a little quiet time." Message sent. Leave me alone. Go away. Don't you know the rules of New York?

The woman sighed. "I haven't ridden this in twenty years."

Joni hadn't either, not in the twenty-one years since her twenty-first birthday, when her mother brought her to the carousel, presented her with a round trip ticket to Paris, and hopped on the merry-go-round with her daughter so Joni would never forget her milestone birthday, which she never did.

"Let's do it," the woman urged again. "What the hell, right?"

"You must have me confused with somebody else," Joni said. Please. Get. Lost.

Instead of acknowledging the chill Joni sent her and stepping away, the woman moved closer, warmly squeezing Joni's arm. Joni had not been touched by another human being in so long. She hadn't cried once since Doug walked out, but there in Central Park, the touch of that intrusive stranger unleashed every tear she'd been too afraid to cry, making a complete mess out of that beautiful mascara job she'd applied in the morning for the sake of Tammy Faye. *Get a grip, get a grip, get a grip,* she told herself, but she could not. The first tear dropped from her eyes, and then others streamed out.

The woman reached for her and Joni succumbed, burying her head in the woman's shoulders, sobbing out loud like a nutcase in front of the carousel. And rather than pushing Joni away as Joni most certainly would have done if the situation were reversed, the woman held her closer. Right there, in view of all of New York, Joni Herrschwitz, a spinster, a forty-two-year-old starting-to-wrinkle romance writer who would likely never have a real man to love, honor, and cherish, let it all go.

"Now, now," the woman said, handing Joni a tissue. "It can't be that bad,"

Sympathy made Joni feel even more pathetic.

"I don't even know your name," she sniveled.

"Ruby," said the woman. "Ruby Witherspoon. Honey, what on earth is the matter?"

Joni couldn't even get the words out. She fell into Ruby's arms again, sobbing and blubbering like a hysterically fool woman who couldn't get a grip, and she cried for twenty whole minutes. Ruby didn't appear to mind and Joni couldn't help it. After the bawling turned to weeping and the weeping turned to sniffling, Joni pulled away, blew her nose again, and warmly hugged Ruby in gratitude.

Gardenia. Ruby smelled of gardenia, and that made Joni tear up again because her mother used to wear gardenia, probably because that was what *her* mother had worn. For one intoxicating moment, Joni pretended. It was her birthday, she was twenty-one, her mother was still alive, and life was just beginning. She'd go to Paris, find a handsome French lover, and eat croissants beside the Seine while he regaled her with his poetry, professed his love, and begged her to marry him.

You want fantasy, buy a romance novel. Fantasies never happen. One day, you wake up in your forties and know full well that what you have is all you are going to get. Forty-three isn't going to be any better than forty-two. How could it be?

Ruby paid for two tickets to the carousel as Joni gave herself permission to forget all those worries for five blissful minutes. It is amazing how that works. Give yourself five minutes to forget, and you will.

But only for five minutes.

Chapter Two

The distance between Central Park and Weeki Wachee is exactly 1,111.8 miles and it takes nineteen hours and eleven minutes to drive there—if you don't stop. Ruby had two weeks to make the trip and lose fifteen pounds. By age seventy-eight, appearance shouldn't count quite so much, but a Weeki Wachee mermaid's figure always matters to her—especially when she has to squeeze back into her old tail and perform for hundreds of spectators at the classic underwater theme park in Florida. Ruby's fin was tight at the twenty-fifth reunion of Weeki Wachee's opening, *really* tight at the fiftieth reunion, and she felt certain it would give her a lethal pinch at the upcoming sixtieth if she didn't start gulping Slim-Fast. Of course, weight comes off a lot slower after the change, and Ruby wondered why the stuff wasn't just called Slim-Slow for Seniors.

Millie would be there, all liposucked into place by some plastic surgeon whom she paid quite well to make sure she upstaged every other mermaid—as always. Shameless. Alma would come, for sure, but she wouldn't care that she'd be the fattest mermaid—she always was, always had been, and since she was the least threatening, she was also one of the most popular. Edie sent Ruby a note that she'd pack the park with all her grandchildren and great-grandchildren— and that rubbed Ruby wrong because, since she wasn't a grandmother by now, she never would be. Iris would come, for sure, and it would be good to see her. Ruby wondered if Iris had yet let go of the fact that Trudy stole her boyfriend more than a half a century ago, but she knew the grudge would still be there. And Martha. It'd be great to see Martha, simply because Ruby loved her the most, even though they never talked anymore.

Ruby kept a picture of her costumed young self in her wallet because there is a saying—"Once a mermaid, alllllllways a mermaid"—and it is always good for a mermaid to remember from whence she came. To honor her truth, Ruby still sung the official mermaid anthem at bathtime: "We're not like other women…We don't have to clean an oven…And we nev-er will grow olllllld…We've got the world by the tail!" It was a really dippy song, but Ruby liked the part about never growing olllllld, and even though the rest of the world might label her as a paunchy old bag, she knew that inside her soul lived the graceful Weeki Wachee ballerina she always was. Back when, she could hold her breath for more than three minutes while changing her costume, drinking an RC Cola, or eating at fifteen feet below as tourists watched, mesmerized, from the underground theater. Ruby spent three years in that first job—her favorite job in life—and only gave it up because a man named Walter stole her heart after the show one August day and moved her to Queens, where he owned an appliance store. They had two daughters and some dogs and cats, and, after he'd opened his sixth store and made his first million, a lavish apartment overlooking Central Park in the city. The twosome went everywhere together, best friends, best lovers, best mates, married for thirty-three perfectly blissful years until the afternoon in the Grand Tetons when Walter rose from the dinner table, grabbed his chest, and suffered a fatal heart attack at the Jackson Lake Lodge.

He passed when Ruby was just fifty-two, and she spent the rest of her life missing his corny jokes and precious kisses. Even though her heart was broken, Ruby kept living. She never once took his ring off—not even when ordered to by a cracked-out mugger on the New York subway who wrapped his filthy hands around her neck and tried to choke her.

You can't strangle a mermaid—everybody knows that. Ruby kneed the bastard in the balls so hard that he doubled over, then fainted. A half-dozen others in the subway car had pretended not to notice the crime when it was happening, but when Ruby took care of business, they gave her a standing ovation. She turned away, embarrassed, then got off at Grand Central Station.

"Son of a bitch," she'd muttered to Walter in heaven. "You never should have left me like that." But she knew he hadn't *really* left. She always felt Walter watching her, and she didn't want to let him down. She wanted to give him something to laugh and smile about—plenty of material to discuss when they got together again, later on. And so she lived with great style.

Why do they call old ladies "bluehairs"? Even if their hair doesn't have the slightest blue tint, young people call them that. Ruby was not a bluehair. She was a whitehair. A gorgeous, five-foot, six-inch, slightly overweight woman with shocking white hair, who at seventy-eight knew how to mix pearls with silver, funky broaches, silver bangles, hoop earrings, geometric belts, and flashy scarves. She knew about the rules of haute couture, about things like A-lines, Basque waists, and hankie hems, but she embraced fashion as sport, a way to re-create herself daily by mixing and matching a little of this and a little of that, with the ultimate goal of most definitely *not* looking, acting, or thinking like a bluehair.

Ruby *was* an original. She pioneered her life by being more than a little imaginative about going where no other seventy-eight-year-olds dared to go. Life for Ruby had changed forever the day she stumbled into Ben's Kosher Delicatessen's annual Matzo Ball Eating Contest. She'd seen enough ordinary, and this contest marked the moment she stuck her first tiptoe in the great basin of the bizarre as she watched a 395-pound subway conductor wolf down twenty-one matzo balls in five minutes and twenty-five seconds—without even barfing. Ask her if she'd rather meet the Queen of England or go watch a guy who could bowl backwards (with an average score of 184 and a high score of 279), she'd go to the bowling alley. Actually, she'd run there if her knees weren't bothering her.

Before the matzo balls, Ruby was bored. She loved the shockers and whammies of life, and those always seemed to come in the form of some display of how far people would go in order to receive a little attention. It impressed her when a tiny Mary Kay Cosmetics saleswoman devoured sixteen hot dogs in twelve minutes at one event, but it floored her when the same woman's husband ate (this is no lie) *ten pounds* of chili in twelve minutes. How could anyone eat ten pounds of chili in twelve hours, much less twelve minutes? She had to know.

She never *entered* such contests, for God's sake. Ruby had enough problems, what with the stroke recovery, the osteoporosis, and the arthritis. But she'd claimed her own piece of eccentric glory in her day, once stuffing herself into a Charleston telephone booth with ten other people back in the 1960s, which seemed like an achievement at the time until twenty-five people crammed into a booth in South Africa and the world record was set without her. Once she was married with children, she tried to be more June Cleaver-like, but never really pulled it off. Ruby lived to experience. In her day, she wore bell bottoms and bouffant hairdos, miniskirts and go-go boots, pillbox hats and poodle skirts, tie dye and turtlenecks. She'd done the hula hoop, the limbo, the twist, the hustle. She once had a black light and lava lamp in her bedroom, wore a mood ring in the seventies, invited friends over to consult the Ouija Board, and could kill anyone at Ms. Pac-Man. She read the gossip column every day and kept up with Liz Taylor and Jackie O., and now kept current about the partying ways of all the twenty-something starlet du jours who dominated the news.

Know the type? Of course not. There was and is only one Ruby Witherspoon.

Once you've seen the sites you are supposed to see on this earth—the Grand Canyon, the Eiffel Tower, the Golden Gate Bridge, and the like, there becomes something far more alluring about taking in a monster truck rally or lawn mower drag racing competition (which, incidentally, was coming up in a couple of weeks, and, incidentally, was sponsored by the National Drag Racing Lawn Mower Association, which was a real thing even though it sounds very made up).

Ruby went to the Spamalympics one year and even competed in the Spam Toss, where she and her friend Maybelle tossed a clump of Spam back and forth—having to spread farther apart after each toss until one of them dropped it. Maybelle dropped it, they lost, and Maybelle died one month later. But Ruby felt certain that Maybelle died a happier person because she'd tossed that Spam.

So far, the biggest adventure occurred when she, Doris, and Helene vacationed in the Catskills and got creative one Saturday when they didn't have much of anything to do except the usual walk in the forest, sunning by the pool, or reading a good book.

"Hey, why don't we go to that *other* resort on the other side of the lake?" Ruby urged. "I'd sure like to take a look around." It was all very hush-hush, and even now it shouldn't go much further than this, but after much consideration, the girls drove to the other side of the lake for the free one-hour tour of the Catskills Paradise Lost Resort. That's a deceptive name because what it really should have been called was the "Catskills Expose-It-All-to-the-Sun Nudist Colony." Ruby and her friends kept their clothes on as a naked man escorted them around the property on a golf cart and explained that "the lifestyle has everything to do with freedom of expression and nothing to do with voyeurism, exhibitionism, or sex."

"Yeah, right," said Ruby.

He rode them past the nude volleyball players, nude weight lifters, nude sunbathers, nude barbecuers, nude square dancers, and nude bartenders. Ruby couldn't help but stare and the tour guide told her, "You appear to be very interested in what you're seeing here"—as if there were something wrong with that.

"And you're not?" Ruby countered.

"I'd thought I would never see another penis," said Doris.

"Me either," said Helene. "There are penises everywhere!"

"Big ones, little ones, skinny ones, fat ones, brown ones, purple ones…" Doris said.

"Soft ones and an occasional, how shall we say, not-so-soft one?" Ruby giggled.

"Chubbies!" laughed Doris.

"Woodies!" offered Helene, who sounded the call of Woody Woodpecker, then laughed with the girls.

The tour guide kept trying to wipe the grin off his face, but it was tough. He was falling in love with these old ladies, just like everybody always did because they were so very cool, so very original. In fact, it was on this trip that Ruby named her clan "The Originals."

Two months later, Doris died. A year later, Helene. Again, Ruby felt certain they died happier because of that trip to the Catskills, but their deaths were devastating as it became more and more apparent that time was running out for Ruby, and that whatever time she had left was going to be lonelier by the minute. The pure pain of aging comes from losing lifelong best girlfriends and loved ones and being forced to replace them with meaningless conversations with strangers. Ruby ached for a night out with her friends, where they could laugh or reminisce or say something shocking to the waiter. She wondered who was better off, the friends who died first, or she, who lived—even though she was left to live alone.

Getting old really stinks. When her oldest friend, Scarlet, died, Ruby's daughter Nina said, "God, Ma, that's a lot of your friends going all at once. Are you depressed?"

"Well, I figure, better them than me, right?" said Ruby, trying to joke about something way too painful to laugh at. As you age, your body falls apart, and worse, the world around you falls apart. Suddenly, there is no one who *knows* you, and no one you truly know.

Her daughters, Nina and Jacqueline, both were busy, busy, busy girls, but they loved their mama and made sure they called weekly and saw her every Christmas. Both were quite successful—Nina graduated with honors from law school at Stanford and quickly made partner in a major civil rights firm in Seattle, and Jacqueline became one of the most sought-after interior designers in Portland. Nina was now forty-three and in a long-standing relationship with her partner, the simply stunning Sarah Simmons, a horse trainer. Jacqueline was forty-five and living with Julien Bedeau, whose name made it sound like he was her handsome French lover, but who was actually quite the French nerd. Ruby had no problem with Nina's choice in a female soul mate, but did think Jacqueline deserved far better than Julien. Regardless, she never figured out why they both moved so far away.

Ruby tried making new friends, but couldn't find a single younger person eager to bond with an old lady, and the old ladies who, like her, were looking for friends, weren't like her. They were old. They played cards. They talked about their aches and pains and doctors and medicines.

So there was Ruby's dilemma. Too hip to be old, and too old to hang with the hip. And oooooh, don't mention her hips.

August 26, the day Ruby met Joni, would have been Ruby and Walter's fiftieth wedding anniversary, and she remembered it, bittersweet. She had filled the years since Walter's death with life and adventure and joy and passion. She refused to live a life of mourning, but she never did remarry. She rarely dated.

On her anniversary, Ruby looked to the sky and invited Walter to join her on an anniversary stroll through Central Park. She stopped to buy a knish and she walked around the pond near the nature sanctuary, then the Heckscher playground, and then over to the carousel. Way back when, she and Walter were on the carousel for a midnight whirl at the South Carolina State Fair when she dropped the bomb on Walter that they were expecting. The carousel played "Let Me Call You Sweetheart," and Walter sang with it.

The memory always made Ruby smile. She sure had put a lot of years on her body, but she mounted that wooden Central Park carousel horse with such ease that Joni looked self-conscious as struggled to get her own leg over the top. When the Wurlitzer happened to play "Let Me Call You Sweetheart," Ruby knew Walter hadn't forgotten their anniversary. She winked at the sky, blew him a kiss, then sang out loud. Joni heard herself singing it too, singing loud and feeling a little—huh?—joyful. She didn't notice when her five minutes of peace slipped into a sixth minute of joy, and when the carousel stopped, Joni embraced her new friend. Ruby twirled Joni around and then coaxed her into trying a little soft shoe right there in front of the merry-go-round. The ever-uncoordinated Joni had never even seen anybody dance a Vaudeville soft shoe, so she paid close attention to her tutor.

"Sliiiiiide," Ruby said. "Sliiiiide, lift, point…"

"Sliiiiide," Joni said, trying to slide her foot along the pavement, trying not to feel self-conscious because never in her life had she done anything so publicly silly, trying to just enjoy the joy she finally felt again. "Sliiiiide, lift, point…"

"C'mon! C'mon! Don't stop!" Ruby urged.

Joni caught herself laughing again, as she began to fake it, lookin' good as moms pointed out the silly ladies for the entertainment of the little ones.

"Hey, look at the fat one!" hollered a little boy.

"Who you callin' fat?" Joni fired back as she slid, lifted, and pointed over to the tot. Shocking behavior for someone as self-conscious and inhibited as Joni. "You callin' me a fatso?"

The little boy stood there, wide-eyed and helpless. "I wasn't talking about you," he said, nervous.

"Oh yeah? I think you're talkin' 'bout me!" she chided.

Weakly, the youngster pointed at his oh-so-slender mom. "No. Her."

Joni and his mother laughed, then Joni took the woman's hand and cajoled her into joining the soft shoe routine. "Sliiiide…sliiiiide, lift, point…" The boy joined in too, and soon, nine New York strangers danced soft shoe together like their own little Rat Pack. After ten minutes, they stopped for a few exhausted hoots and guffaws, then went back to being NYC aloof. Joni's heart once again beat with life.

The Wurlitzer played "The Stars and Stripes Forever" and Ruby grabbed Joni's wrist, trying to entice her back onto the carousel.

"Time out!" Joni finally called. "You tryin' to give me a heart attack on my first day out?"

Ruby looked perplexed. "First day out of what?"

"First day out of my apartment. I'm a little embarrassed to say this, but I guess I've been in self-exile for sixteen and a half days."

"That must've been some case of the flu."

"Don't I know it."

"Hey, what are you doing for the rest of the day?"

"Taking it a minute at a time. I've been waiting for the panic attack, but aside from my little outburst with you, it hasn't come."

"Good. Let's go to Coney Island."

"Coney Island?" Joni looked incredulous. She hadn't been there in a zillion years.

"Coney Island." Ruby had been there more recently—actually, a week ago, for the Houdini celebration.

"No, no, no," Joni said, not very emphatically.

"You have other plans?"

"I need to get back to…"

"Oh, think up a good excuse, because if you've been trapped inside for sixteen days, it's going to need to be a doozy to get out of this."

"I'm not thinking of an excuse. It's just…"

"Your mother told you never to talk to strangers."

"That's it." Joni smiled.

"Well, once we've danced the mambo in Central Park, we aren't exactly strangers."

And that was kinda true. Ruby marched Joni to Fifth Avenue, where she hailed a cab and announced, "My treat" as they rode so casually out of the city in a hot summer midday cab ride that lasted forever in traffic. Ruby gave the cabbie a hundred dollars from an astounding wad of cash in her wallet, and told the guy she hoped he would be able to cut out a little early so he could make it to his son's baseball game.

Coney Island with Ruby was beyond exhausting. Ruby had no problem on the Cyclone (Joni did), bumper cars (Joni did), or Tilt-A-Whirl (Joni did).

"I can't believe I can't even ride the Tilt-A-Whirl," Joni said as she practically collapsed on a bench and dry heaved. Her center of gravity sure wasn't where it used to be.

She deliberately distracted Ruby from the amusements by suggesting they visit the "Sideshows by the Seashore," billed as *"the last place in the USA where you can experience the thrill of a traditional ten-in-one circus sideshow…Freaks, wonders and human curiosities—another Coney Island gift to culture."* The whole concept was so utterly un-PC. Joni'd never seen a bearded lady, never wanted to see a bearded lady, and never would have seen a bearded lady if Ruby Witherspoon hadn't come along.

Something about the woman. She didn't have to coerce Joni into doing anything, even though her suggestions were so far out of Joni's realm.

Like checking out the fire-eating, sword-swallowing, razor blade- and glass-eating magician who took a swig of kerosene, then spat it at a lit torch that exploded toward his face in a ball of flame that traveled straight to his lips. He called out for a volunteer among the sparse crowd to swallow a sword, and when Ruby started to raise her hand, Joni yanked it back down.

"Don't be crazy. Are you nuts?"

"Don't egg me on," responded Ruby.

Don't egg Ruby on. Ruby. Will. Do. Anything.

"I wonder what makes somebody decide they are going to do that for a living," Joni said.

"It's certainly a lot of talent," Ruby said, looking amazed.

Joni thought about it, and it certainly was a lot of talent. Among other things.

After him, they went to see Carmen Le Mermaid perform her pure Burlesque review, wearing only a sparkling green mermaid tail and sequined pasties. The poster said she was straight from venues like "The Girly Shower of Freaks" and "The VaVa Voom Studio," but Ruby was not impressed at all. Mermaids should not be wearing pasties or acting like trollops. Coney Island has an annual mermaid parade, where Carmen Le Mermaid was heralded as the queen of the mermaids, nipples to the sky, service with a smile. Ruby never went to the parade and could not hide her contempt for the disservice perpetrated by the faux mermaids of the world.

"An insult to all mermaids!" said an indignant Ruby.

"What do you mean?"

"Mermaids are not to parade around like tarts."

"There are rules for mermaids?" Joni chuckled.

"Of course there are," Ruby snapped. Serious. Offended.

"I didn't know."

"That floozy is a *sideshow* mermaid—not a *real* mermaid. A total trailer trash version of a mermaid. A disgrace to the profession."

"A trailer trash version," Joni deadpanned.

"At best."

"So there is a cultural hierarchy of mermaids? How do you know so much about all this?"

"I'll explain later," Ruby said.

She figured they would need conversation for their cab ride to Atlantic City.

Chapter Three

Ruby prided herself on being an act first, get permission later kind of woman, so she never even mentioned that they were headed to Atlantic City, but they were because Ruby absolutely had to play tic-tac-toe against the world-famous gambling chicken in the casino at the Tropicana. That's right. She'd stand in line for an hour or two and all she had to do to win ten grand was outsmart a chicken.

Thing was, the chicken got the first move. That matters in tic-tac-toe.

Only five people have ever won in history, not that those odds mattered to Ruby.

When she boarded the yellow taxi with Joni, she waited until the cab was moving before calling out to the young woman driver, "We're going to the Tropicana."

The Tropicana.

Okay, the Central Park carousel ride and boogie was a little unusual. The trip to Coney with the old lady was enjoyable, though that was pushing things waaaaaaay beyond Joni's comfort zone. But getting in a cab and riding to Atlantic City with her? The events of the day had somehow crossed over from exciting adventure into bad judgment territory. You don't just get in a cab with a stranger, you don't just do what someone else tells you to do just because you don't have a better idea, and you don't just walk away from your own little world because you are unhappy and have been unhappy for a very long time.

Or do you?

"You're out of your mind," Joni said. "I'm not going to Atlantic City."

"Sure you are." Ruby motioned to the driver to get moving. The cabbie accelerated.

"No, Ruby," Joni said, trying to sound firm, but not pulling it off because her tone was a touch playful. "Stop the cab, please."

"Oh c'mon," the driver whined, fully aware that a fare to Atlantic City did not come along every day. "Let the lady have her fun."

"Yeah," Ruby said. "Let the lady have her fun."

Who takes a cab all the way to Atlantic City to play tic-tac-toe with a chicken? Who picks up a stranger and takes her to a freak show? Who dances in the middle of Central Park? That kind of behavior was not adult behavior, Joni thought. Real people do not behave in that way. They just don't. It's not…it's not respectable. Or acceptable. Or normal. It's just not normal.

"I'm tired."

"I'm almost twice your age. I'm not tired."

"I don't feel comfortable just leaving…"

"Leaving what?" Ruby asked.

The question hit Joni in the gut, because she wasn't leaving anything. She didn't have any pages due to her editor for another two months. She didn't have any appointments on her calendar. She didn't have a boyfriend anymore—she didn't even have a cat to feed. All she had was that nice two-bedroom apartment filled with books and antiques and a twenty-seven-inch flat-screen television across from her bed that kept her company.

"Come on," Ruby said. "Or don't. If going home and staying home works for you, then great. If it doesn't, maybe you should loosen up and stop acting like a dead person."

Well, that statement hung there in the stale air of the cab. Joni thought about resisting again, but she knew that Ruby knew that there wasn't a damned thing back home that needed her tending, and so what if it did? Joni really was in no rush to return to her funk. Ruby was a little different, but she promised a way out of the dark.

"It's almost eight o'clock and I am starving," Joni said, relenting.

"There's plenty of food at the Trop," Ruby smiled. "We can eat at the buffet."

"But we're on fast food row," Joni said. "I'm hungry *right now*. I'm eating *right now*. Pick your poison. *Right now*."

"I say Wendy's," chimed the driver, who hadn't been asked and didn't wait for approval before zipping into the drive-thru lane and ordering herself a Biggie single combo meal before calling out to the back seat, "You guys want anything?"

"I want you to turn off that noise," Ruby said, rubbing her palm against her forehead to ward off a headache from the rap music on the radio that was not blaring, but was still annoying. "How can you listen to that?"

"It's good rap, nothing too nasty," said the woman.

"It is nasty to my ears," said Ruby. "So could you please turn it off?"

It was off before Ruby finished her sentence. The driver knew this would be an especially tricky situation tip-wise, because there was no way those two wacky women were going to be happy about spending almost five hundred bucks to travel just two-and-a-half hours away. They could have flown to Florida for that much. She wondered why they hadn't just boarded a gambling bus like the rest of the old people of New York who paid thirty-nine bucks for the ride and got twenty-two dollars back in gambling tokens. Some people have money to blow, and cab drivers see that every damn day. But a situation like this was especially tough. People will tip a bartender a buck for spending four seconds pouring a drink, but completely stiff a cab driver who fights for a hundred minutes of rush "hour" or a snowstorm in midtown Manhattan.

"You been doing this a long time?" Joni asked. Actually, she knew from the license posted in the back seat that the woman, thirty-year-old Maria Muñoz, had been licensed for just six months.

"Long enough to know that I don't want to do it for the rest of my life," she answered.

Driving had its shortcomings, but it was blessedly safe for Maria. Blessedly safe.

Other drivers feared the strangers who might get in their taxies armed or deranged, but losing one's self in a sea of almost thirteen thousand yellow cabs in New York City was the very best way for Maria to live in peace and shake the stalker who had taken over her life and forced her from her old, secure life in Atlanta, where she'd always lived. The one way she could make sure her stalker couldn't find her was to never be where she just was. That meant driving a cab.

Joni looked at Maria's picture on her license. It sure wasn't a very good one. It made her look seven or eight years older and a little hard in the face. In the photo, her hair was tied back and her eyes stared vacantly at the camera. The perfectly proportioned woman in the driver's seat had much softer features than the lifeless woman in the photo. Deeply set, dark brown eyes, stunning straight black hair that fell to the middle of her back, and a smile that suggested she was in on some kind of joke.

"You all need anything else before I hit the highway?" she asked. "Need a bathroom break? Something to read?"

Cab driver talk. Professionally superficial. Usually, the passengers have some sort of class thing going on where they think they deserve points for making small talk with the lowly, pathetic, uneducated driver. Maria was hardly a lowly driver. She had a college degree, money in the bank, investment property, and a stock portfolio. Driving was not her career—it was her refuge. It was either lose herself in New York or be killed. That simple, that terrifying.

They said nothing, so off they went.

Twenty minutes down the road, Ruby reached into her pocketbook and pulled out her wallet, then removed the photo of a nineteen-year-old Ruby dressed in a mermaid costume. "I don't ordinarily show this to other people," she said, presenting Joni with the photograph. Ruby as a mermaid. Swimming underwater with a stunning pink mermaid tail, surrounded by bubbles and drinking an RC Cola. It was one of those black-and-white photos that had been water-colored. "I am a mermaid."

Maria glanced at her through the rearview mirror, trying hard to maintain professional disconnect, but giving up.

"Can I see?"

Joni took another look, then passed the photo up front.

"You were a mermaid?" Maria asked.

"Still am, actually," Ruby said.

There's not much you can say to that.

"I've never had a mermaid in the car before," Maria said.

"A mermaid?" asked Joni.

"That was my fairy tale life," Ruby said. "My 'Once upon a time' moment. Once upon a time, I was a starry-eyed young mermaid frolicking in paradise. It was the most mystical and magical time."

"A mermaid." Joni knew Ruby wanted her to ask for more, but she didn't. "That's a nice picture." She handed it back.

Joni figured Ruby was a tad nuts.

The cab arrived at the Tropicana just as the ten o'clock crowd began to overwhelm the casino. Although exquisitely decorated, the cavernous resort, with its 4,000 slot machines, $14 million in German crystal chandeliers, and more than 6,000 employees, was always a great equalizer. It doesn't matter if you are Donald Trump or Maria Muñoz. You got a buck? You can play. Blackjack, craps, poker, chicken tic-tac-toe—whatever. Figure the games out and your chance of winning is about the same as the next loser's chance of winning: not good. It just doesn't matter if you adorn yourself in silk or polyester. Your money goes down the toilet just as fast.

"You want me to wait so I can drive you back?" she asked.

"That'd be so nice," Ruby said. "But we'll be awhile."

"I don't mind," Maria said. "I might even play a little blackjack."

"I've never even been to a casino," Joni said. "In all these years. Never been to Vegas, never even been here."

"One born every minute," Maria laughed as she helped Joni out of the taxi. "You'd better stick to the slots."

So there Joni was, lost in an ocean of one-armed bandits. She walked up to a Betty Boop slot machine, dropped in a token, and yanked the crank.

"Wait!" yelled a furious eighty-something woman who'd dared to take two steps away from her machine to flag her substitute over so she could go to the bathroom to tinkle. The woman elbowed Joni , nearly knocking her to the ground. "That's *MY* machine!"

"*Your* machine?" Joni asked.

"Don't you know the rules? I've been taking care of this machine for the last nine hours, and you can't have it!"

Joni had no idea that men and women like that lady guard their machines forever, as if they own them, because they have already pumped in their own fortune and aren't going to surrender *their* jackpots to an interloper. They know that all it takes is for them to step away for two minutes and some stranger will drop in a quarter and win the jackpot they've been priming all night.

"I want it back," the woman said, so Joni moved over because she couldn't figure out what the big damned deal was. Joni scanned the rows and rows of slots. Everyone knows how to use a slot machine. Really. How hard is it to plug a few tokens in a machine and pull the handle or push the button? She remembered reading how one person won $35 million playing the Megabucks slot at the Sheraton Desert Inn, Las Vegas. It doesn't take one heck of a lot of skill, now does it?

Of all those slot machines in the casino at the Tropicana, Joni picked the Elvis slot machine next to a five-foot-three bearded bald guy named Thomas J. Love, who dropped his last dollar into his machine, then slapped it when he lost. He turned toward Joni, and eyed her as she awkwardly played her tokens, one at a time, one at a time. At her rate, Joni'd be able to play that same bucket of tokens for two weeks.

"You're doing it all wrong," he advised her as she scooped a whopping $4.75 in winnings from her tray and put it in her bucket. "Don't play one at a time. You're never going to get any action playing twenty-five cents at a time."

"Well, this is how I…"

Before she could finish her sentence or even voice a protest, he grabbed a fistful of tokens from her bucket. "Do it like this!" he said. "I'll show you."

He plunked four tokens into his machine and pushed the spin button. *Seven. Seven. Seven. Seven.* Lights flashed—ONE THOUSAND DOLLARS! Without waiting for it to register with Joni, he plugged another four tokens into the machine and spun again. By the time the word "Wait!" came out of her mouth, one Elvis, two Elvises, three Elvises, then FOUR ELVISES came up on the lucky slot. Sirens blared, a speaker screamed "WE'VE GOT A WINNER!" lights flashed SEVENTY THOUSAND DOLLARS, and Thomas J. Love danced a wild jig in the air like a lucky leprechaun. "I FUCKING WON!" he shouted. "I FUCKING WON!"

"WE WON!" Joni shouted, joining him in his jig. "WE WON!"

"I WON! I WON! I WON!" he shrieked.

Joni kept dancing. Two casino pit managers approached Love for the presentation and eventual escort back to the office where he'd have to sign for his winnings and sacrifice his chunk for Uncle Sam.

"Congratulations are in order!" manager Mick Danville announced to the gathering crowd as he reached for Love's right hand and shook it. That's when the scene started playing out in slow motion for Joni. For one long, helpless moment, she froze as she watched Love stake his claim on her winnings. Really surreal, because at first, it was like watching a movie, but the next second it was like real life again. There's Joni. Fucked again. Perpetual victim. It was living her most recurrent dream, the one where she is being chased and she tries to scream but her voice fails, or she tries to run but can't move. He'd used *her* tokens! It was *her* jackpot!

Across the way, Maria saw the commotion and rushed to Joni's side, mouthing, "What happened?"

"He's stealing my money!" Joni told her. "He played *my* tokens, he won with my tokens, and now he's telling those people that my winnings belong to him. They believe him!"

"He played your tokens?" Maria asked. "What do you mean, 'He played *your* tokens'?"

"He just reached over and took them from my bucket," Joni said. "He was teaching me how to play the slots, like he was doing me a favor. I didn't even ask him to or anything."

"Why are you telling me this?" Maria asked. "Tell *them!*"

Joni froze, helpless. "What should I say?"

"Oh, forget it," Maria said, rolling her eyes. "Excuse me," she said to the pit manager.

Danville either didn't hear or he ignored her because he was so busy demonstrating for the spectators how easy it was for a regular guy like Thomas J. Love to win at the slots and walk away with a life-changing fortune by just investing a few coins.

"Excuse me," Maria said a little louder.

The guy didn't even glance her way, and continued slapping Love on the back. "And this is our second big winner tonight!" he announced.

"EXCUSE ME!" Maria shouted to him. "Cut the backslapping for a minute. That's *her* jackpot!" She pointed to Joni.

Danville finally looked at Maria, then at Joni, and then started to laugh. In fact, everyone around her started to point and laugh. Some held up the L-is-for-loser sign. "Yeah, lady, mine, too!" one man chortled. "Drunk!" cackled another. Danville began to escort away from her, but Maria lunged forward and clenched his red cummerbund.

"Look!" she yelled. "He used *her* money to win that jackpot! Those are *her* winnings!"

"Ma'am, take your hands off of me," Danville snapped.

"Listen to me," Maria said, firm, calm, and certain. "This gentleman used this woman's money to place his bets. He was at the machine next to hers, and took his playing money right from her winnings, without her permission."

Love, composed and acting quite the professional, shook his head. "Ma'am, you are hallucinating."

"LOOK!" Maria shouted to Danville. "WE GOT A PROBLEM HERE. ARE YOU CATCHIN' MY DRIFT YET?"

"Hysterical female," Love muttered.

"I HEARD THAT," Maria shouted. "YOU'RE AWFULLY SMUG FOR A THIEF."

Joni cringed at the crude force of Maria's voice, but she was glad that if anyone was on her side, it was the cab driver. Joni would rather die than make a Superbitch scene like that.

Danville motioned for security, and instantly, she and Maria were flanked by three 275-pound goons, one of whom ever-so-kindly told Maria, "Ma'am, we're going to have to ask you to leave."

"GO AHEAD AND ASK US TO LEAVE. MY FIRST CALL WILL BE TO THE NEW JERSEY DIVISION OF GAMING ENFORCEMENT. MY SECOND CALL WILL BE TO AN ATTORNEY. YOUR MAKING US LEAVE WILL ONLY MAKE THE LAWSUIT EVEN BIGGER, AND YOU KNOW FOX NEWS IS GOING TO BE ALL OVER THIS!"

They gave each other the "what a wacko" look.

"See all your cameras?" Maria asked Danville. "I want you to look at your security videos and see what happened here. He took this woman's money, pushed her aside and played it on her machine. She didn't give him permission. But it was her money."

"Good God, lady," Love said. "This ain't the flippin' NFL. No instant replay." He looked at Danville and said, "What a nut-ball."

Maria's eyes blazed. She wasn't about to back down. "You need to get the casino manager. Either that, or I am going to the organized crime unit tomorrow and then I'm getting a lawyer who is going to file a nice civil suit like you've never seen before. And it kinda sounds to me like racketeering, right? Those organized crime cops love stuff like this."

Racketeering. Lawsuit. The two magic words that could silence any casino. If the videos backed her up, there would be serious trouble. Bad publicity. And investigators would come in and, perhaps, see too much.

"Hang on," Danville said. "I'll get someone."

In a flash, the casino manager, Brian Allies, was right there. By that point, about a hundred people crammed into that slot area to see what was up.

"It wasn't her quarter, it was mine!" chided a sixty-something man.

"No, it was mine!" laughed a woman.

"It was mine!" screamed another.

"That bitch is outta her gourd," Love said to his crowd. Nevertheless, Allies heard Maria and Joni out as they recounted very specifically how Love had taken Joni's money to "teach" her how to win at the slots.

"Absurd," Love said. "That's just ridiculous. My money, my jackpot."

"¡Qué paqueté!" Maria muttered to herself. *What a pack of lies.*

"Just get me half," Joni told Maria. "Fair is fair." If she sued, she'd probably walk away with the whole $70,000, But how long would that take? How much would the lawyers take? Besides, fair was fair. She wouldn't have won without Love.

"We can compromise," Maria started.

"No way," said Love. "It's all mine. The most I owe you is about ten bucks in tokens, but no more than that because this was *my* skill and *my* luck. I'd been on that machine for four hours. If I hadn't played that money the way I played it, there wouldn't be any jackpot."

He sounded shrill, like someone in a car crash who jumps out of the car right after impact, screaming real loud, no matter who was at fault.

, "You used her money," Maria said. "You just admitted it."

"I am willing to split it," Joni offered meekly. "Fifty-fifty."

"Like hell," Love said before anyone else could appraise the offer. "That's my seventy grand."

"She may be giving you a very good offer," Allies said.

"It's *all* mine," he said.

"Well then," said Maria, "we will contend that it's *all* hers."

"It's *my* jackpot," he whined. "She doesn't know jack shit about slots."

"And you don't know jack shit about felony theft," Maria snapped.

"S-s-s-s-s-s-s-s-s," mocked someone from the crowd.

"S-s-s-s-s-s-s-s-s," a half-dozen others chimed in chorus.

"Let's move this into my office," Allies said.

Any PR value for the giant jackpot had been long lost, because this battle royale had gotten way too ugly and was unlikely to resolve itself easily. Moving the players out of the limelight would let the spectators get back to losing their own money in the casino, so everyone followed Danville to the back.

For a full hour, Joni, Maria, and Love sat across from each other, waiting as the managers reviewed the security tapes. Out in the casino, gamblers bet each other on who would prevail. Most said they sided with Love, who was a familiar face around the Trop. But it was an interesting question. When you win with stolen money, who gets the jackpot?

Meanwhile, Ruby never saw one bit of the commotion, mesmerized as she was at first by the tic-tac-toe with the chicken (she tied) and then with the tokens that kept flowing from her "I Dream of Jeanie" nickel slot machine.

Two lawyers convened with Allies and Danville and finally everyone sat around a long conference table to hear the verdict.

"The video does show that you were betting for Ms. Herrschwitz as her surrogate," one of the men in suits informed Love, whose right eyelid began to twitch. "So we suggest you reconsider Ms. Herrschwitz's offer of splitting the jackpot. We don't think you are going to get a better deal."

"That's bullshit!" Love shouted. "I'll give her the freakin' ten bucks back!"

"Look," Maria told him. "I can see you are a little disappointed, but she's made a generous offer—far better than I'd offer. You can have thirty-five thousand dollars—or nothing. You aren't getting screwed," Maria said boldly. She looked at her watch. "You've got two minutes to take it or leave it. Thirty-five grand or zero."

His breathing grew faster and deeper, and his face reddened even more. His eye kept twitching with embarrassing rapidity. Five foot, three inches tall. He looked like such a pipsqueak. An angry dwarfish man with a real grudge.

Checking his watch, one of the lawyers spoke. "Mr. Love, it was her money and you volunteered your assistance. If you plan to challenge this, we'll need to put everything in an escrow account until your claim can be reviewed in court. You'll need a lawyer. By the time you are done with this—even if you get a ruling in your favor—you won't get much more than she's offering. It will take you at least a year to get it resolved. Probably two, maybe three. And you could well wind up with nothing at all, plus that stack of legal bills."

Love seemed unmoved.

"You got forty seconds, Mr. Love," Maria said. "Why don't you just go and celebrate winning a lot of money. Thirty-five thousand is nothing to sniff at."

He looked at his watch. Forty seconds. The second hand on his watch moved forward, and finally he choked out the words, "I'll take it," he surrendered.

Maria looked over at Allies.

"I'm glad we got this worked out," he told her as the cashier counted out Joni's $26,250 after-tax winnings in the crispest bills available. Joni watched the counting down to the last fifty, then took her stack and counted again. She peeled off five one hundred dollar bills and folded them in half, then pushed them down into Maria's right pocket. Maria smiled politely. Grateful, even.

"I do have a few other concerns," Maria said to Allies, continuing to argue for Joni even though Joni had been rather stingy with the reward.

The casino manager rolled his eyes—what now?

"This has been a little stressful and it seems to me you gotta give us one of those suites you keep reserved for all those high rollin' types—for free. What is it you call those big players? Whales?"

"Yes."

"We want to be whales."

"Good grief," he said, then smiled. Maria and Joni did not fit the stereotype of the high-rolling, big money whales whose asses casino managers so endlessly have to kiss.

"Exactly what kind of whale suite did you have in mind?" he asked.

"The kind with a Jacuzzi," Maria said. "And three bedrooms, because there are three of us, not two."

"Mmmm hmmmm," Allies said.

"It's only fair."

"Yes. Only fair," he said, pursing his lips and nodding his head.

"And, a butler. We need a butler. That's only fair too," Maria said.

"No butler." He smiled. He motioned to an assistant who left, then returned in a flash with three plastic keys to their own hotel paradise in the Trop.

"Enjoy yourselves, ladies," Allies said. "It's been a pleasure."

Thomas J. Love didn't wait around to demand his own suite or share small talk. By the time they released his winnings, he raced back into the casino so he could lose everything by sunrise, which he did.

It was 12:45 a.m. when Maria and Joni headed back into the casino.

"Do Ruby and I have to pay rent to stay overnight in your suite?" Joni asked.

"No. Your cab fare is all-inclusive. Includes accommodations I might wangle along the way." She smiled. "But don't forget me in the gratuity!" She hated joking about the tips. It seemed so desperate, but after that $500 "reward" from Joni, Maria didn't hold back.

"Mmmm hmmm. How much is this tip going to cost?"

"Millions," Maria said.

Joni hugged her guardian taxi driver angel. Minutes later, they found Ruby cashing in a bucket of tokens, elated.

"Look!" Ruby shouted. "I won!"

"You beat the chicken?" Joni asked.

"Of course not," said Ruby. "That chicken beats everybody or it ends in a scratch. But I really scored on the slots!"

"How much?" Maria asked.

"Three hundred and thirty-seven smackeroos!"

"Wow!" said Joni.

"I could go all night, but I figure it's best to quit while I'm up," Ruby said. "Besides, we ought to hit the buffet."

"Isn't it kind of late for that?"

"You crazy?" Ruby asked.

"Maybe we should get room service," Maria said confidently.

"Now that's a thought," Joni said.

"Why room service?" asked Ruby. "We don't even have a room. Let's hit the buffet, then see a show."

"You enjoy the action," Joni said. "Maria and I are going up to our suite."

"Suite?" Ruby's ears perked up.

"Long story," said Maria. "But there is a six-person private Jacuzzi just waiting for us. And our own bedrooms. And room service. But if you want to go to the buffet…"

"Well, I *am* on a diet," Ruby said. "Hey, how did you all do in the casino?"

"Not bad for a beginner," Joni said. "Not bad."

The women headed up their suite, finding a fruit and cheese platter and not one, but *two* bottles of chilled Dom Perignon, with a personal note from Brian Allies that read, "Good work, ladies. Enjoy the evening with our compliments." The corks flew, the girls laughed and danced to swing music from their suite's state-of-the-art Bose surround sound, and in an hour, had regressed to the point that even Ruby jumped up and down on one of the king-size beds, careful not to hurt herself.

At five a.m., Maria finally fell asleep, into a deep, therapeutic sleep for the first time in at least a year. Only Ruby, Joni, and Brian Allies knew where she was, and she felt safe and insulated.

She dreamed.

Maria is back in her bedroom—her real bedroom—home in Sherwood Forest in Atlanta, on the bed with the fluffy white goose down comforter and the smooth Egyptian cotton sheets, and pillows—lots of pillows, pillows everywhere in the all-white room where she is finally safe and sleeping deep, so deep, for the first time in years because it's okay now, she can be there, he can't find her. But the door opens and she tenses, tenses right up into a panic, and she doesn't know whether to scream or just lie there like she doesn't know, pretending like she is still asleep, but she knows what is coming and he is there and she doesn't know what to do. He pulls back the covers and slides into bed with her, like it is his bed too, like he belongs there, like he is the husband and she is the wife, and he moves close to her, then wraps his arms around her, then shakes her awake. She can't pretend she's asleep anymore.

"Look at me!" he yells, and she opens her eyes and he clears his throat twice. He is there, it is him, but he has no head, no head at all. His body stops at his shoulders, but his voice booms throughout the room. "You know what to do, baby. Do it. Do it, baby. You know what to do!"

But she doesn't know what to do, not at all, because it is him, he terrifies her, and besides, he has no head, so she pushes him back and he beats his arms down on her, hard and violent and she pushes again, but he rolls on top of her and she takes her arms and pounds on his back, but he likes that.

"I like it that way," he said. "You know what to do, baby!"

"What will it take to make you leave me? Please leave me…"

"You know it doesn't work like that. We're together forever. You can't get rid of me because I will never leave you."

Maria pushes him away and screams, "Get out of here! Get out of here!"

"Maria? You okay?"

Maria's scream was so loud that Joni had heard it and knocked on Maria's bedroom door.

Maria opened her eyes, so groggy it took a long moment to even know she'd been dreaming and another long moment to figure out where she was.

Joni walked in without being invited.

"Maria?" She saw Maria in the bed and looked around—no one else in the room.

"Bad dream, girlfriend. Nobody in here but you and the boogeyman."

Maria's heart pounded like it might explode. "God, I need a vacation," she said.

They got up two hours later, at which time the threesome called for room service and dined on fresh fruit and the lightest pancakes ever flipped. Once again, Ruby counted out her gambling winnings—just to be sure she'd counted right the night before. "Yep. Three hundred and thirty-seven smackers."

"Nothing to sniff at," Joni said.

"Enough to get us over to the Polkamotion by the Ocean, right?" she asked Maria.

"Polkamotion?" Maria asked. "By the ocean?"

"Noooooo, Ruby. This is the end of the line," said Joni.

"Yesssssss," Ruby said, singing, dancing, and bouncing her way through the room as she hummed the "Pennsylvania Polka" in their living room. "We gotta go. I'm serious. How much to get a cab to Rehoboth Beach? The Polkaholics are playing." She hooked Joni into her polka, and after initially resisting, Joni finally started to dance quite clumsily.

"I'm going to sit this one out," Joni said.

"Look, you already won thirty-five grand because of me. Just live a little. It isn't going to kill you," Ruby said.

"I'm going back home," said Joni.

"No you're not," Ruby said.

Joni nodded. "Oh yeah. You might die without attending the damned polka festival and I would be distraught for the rest of my life for having deprived you, so you are actually doing me a favor by dragging me along so I'll be able to live with myself."

"Exactly," said Ruby.

"Makes sense to me," Maria said. "But it's only seventy-five miles to the festival. You are going to pay me three hundred thirty-seven dollars to go seventy-five miles?"

"No. Not seventy-five miles. We'll have to go down to Florida too."

Maria and Joni laughed. As though Ruby were kidding.

Chapter Four

You shouldn't have regrets in life, but Ruby had a nagging list of unfinished business. With both hips wearing out, odds weren't good that she'd dance onstage in Madison Square Garden or trek to the top of Mount Everest. But she still had to "See Rock City," do Dollywood, and pet an orangutan at the refuge in Zolpho Springs. She needed to visit her cousin, Camille, in the nursing home and go back to Hawaii. Someday. Ruby ached for a road trip. It'd been at least a dozen years since she'd feasted on the pecan divinity at Stuckey's, and it ticked her off that now she could only have one piece, lest she risk splitting her tail fin when she bent over.

She gave herself a good look-see in the mirror before joining the others in the Tropicana suite's living room. Considering how worn out she should be, Ruby felt wide awake and alive, and she danced a little jig for herself in the mirror while singing "I've Grown Accustomed to Her Face" from *My Fair Lady*.

"I've grown accustomed to her face, She almost makes the day begin, I've grown accustomed to the tune that, She whistles night and noon, Her smiles, her frowns, Her ups, her downs, Are second nature to me now; Like breathing out and breathing in..."

Ruby *had* grown accustomed to her face. She looked her age, but was absolutely unapologetic about it because she believed she had earned every wrinkle and white hair. She had friends who went to plastic surgeons, tried chemical peels, and did whatever they could to make sure they looked younger than their years, but after awhile they all started looking stretched and freaky. Ruby didn't mind looking seventy-eight because that was the magic number in her life, so big damned deal! She felt euphoric—intoxicated with the moment, because whatever happened that day it would be far better than what would have happened if she hadn't found Joni or hailed the cab. Ha! Ruby danced some more. *"I could have danced all night! I could have danced all night! And still have begged for more. I could have spread my wings, and done a thousand things I've never done before…"*

"Somebody needed to get out of the house," Maria said, nodding her head toward Ruby.

"I sure did," Joni said.

Ruby emerged from her wing of the suite singing "Skip to My Lou" to the others.

"We gotta hit Wal-Mart before we go to your polka party or anywhere else," Maria announced as she grabbed the lotion, conditioner, shampoo, sewing kit, and Q-tips from the front bathroom. "I need clean underwear and I need a toothbrush."

"Me too. Underwear and a toothbrush," agreed Joni. "And a clean shirt."

"All you need to vanish without a trace," Maria said knowingly. "Don't forget to clear your bathrooms of the toiletries."

"Will do," said Joni. "When do you have to get your cab back?"

"As long as the meter's running and someone's paying the bill, I can have the cab," Maria said. "I just have to arrange it. But Ruby, it's not that I'm not enjoyin' the work or the company, but there are cheaper ways to travel than hailing a taxi."

"Maybe, but I travel in Technicolor, not black-and-white. This is my Technicolor road trip."

"Well, I'm only on board for one more day of your harebrained Technicolor adventures. You wear me out," Joni said.

"Yeah, yeah, yeah…" Ruby droned. "You act like you're the seventy-eight-year-old, not me."

Joni thought for a minute and knew there was some truth to what Ruby said, but she wouldn't admit it. "I'm serious. Polka festival, then I'll take Manhattan."

"You have no sense of adventure," Ruby said.

Joni just shook her head at Maria.

"Let's just take the lady to her Polkamotion," Maria said to Joni. "I could use a break from the city and this is the only fun I've had in way too long."

"Well, me too," said Joni. "But I'm not the kind of person who just takes off without a plan." And she wasn't. If Joni left the city for anything, it was with a strict itinerary that mapped out the who-what-where-when-why-how of the trip, whether it was business or pleasure. So rigid, so predictable, so safe.

"Plans are good for nothing," Ruby said. "Let's go live."

So they got in the cab and headed to Rehoboth Beach.

In Ruby's mind, travel by cab was the only option for her trip to Florida. She didn't want to fly because that meant going alone. She couldn't drive—not anymore—and trains made her want to hurl. Eighteen months had passed since she arrived at the St. Mary's ICU and the nurse told her, "Mrs. Witherspoon, you've had a stroke." The doctors predicted Ruby would never talk again, walk again, eat again without a stomach tube, or be independent, but Ruby would have none of their nay-saying, and set out to prove them wrong. After a three-month incarceration in the hospital and rehab unit, Ruby could talk, walk, eat, and be independent. The paralysis on her left side was completely gone. But she couldn't get her driver's license back. You have a stroke or seizure and the state takes it from you, and what hurts is the principle of the whole thing. If you'd asked Ruby whether she'd want a hundred thousand dollars or her driver's license, she'd pick the driver's license every time, and so would just about every other senior citizen forced to make the choice. It's not about being able to drive any place in particular, it's about having the option.

As much as she tried to talk herself into flying, it just didn't seem to hold any adventure. What kind of fun was that? She'd get on an airplane and two hours later she'd be in Florida, just sitting there at the airport waiting for some shuttle van to pick her up and take her to some motel where she wouldn't know anyone or have anyone to talk to or dine with. She would miss every bizarro site along the way and would probably only get one or two conversations—on the airplane—before the other mermaids arrived, which almost always was right before the first practice session the day before the reunion show.

Ruby was going to that mermaid reunion, dammit. She just didn't quite know how to pull it off. But dammit, she was going—and she was going with style.

The standard cab seating arrangement began on the road to Wal-Mart and was quite functional and fine from then on. Maria driving, Joni on the passenger side up front, Ruby taking the whole back seat. Driving Miss Mermaid.

Ruby's main reason for going to the Polkamotion by the Ocean was very simple. She liked saying the word "Polkamotion" and especially liked saying "Polkamotion by the Ocean." She liked to polka. None of them had ever attended a polka festival before, much less one of such prominence.

Twenty-nine hours earlier, when Joni had tuned into the *E! True Hollywood Story* and watched Tammy Faye implore her to put on her lipstick, she never expected she'd go to Coney Island. Or win $35,000 in the slots at Atlantic City. And she especially didn't figure that she'd find herself trying to polka with a 350-pound, sixty-four-year-old Polish immigrant named Bazyli at some harebrained polka festival in Delaware.

"I don't like this!" she shouted to Ruby as Bazyli swung her past.

"Stop making it so hard! Just go with him. You dance the circle with him and keep turning around until they call for a change in direction."

"This isn't worrrrrking!" Joni called to Ruby on the next pass.

"Keep moving! Let one foot chase the other. Three small steps. Keep moving!"

"I made it all these years without knowing how to do this! I don't need to know how to polka," Joni said, trying not to let Ruby see her laugh.

The next guy who asked Joni to pair up was a seven-foot, one-inch skinny giant named Vavrinec, resplendent in a red, pink, green, and black vest, and pants as red as Santa's. Just as Joni thanked God that no one had a camera, she was blinded by a flash from the photographer from the *Cape Gazette*, who then danced behind her and asked her to spell her name so she could be identified in the caption.

"My name is Ruby Witherspoon," said Joni. "From Manhattan."

Vavrinec took Joni's hand and swung and swayed and swished and sashayed in God knows which direction to the band's clarinet, accordion, and trumpet version of the "Hoop Dee Doo Polka." Vavrinec was all business, so his shoulders tensed up and his face morphed into a scowl every time Joni cheerfully laughed when she tripped. He thanked her when the song ended, but Joni knew he was making a mental note to never ask her to polka again—not this year or next year or the year after.

For the first hour, Maria managed to sit out every polka by hiding behind the invisible professional wall between cab driver and passenger. She was the driver and, therefore, not under any particular obligation to perform as a polka dancer. But that only worked for so long with Ruby, who finally directed an eager octogenarian straight at her, imploring him to "Go get 'er, Kazmer." Kazmer went and got her, and did not give Maria a break for more than two hours, proving something that is not generally known about polka dancers: They are a little off.

"Tell me how you polka, and I will tell you how you love," Kazmer said in an accented whisper.

Maria took another look at him. Eighty-plus years old, and he's whispering about love in her ear? Was this the best she could do?

Joni fared much better.

"My name's Buster," a definitely un-polkaish-type said to Joni. "Care to polka?"

"I don't polka," Joni said.

"Polka snob?" he asked.

"Polka clod," she giggled.

"So why are you at a polka festival?" asked Buster, who Joni sized up as slightly older than she, and relatively tame. Nice build, a little hairy (but the salt and pepper beard worked and it was a treat to find a middle-aged guy with such a full head of hair), and good and tall.

"I have no idea why I am at a polka festival," Joni said. "It was never on my to-do list until this morning."

"Why *are* you here?"

"I was coerced. I realize you won't believe that, but it is the truth."

"Naw," said Buster. "I saw you and that other dude dancing, Twinkletoes. Didn't look too forced to me."

"See that lady over there?" She pointed to Ruby. "She's the one. She abducted me from Central Park yesterday, and since then, I haven't been right. In fact, please go to the police and let them know where I am."

He laughed.

"That your mom?"

"No. Actually, I think she is my guardian angel."

"Sounds like you all are on quite an adventure."

"You have no idea. So, Polkabuster, why are you here at the Polkamotion?"

"Saw the story in the paper and figured I'd stop for kicks. I'm living spontaneously right now."

"Good place to pick up chicks?"

"Sure, if you're looking for chicks over sixty."

"Where are you headed next?"

"Don't know, don't care. I'm taking some time off to see the country and read all the books I swore I'd read one day."

"This is the 'one day'?"

"It is."

Joni realized it was the "one day" for her, too, because she'd never given herself permission to even dream of a day, or even an afternoon, away from her apartment, without structure.

"What is your regular job?" she asked him.

"B-b-boooooring. CEO for a textiles company. I gave myself an indefinite leave of absence. The job makes me crazy."

"I can see why," Joni said.

"How 'bout you?"

"You'll never guess."

"Okay, let's see. Gourmet chef."

"No. If it can't be microwaved or doesn't come in a can, I can't handle it."

"Magazine editor."

"No."

"Accountant?"

"No." She smiled, as she hadn't balanced her checkbook since 1989.

"Graphic artist?"

Joni smirked. "No, no, a thousand times no."

"Okay, maybe you are the 'Diva of Desire'?"

Lord.

"You gotta be kidding me," Joni finally said. "How'd you know?"

"Saw you on Oprah," he said. "I was going to the beach for a week, so I even bought one of your books."

"Which one?"

"Oh, I dunno, passion's something. It was about that woman Arielle and that guy, what was his name? Andre? And he went off and all appeared lost but then they wound up together."

"*Passion's Witness.* I can't believe you read a romance novel. Or that you forgot the title."

"I liked the sex scenes. Pretty hot stuff. Nice to have a face to attach to all that nice hot stuff."

Joni liked him—plenty—so she took his hand, led him out on the dance floor, and let him whisk her around, letting one foot chase the other, just three small steps.

"How long will you be traveling?"

"Dunno," Buster said. "I think I've retired myself from the real world and I am planning not to plan."

"Good plan if you can afford it. That's how Ruby lives."

Ruby and Maria danced around the room to Joni and Buster, then Ruby pointed to her watch and mouthed, "Let's go." As impossible as it sounded, Ruby was all polkaed out, and Joni was just beginning.

"My friends have such lousy timing," she said to Buster. "I'm so sorry."

"My Cinderella is turning into a polka pumpkin? This is my loss. It was such a pleasure meeting you."

He kissed her hand. She couldn't believe it. Did men even do that anymore? Buster did, not that it mattered. He was history the minute she got back in the cab. She didn't even know his last name.

Just as Maria turned on the light and started the engine, a hand tapped loudly on the window of the passenger side, startling Joni, who saw Buster and rolled the window down.

"One more thing," he said. "This is for you." He passed her a copy of the Polkamotion program with a note scribbled on the front. "Enjoy your road trip," he said.

He smiled, then scooted off with his own polka motion.

Joni read the note. "I'll never see you again," it said, "so I think you should know that you are a very beautiful woman. Spectacular, actually. Best, Buster."

No last name, no phone number, no e-mail, no fax.

Just "Buster."

Three weary women pulled into the parking lot of the Salisbury, Maryland, Microtel. By that point, their "luggage" consisted of two large Wal-Mart shopping bags. Being the driver, Maria took responsibility for the bags because, after all, it was still technically baggage. Joni headed straight for the front desk because she needed sleep—bad.

Now, Ruby was mighty exhausted, but she wasn't blind and when she saw Maria remove a handgun from a pocket in the driver door of the cab, she bolted to full attention.

"What the hell is that?" Ruby demanded.

Maria put the gun in the Wal-Mart bag and didn't answer.

"Maria, I saw that. What are you doing bringing a gun with us?"

Maria put her finger to her lips. "It's not a big deal."

Like hell.

"You have to get rid of that gun. I won't travel with it," Ruby said as they closed the door to their motel room. Joni, who'd already collapsed on one of the beds, sat upright.

"Ruby, trust me on this, okay? It's not a big deal. A lot of drivers carry guns."

"Not my driver."

Maria looked at her, a little stung by the class distinction. Now she was just Ruby's driver. Harsh.

"You've got a gun?" Joni asked.

"No big deal."

"Is it loaded?"

"What good is an unloaded gun?"

"Then it is a big deal," Ruby jumped in.

"Just unload the thing while we're on our trip," Joni said. "That ought to be good enough. The goons of Manhattan are miles and miles away."

"It's not good enough," Ruby said. "I want it gone."

"I'm not unloading it and I'm not getting rid of it."

"What are you so afraid of?" Ruby asked.

"Nothing," Maria said. "I don't have to be afraid of anything because I have the gun."

Some American dream. It sure had unraveled fast, hadn't it? Only a year ago, she was a celebrity of sorts. Busy, successful, high-profile, and rolling in cash. Now she'd slipped to driving a lousy cab and citing her constitutional right to keep and bear arms. Maria'd sure fallen fast.

Actually, that wasn't entirely accurate.

She'd been pushed.

Chapter Five

How the hell did he find me here? In this motel room? In Maryland? How? I didn't tell anyone I was going to be here. Christ, I didn't even know I was going to be here until I pulled in the drive at ten o'clock.

Maria sat upright in bed. The headless man hovered in the doorway, waving her to come with him, saying nothing so as not to wake Ruby and Joni. Just waving his arms out and back, come with me, come with me, and then more insistent, come NOW, come now! Come. With. Me. Now!

Maria needed to wake the others, but what if it made him mad? He might… Who the hell was he? Why wouldn't he leave her alone? He cleared his throat, impatient.

"¡No jodas!" Maria whispered loudly, ordering him, "Get out of here!" She tried to figure out what to do, tried to get a minute to get her head together, because she couldn't go with him, but he was there and she was scared and what options did she have?

And then there was peace again, when she woke and saw the light coming in through the motel window and Ruby and Joni and all things normal. God, running was so exhausting.

Maria glanced at herself in the rearview mirror of the taxi and remembered being told how beauuuuuutiful her deep brown eyes were, how they sparkled. Now they just looked so damned tired. Her face, pale. Two days of unwashed hair! No make-up. What an astounding transformation, considering. If anyone would have told her that her life would have amounted to this—driving a yellow cab with such a prickly paranoia—after so much career success—she would never have believed it. Impossible. Maria had never considered herself judgmental or classist—not till she had to demote herself several classes, from "trend-setting oh-so-hip stylist" to invisible cab driver.

In Atlanta celebrity circles, Maria was her own celebrity who instinctively knew how to spiff a man or woman—the hair, the clothes, the style, the aura. She attended a style institute to learn hair, but soon figured out it was all about essence. By age twenty-five, she was featured in *US Magazine* as the nation's not-so-secret "Image Wiz," who "grooms political candidates, anchor people, musicians, fashion models, and movie stars—all from her home base in Atlanta. *"They* come to *her,"* the story emphasized. Once the article ran, real money poured in. By the time Maria was twenty-nine, she was so in the money that she bought a four-bedroom antebellum home in the Sherwood Forest area of Atlanta, amazed that the daughter of two Cuban "boat people" could have come so far, so fast.

She looked in the mirror again and smiled at the incongruity of her life, of what she'd expected and what she wound up with.

Motherfucker.

Maria couldn't help but be a little flattered by his first note. *"Maria, I thought you'd like to know that I am a secret admirer who would love an opportunity to get to know you better. I have never fallen like this before— from a distance, in silence. Could this be love? 'For stony limits cannot hold love out…And what love can do that dares love attempt.'"*

Romeo and Juliet. A little much, to be sure. But it was nice— definitely different. It broke the monotony of being hit on by her male clients (and sometimes the females) who prattled on about her sultry eyes.

The next letter came with a fourteen-carat gold puzzle necklace. Her half said, "LOVE YOU," and the note said, *"I've got the other half. Meet me at 1 p.m. at Downie's and I'll show it to you over a romantic lunch."* Maria did not go. That was when he graduated from secret admirer to anonymous stalker.

The next day, Maria found a rusty knife hammered four inches into the hand-carved wooden front door of her studio. A letter came in the next day's mail telling her, "*I only want you to know how much I love you. Let me show you. Why won't you give me one chance?*"

Detective Larry Smith had no suspects, so he told Maria to "keep your eyes open, but don't worry too much." She didn't, really, until another letter came that said, "*I will fuck you so hard you will scream for your fucking life.*" It terrified her, but the detective said that, again, there wasn't anything he or anyone else could do without a fingerprint or a tip or some sort of evidence. The suspect was the entire population of Atlanta—or more. About all Maria could do was hope the sicko would lose interest.

But another note arrived, this one the most chilling yet. "*I know you down to the little mole on your hand, next to your thumb. I know that photo of you and your mama at Stone Mountain—the one you keep in front of your styling chair in the salon. I know your home because I go there sometimes, just to feel near you. I know you spent 32 minutes in Nordstrom on Saturday, 11 minutes in American Eagle Outfitter and that you and that skinny chick did lunch at The American Café that day. Oh, I just love that Kandinsky print on your bedroom wall. And the quilt on your bed. Did your granny make that? It'll be oh-so-comfy when I fuck the shit out of you. Till then, I'll see you in all your dreams.*"

It really could have been anyone. It could have been someone from the work crew that gutted and renovated her home before she moved in. It could have been a repair person or her accountant or the president of the neighborhood association or her old high school principal. It could have been a client. Maria clicked on her brain's computer and endlessly searched her memory files to guess who should be suspect, but hours of that made her realize how futile it was because it could have been anybody she had ever met, or anybody she hadn't.

She thought of the neighbors, one at a time, and wondered if any of them seemed peculiar. And she thought of friends and old acquaintances. Like it would have mattered. It's not like stalkers hand out business cards to market themselves. And you know what they say every time a psycho surfaces and the media starts reporting about him. The neighbors will go on television saying, "He seemed so normal," or, "I never would have imagined him being capable of doing something like this." She wondered why she was spending any time at all imagining who was a qualified candidate for the weirdo.

Who the hell was he?

"I've got more than fifty cases like yours in my case file right now," Detective Smith told her. "I know this is very alarming, but you aren't alone in this."

Like that was supposed to make her feel better?

The first time she realized he'd broken in, she called the cops and a full team of technicians came out to fingerprint and take evidence from the house. They came up with nothing.

"You shouldn't stay here for now," Detective Smith warned her. "I don't want to scare you, but you aren't safe."

And that, of course, scared the hell out of her. She roomed with her cousin for six nights and invested in the most expensive home alarm system she could find.

"You should have a gun," Smith told her. "You definitely should have a gun."

Hysterical people have guns, she thought. Victims. NRA fanatics. Criminals. Not social liberals who believe gun control is absolutely necessary in order to maintain what little semblance of civilization still remains. Faced with two choices—going home feeling powerless or going home feeling at least some measure of control— she listened to the detective and bought a Ruger .357 magnum. Her father took her to the gun range and started with the basic safety rules.

First, always keep the thing pointed in a safe direction. Maria felt there were no safe directions anymore. Second, keep your finger off the trigger until you are ready to shoot. Would she ever be ready to shoot? Third, always keep the gun unloaded until you are ready to use it. Well, gee. If you keep the damned thing unloaded until you need it, it is not going to do you much good.

But she listened carefully and watched as her father very paternally guided her through the loading, aiming, and firing lessons. He shot first, right into the chest of the man's body on the target. She held the gun firmly, aimed it straight for the man's head, and blew out his brains. Every time. No shaking or wavering. She aimed, she fired, and she hit her mark. After that, she carried the weapon with her everywhere, and she felt sure she'd be able to use it if the time came.

Probably.

It didn't make her safe, but it did even out the power balance a little.

"Hello?"

It was three weeks after she'd dared to return home, and the phone had rung just after four in the morning.

"That black nightgown is your sexiest one yet," a deep-throated man whispered into the phone. He cleared his throat. "Makes me hot. You make me hot. You know what to do, baby. Take care of me now." His breathing was heavy, and it disgusted her. "C'mon, baby, you know what to do."

"What?"

He cleared his throat again. "Enjoy the flowers," he whispered before abruptly hanging up.

Maria lifted the covers a few inches and realized she *was* wearing her black nightgown. Her heart raced even faster as she leaned over to turn on the light, but then she wondered: Would that make her more vulnerable to him? It took a moment for her eyes to adjust, then focus, then process the fact that another dozen dead roses sat on her nightstand in a lead crystal vase. The card read, *"Next time, my woman. I'm really going to fuck you, baby. I've told you what's coming. You know what to do."*

"You can hire bodyguards," the detective told her. "It is expensive and it takes some getting used to, but he may get discouraged and if he doesn't, they could well give you the protection you need."

"I can't live like that."

"Hopefully you won't have to for very long," he said.

"What are my other options?"

He put his hand on her shoulder, protective and fatherlike.

"Get lost," he said.

"What?"

"If you were my daughter, I would want you leaving town in the middle of the night and getting lost for a good year or two," he said. "I'm not allowed to say things like that. But I am so tired of women having to be so victimized. You need to get lost."

Her life had sunk to the point that she needed an expensive security system, a handgun, three double-cylinder deadbolts, and two door slide security locks to make her feel secure—and that still was not enough. Every time a male client walked into her studio, she wondered if it was "him." If she glanced in her rearview mirror and saw a car following too closely she wondered if the driver wanted to rape or kill her.

"Get lost," the detective had said. She knew it was the best option, and really, the only solution. Put the career on ice, disappear from Atlanta, and pop up in some other context in some other part of the world where the odds of running into "him" would be zero. Wait awhile, a good long while, and maybe "he" would forget about her or, at least, lose interest.

New York called to Maria. Big city, eight million people, and thousands with the last name of Muñoz. In fact, there were probably more than a hundred Maria Muñozes right there in Manhattan.

He'd never find her.

Chapter Six

Joni leaned out of the taxi window for some fresh air and caught a whiff of the Maryland farmland where they were driving. That's one thing about escaping to the country. Sometimes, it smells like shit.

"I dub this 'Shitfilledcowfield, USA'!" Joni shouted, as Maria glided past the odiferous cow pastures at forty-five miles an hour.

"Roll up the window!" Ruby commanded.

They were sooooo far from Gotham City.

"So Ruby," Joni asked, "what are we doing? Why are we aimlessly riding through all these pastures?"

It may seem odd that it took so long for someone to call the question and ask Ruby what the hell they were doing, but that was just how it went—largely because all three had good cause to run away, and Ruby just gave them the excuse.

"We've been gone for three days," Joni said.

"Is that all?" Maria said, and started counting the days on her fingers to be sure.

"When are we going home?" Joni asked.

Ruby thought about snappy responses, but instead watched the farm scenery roll past and didn't say a word.

"Ruby, are we *ever* going home?" Maria asked.

"Of course. Just not today. Or tomorrow. Or the next day, for that matter," Ruby finally said.

"Ruby, *where* are we going?" pushed Maria.

"South," Ruby said.

South was better than north, which was home, but "south" wasn't a destination. Well, maybe it was, but Ruby hadn't gotten them to realize it yet. All of them needed an excuse to change direction in their lives, so it was good—healthy—to see they still had the power to walk away and be in charge for themselves, even if it was just for a few days and even if it was only to go "south." That was what brought them together and gave Ruby such huge license to look at the Rand McNally map she bought at a convenience store and select the next back road or destination on a whim.

"Is there a plan?" Maria asked.

"Well, if you are asking if I know where we'll be tomorrow at three o'clock, no," Ruby said. "Do we need to know that? What difference does it make?"

"Is there a final destination? Where are we heading?" Joni asked.

"Well, if you must know, I need to be somewhere in ten days."

"Where?" asked Maria.

"*Ten days?*" Joni exclaimed. "I can't be gone for ten more days."

"Why not? You locked yourself away in your apartment for sixteen days and the world didn't end."

"Where?" Maria asked. She calculated the financial incentive of being on the road so long, and it was substantial. But it was unsettling. And fun. But unsettling.

"Ruby, really. I can't just vanish," Joni said.

"Missy, is there some place you need to be? Because it sure didn't sound like it to me. From what you told me, it sounds like your dance card needs to be filled, and I'm going to help you fill it."

"Very funny."

Maria tried again. "Ruby, cut the crap and stop teasing us. Spill it."

"We're going south."

Ruby had gotten the idea for the trip when she read in *The National Enquirer* the true story of an epileptic Jacksonville, Florida, woman who hailed a cab because she wanted to see the country. Sixteen *thousand* miles and $20,798 later, the woman felt she'd seen America. The article referred to the woman as an "eccentric," and the concept appealed to Ruby because she wouldn't have to fly, she could stop at all the places she'd secretly wanted to stop before, and she'd have traveling companions. That last thing—the companionship—was a huge deal, particularly since Ruby's closest friends were all dead and her daughters would not do a road trip with her. She'd asked, plenty of times. The cost of it was irrelevant to her. Not that she liked to blow through money, but she had money. Walter left it to her. Walter would have approved of her spending it this way—a hundred percent.

Maria called in to her manager and they negotiated a special rate with Ruby—$700 a day, no matter how short or far, fast, or slow they drove. Ruby had to fill the tank too, and pay all tolls, expenses, and incidentals. That included food and hotel bills, with the understanding that the threesome would bunk in the same room. That seemed more than fair to Ruby, who would much rather spend on Maria's chauffeuring than on assisted living arrangements. Joni coming along was just the bonus.

Joni hated Ruby playing coy about where they were going, but she knew the older woman enjoyed being begged for details, so she stopped begging. For a moment. Ruby could not stand it.

"I am concerned about fitting into my tail," Ruby finally blurted out.

"'Beg your pardon?" asked Joni, taking a swig from her Diet Mountain Dew, knowing she'd definitely need caffeine for this conversation. If not something stiffer.

They'd been to Coney Island for the freak show, Atlantic City for tic-tac-toe with a chicken, to the Polkamotion by the ocean, the seashore, and plenty of stops in between, but it was in this moment that Joni finally asked herself if Ruby might be certifiable. "Nuts" was the word here—not eccentric. Maria glanced in the rearview mirror as Ruby continued.

"I won't fit into my tail. I'm sure of it."

"What the hell are you talking about?" Maria asked.

"The sixtieth reunion show at Weeki Wachee," Ruby finally said. "Rehearsals start in ten days. I know I won't be able to zip my tail when I get there. I've gained too much weight. I am a corpulent mermaid and I don't like it. I'll be self-conscious."

"Ahhhhh," said Maria. *"That's* where we're going? Weeki Wachee? That's the old tourist trap in Florida, right?"

"Tourist trap?" Ruby bristled, offended.

"I thought they closed that place," Maria said.

"Don't insult me. It is still open. Of course it is."

"Well, I thought all those pre-Disney parks like Weeki Wachee and Cypress Gardens were already dead," Maria said.

Well, sort of. Walt Disney entertained more visitors in an hour than the mermaids of Weeki Wachee wooed all year, and it was pure injustice! Ruby winced every single time she thought of the magnitude of the insult, because it so minimized the most magical place and moment in her life. People dismissed Weeki Wachee as fading roadside kitsch, but it wasn't kitsch, not to Ruby or any of the mermaids who swam in the spring. Going back wasn't about reminiscing about a B-list tourist attraction, but rather, about frolicking again in the most blissful moment of freedom she'd ever known. For Ruby and the others, it was their first job, but not only that. It wasn't much like a job at all. It was more like a paid summer camp where they dove in as teenagers and emerged as confident women. And though, from the surface, it was all about the nine shows a day to the ticket-takers, for the mermaids, it wasn't acting like mermaids at all. They *were* mermaids. Not pretend mermaids, but real ones. Even after each of them grew out of their jobs and went on to live in that "real world" where they did what women of that generation did and married and had children and cleaned house, the longing never left. Ruby always said that Weeki Wachee was the worst first job a person could have because, after that kind of freedom swimming and dancing and living in that seventy-two-degree crystalline spring, *everything else* was "less than." They all wanted to go home to Weeki Wachee. That clear spring water, so full of life, called to them. They craved the privilege of swimming there again.

Ruby swam from 1950 to 1952. Her years with Walter were the most satisfying of her life, but her years at Weeki Wachee were the most treasured. She couldn't wait for Joni and Maria to meet Barbara Minns, the most important mermaid of all, who mobilized the alumni mermaids back for the twenty-fifth and fiftieth and now the sixtieth reunion to generate some much-needed cash and publicity to keep the place alive. All the former mermaids were coming back.

"So you're going to go to this reunion? You're paying a million dollars to swim like a mermaid?" Joni asked.

"Once upon a time," Ruby began, "there was a young woman named Ruby Lane. Ruby grew up in Spring Hill, Florida, a small town with a small town school and a small town view of the rest of the world."

Back in those days, women were called "girls" and all girls aspired to be among the mermaids of Weeki Wachee. These days, you could over-intellectualize the sexual objectification of those young women doing their underwater acrobatics in form-fitted bathing suits, but people did not over-intellectualize such things in the 1940s, 1950s, and early 1960s. Those were the days when feminine mystique really was a young, attractive mermaid frolicking in the springs of Weeki Wachee because there was something mystical and magical about it. And there still is.

"Those were the days," Ruby said. "We all lived together on the grounds and we'd shortsheet the beds, put peanut butter in the toes of each other's shoes, leave 'messages' from guys with the phone number for the zoo, put toenail clippings in each other's beds, steal each other's boyfriends—the usual."

But, Ruby said, they all learned to count on each other in ways that ordinary showgirls wouldn't. No matter what kinds of rivalries or jealousies emerged, the mermaids had to work as a team because their work was truly dangerous. There was no such thing as carrying a grudge with another mermaid, Ruby told them. When you are working with a limited air supply, you have to be each other's lifeline.

The mermaids had to be able to hold their breath for well over two minutes again and again, but there were air supplies down there—air hoses and the airlocks. Mermaids didn't wear weight belts, so they had to use the air in their lungs to control their ascent and descent. They didn't wear tanks, but rather, used those air hoses that were scattered in different areas in the underwater theater.

Remembering the techniques might be a tad stressful, but Ruby felt confident everything would come back. The stress here was strictly the more serious kind: cellulite. Ruby's would be in her bathing suit in an underwater theater where thousands of people would see if she still had "it."

"Okay, so let me make this big leap here," Joni said. "Your reunion is in ten days and it's down in Florida at Weeki Wachee. Right?"

"That is correct," Ruby said.

"And somehow you think that we are going to take a cab down to Weeki Wachee to attend this thing?"

"That is also correct," she said.

"You think we are going to drive from central Manhattan to Weeki Wachee *in a taxi cab?*"

"Yes, Joni," Ruby said with great resolve. "I do."

"Ruby, you have lost your mind."

"Maybe. But we're going."

"I like how you don't even ask me if I want to go."

"Of course you want to go," said Ruby.

"I want to go," said Maria. "Joni, you want to go too. Stop being such a pain in the ass."

And that was really all there was to say about it. Joni's two options were to go back to a dead life in that dead apartment or to go to Weeki Wachee and see Rock City and stop for every crazy tourist weirdness along the way.

Ruby wore a self-satisfied look, glad that the formalities were gone and that now all three were working with her toward a common, noble goal.

"You still think you can do it?" Maria asked.

"Once a mermaid, *alllllways* a mermaid," Ruby said. "But I weigh at least twenty pounds more than I did at the fiftieth reunion show, and I'm not saying how much more I weigh than when I was a mermaid in my prime."

"You're still in your prime," Joni said.

Ruby raised her arm and demonstrated how her flab danced with the slightest movement. "A mermaid can't hide her flab. Especially when she's got to get into a tail that is two sizes too small."

Joni had just one pair of jeans that fit, so she related.

But when it hit Joni that she was comparing a pair of tight jeans to a Weeki Wachee mermaid's tail, she realized she might be the one who was nuts.

And that was okay.

That night, when Joni went to sit in the hot tub of the Super 8 Motel (Ruby wasn't springing for anything more upscale), Ruby motioned for Maria to have a seat.

"I don't want that gun with us," Ruby said.

"Not again," Maria said. "It's not negotiable."

Maria didn't know what or how much to tell Ruby, because she didn't want to scare the woman. She needed the gun, she would not compromise on the issue.

Ruby did not like guns, not at all, because they held their own power. To her, it was as though a gun could wake itself up in the middle of the night and go off without anyone touching or even looking at it. There was a meanness to guns.

"I need this gun."

"Oh baloney. Give it here. I am going to unload it right now."

"Ruby, I agreed to do this trip because I needed a nice escape," said Maria. "But I need the gun for my protection. I know everybody says that, but in this case, it's the true story."

"What are you so afraid of?"

"It's not a good story, and I don't like dwelling on it. But I need the gun."

"I don't like guns," said Ruby.

"I don't either," said Maria. "But I know what I'm doing. Drop it, okay?"

Ruby did. But she figured she'd handle the matter in her own way.

Chapter Seven

"You have NINE new messages. First message, sent Tuesday at 9:52 a.m."

"Mom, it's me. Gimme a call." (Jacqueline)

"Second message, sent Tuesday at 2:21 p.m."

"Mom, where are you? You hiding?" (Jacqueline)

"Third message, sent Tuesday at 5:35 p.m."

"Mom, are you ignoring me? I need to talk to you. You're scaring me." (Jacqueline)

"Fourth message, sent Tuesday at 9:32 p.m."

"Ma, where are you? Jackie says she's called about 400 times. Give us a call so I can get big sister to stop bugging me, okay?" (Nina)

"Fifth message, sent Wednesday at 7:01 a.m."

"Mom, if I don't hear from you by nine o'clock, I'm reporting you missing to the cops." (Jacqueline)

"Sixth message, sent Wednesday at 7:45 a.m."

"Mom, call me now." (Jacqueline)

"Seventh message, sent Wednesday at 9:03 a.m."

"If you don't call me in ten minutes, I'm making the call." (Jacqueline)

"Eighth message, sent Wednesday at 9:05 a.m."

"Ma, she's not kidding. Where the hell are you?" (Nina)

"Ninth message, sent Wednesday at 9:15 a.m."

"Ma, I made the call. If you aren't dead, I'm pissed." (Jacqueline)
"Uh-oh." (Ruby)

Since leaving the city, all three of them had turned off their cell phones and gleefully neglected all voice mail. Nobody runs away from home and checks voice mail or e-mail. That's just silly. But Joni made her case that they should call in if for no other reason than to make sure nobody had died, so Maria pulled into a park on the Chesapeake and they each sat on three separate park benches and reconnected with their old world.

Ruby had known her girls would call eventually, but she never expected them to be such frantic, bossy cows about everything and report her to the friggin' NYPD.

She smiled, thinking back to eighteen-year-old Jacqueline yelling at her for waiting up until she got home from a date at two in the morning. "I don't need a babysitter. Stop being so overprotective!" Jacqueline had said. Ruby felt like sending a postcard saying the same thing, but Jacqueline definitely would never get or appreciate the humor. She never did.

"You're going to call your girls, aren't you?" Maria asked.

"I'm not in the mood yet."

"Sounds like you'd better get in the mood," Joni said.

Ruby loved her girls wildly, and missed them madly, but things had grown tense in the past couple of years because they didn't like Ruby being Ruby, and campaigned hard to get her to move closer to them so they could watch over her and make sure she was "safe." As though the word "safe" held any appeal to a woman who believed she'd better act out now, and act out with great pizzazz because her bronco-busting days were running short. They tried to guilt her into giving in, telling her again and again that her insistence on independence stressed them out, and blaming her for their constant worry. They didn't "get" her fascination with the curious, freakish, ludicrous, oddball, off-beat, and peculiar pockets of humanity. "Why do you have to be so weird?" Jacqueline once complained out loud, then asked why her mother wasn't more like other old ladies whose daughters only had to worry about their aging mother's cholesterol.

"Not us. We have to worry you are going to wander off to some hairball coughing contest or some other bizarre event," Jacqueline said.

"There's a hairball coughing contest?" Ruby retorted, and it cracked Nina up.

Ruby told Jacqueline she would never surrender to old age when she had another choice, and as long as there was a hairball coughing contest that she hadn't seen, she might as well check it out. Aging may suck, but it happens and as Ruby will tell anybody, "It sure beats the alternative."

With every passing birthday—and the stroke that came so unexpectedly a year and a half earlier—the girls became more intrusive and insistent. At first, Ruby felt touched by their concern and protectiveness. She needed it when she felt vulnerable, but once she became strong again, their interference ticked her off. They sure knew how to knock her confidence. They kept a documented list of all Ruby's misfires—that little fall at the grocery, the forgotten bills, her trip to the theater with the oven still on (thank goodness the fire hadn't spread to another apartment). Jacqueline wrote everything down and brought out her file whenever she dared speak those three dreadful words, "assisted living facility," as she urged her mother to move west where she and Nina could watch over her. Her own daughters building a case to put her away! Ruby couldn't believe it.

The insult! Ruby had grown those girls up by counseling them through every screw-up, job change, car wreck, or broken relationship, and she'd never questioned whether they were capable of being in charge of their own lives. Of course it wasn't as easy as it once was for her to meet the day's challenges, but that was part of the beauty of aging. The battle meant she was still playing the game. She still mattered. The girls kept trying to wear her down, swearing over and over that they only wanted what was best for her because they loved her.

"But do you love me enough to just let me be?" she'd ask.

They would never answer. They weren't the enemy, and kept trying to show her that, but she did not get it.

No, she did not. Her girls made her heart hurt. Yeah, the old gray mare might not be what she used to be, but so what? When she turned seventy-one she realized it wasn't as easy as when she was seventy. The lesson there was that she'd better enjoy seventy-one before she was seventy-two. And now that she was seventy-eight? She'd enjoy every adventure she could before she turned seventy-nine. And seventy-nine was coming, whether she lived life or shut herself away. Who was she hurting by being a little daring and flashy? Didn't it matter that her choices fulfilled her, or that she felt happy? What was the big crime? Ruby did not get it at all. She had respected their wishes that she not act like an overprotective mother and now she didn't need to be smothered by her overprotective kids.

Ergo, the runaway taxi ride to the South.

Checking out of her day-to-day reality for a while without calling in for permission or updates wasn't that big of a deal in Ruby's mind. She didn't feel like calling in—and that's why she didn't. Maybe it was a bit passive-aggressive. But they weren't the boss of her—she was. She didn't do it to teach them a lesson, although if they learned a lesson, it would be fine by her.

Joni's voice mail box had four messages, all from Doug.

"You have FOUR new messages. First message, sent Tuesday at 6:06 p.m."

"Joni, how are you doing? I know you are pretty angry with me, but I need to talk to you about something and wondered if you might join me for dinner…"

"Second message, sent Tuesday at 8:33 p.m."

"I hope you aren't ignoring me. I would really love to talk to you."

"Third message, sent Tuesday at 11:45 p.m."

"Okay, I know you aren't calling me back, but we really need to talk. Can we get together tomorrow? Maybe I'll just come over there…"

"Fourth message, sent Wednesday at 7:57 a.m."

"You emptied our joint account, Joni. I know that most of it was your money, but some of it was mine and I need it now, so please call me. I'll be on my cell all day."

"What an ass!" Joni yelled from her bench. "Fucker wants money from me."

"Jerk," said Ruby.

"Screw him," said Joni. She leapt up from her bench and yelled, "SCREW YOU, DOUGIE FRYE!" as she ran out on the grass and attempted a cartwheel for the first time in more than thirty years. She never got her legs off the ground, so she tried again, still not getting it. So she just lay flat in the grass, as she next shouted, "Doug Frye is a lousy lay!"

She smelled the clean air and the freshness of the grass, and she could literally feel her heart beating life inside of her.

She smiled.

She smiled?

She smiled.

Those phone messages would ordinarily have derailed her for another two weeks of self-exile in her apartment, but not this time. Something was different in Joni's world as she discovered the greatest symbol of a woman's liberation—the realization that having no man is better than having a lousy one.

Maria said nothing about her voice mail.

"You have ONE new message. First message, left Wednesday at 8:27 a.m.

"Maria, this is Lana in dispatch. You're out of radio range, so I thought I'd leave a message at your apartment in case you check your voice mail. Hon, we got a call from the cops looking for you. Someone broke into your place. It doesn't look like anything was stolen, 'cuz the guy apparently got spooked by a neighbor. Call me and I'll give you the number for the detective.' Don't you worry, okay? Don't blame New York. These things happen."

No, Maria didn't say a word about any of it, and she didn't call for details.

She didn't blame New York.

Stalkers happen.

Chapter Eight

"Well, here's an interesting story on the wire," shock jock Steve Rosenthal announced to his morning audience of millions. *"Worried family members have launched a national search for Ruby Witherspoon, a seventy-eight-year-old woman who vanished last week."*

"And?" asked Sister Liz, his AM sidekick.

"I know. So? Somebody disappeared in Manhattan. That's news? BFD."

Maria turned up the radio.

"Ruby WITHERSPOON?" he mocked. *"Couldn't come up with a better bluehair name than Ruby Witherspoon. So Ruby Witherspoon took a long walk. Well, Ruby, I hope you haven't dropped dead. Your family is worried out there. ET phone home."*

"What a jerk!" Joni said.

Ruby shook her head, supremely annoyed.

"But what gets me about this is that Ruby Witherspoon's family asked the mayor's office to launch a search. I hate to be cruel and insensitive, but…"

"You are the king of cruel and insensitive," injected Sister Liz.

"Well, Liz, you tell me why, with thousands of missing people in this city, Ruby Witherspoon is so damned important that hizzoner the mayor has his press office send out a release to the media."

"You got a point, Bucko."

"Sorry, Ruby Witherspoon, but really, nobody cares about you. You know what I think? I think it's because the mayor's just worried because people are

talking too much about his relationship with that female treasurer of his. He's on his couch boffing the bean-counting bimbo and trying to distract us with some old bag who got lost walking around the block. The mayor's changing the subject."

"That radio announcer is very nasty," Ruby said. "And immature."

"Want me to change the station?" Maria asked.

"No," said Ruby. "Leave it on. I'm a big girl."

"Whoa, did I misspeak?" Rosenthal said. *"Suddenly, all twenty-five lines are jammed with people who are pissed at my candor. Okay, Denise on line one…"*

"Steve, normally I love your show, but I can't help but wonder, what if that was your mother? Wouldn't you do everything you could to find her?"

"Well, if it were my mother, it would be newsworthy because she's got a famous son and people care about her because they care about me. I promise, nobody gives a rat's ass about Ruby Witherspoon except her two publicity-seeking daughters. Just another old lady making life difficult for the rest of us. Line two, you are on the air."

"You are disgusting!" shouted the caller. *"Sometimes you go too far, and today you are a total insensitive ass!"*

Rosenthal disconnected the call. *"Sticks and stones may break my bones but names will never hurt me… Line three, go!"*

"Steve, I have to agree with you. We've got bigger things to worry about than that roaming dinosaur."

"What's your name?"

"Jason."

"Jason, thanks for calling. I can tell you are a very bright guy. Harvard educated?"

"Harvard High School?"

"Go away, Jason."

"Line four?"

"Steve, this is Ruby," said what was obviously a teenage guy imitating an elderly lady's shaky voice.

"Ruby Witherspoon?"

"Meow!"

"Mrs. Witherspoon, what has happened to you?"

"Meow! Meow! Meow! Meow! Meow!"

"You're not right, Ruby."

"Asshole!" yelled Joni.

"Asshole!" yelled Maria.

"Meow! Meow! Meow!" Rosenthal joked.

"Ruby, you should call him," Maria said. "Shut that bastard up."

And that was the moment, the very moment, the momentous instant, when all the chaos started. The turning point.

"Call that asshole," Maria said as she tossed her cell phone to Ruby.

Rosenthal's producer interrogated Ruby for a full five minutes to make sure she was actually *the* Ruby Witherspoon ("Can you give me your home address? What is your date of birth?"). Finally, Ruby met the shock jock live, on the air.

"Ladies and gentlemen, call off the dogs. Apparently, the reeeeeal Ruby Witherspoon has called us to make sure we know she's alive and well. I'm a little nervous now. I think she might be pissed. Ruby, are you there?"

"Yes."

"Have you been listening to the show?"

"I'm afraid so."

"Uh, I guess we were a little hard on you. It wasn't anything personal. It wasn't about you."

"You've got a big mouth."

"Me?"

"I guess that's how you got your job."

"Very perceptive, Ruby," he said.

"But stop calling me an old lady and a bluehair. That's not just disrespectful to me, but to all of your elders. And my hair is not blue. It is white, and very attractive if I might add. I've seen your picture, you are very homely and I don't know what makes you think that you can be so rude about other people."

"Hey, it's my show. Stop insulting me."

"You don't have to be so mean to old people."

"I don't want to get old."

"Well you'll die young, you ass."

Joni and Maria laughed out loud, then high-fived each other.

"Go Ruby!" chuckled Sister Liz.

"Whatever, lady. Why haven't you called your damned daughters?"

"You need to watch your damned mouth."

"I've heard that before."

"Maybe you should listen. Rude Boy. Disrespectful. I'm fine, you can just tell my family I'm fine…"

"Shall we call them together and let you tell them online?"

"No, we shall not."

"Aw, c'mon, Ruby."

"Call them and I hang up."

"But why don't you want to talk to them?"

"Because I don't feel like it."

"I see. A little family dysfunction playing out right here live on the Steve Rosenthal show."

"No, it's functioning just fine with me doing what I'm doing."

"What are you doing?"

"None of your damned business."

"C'mon, Ruby."

"I'm on vacation with some friends."

"What friends? What kinda vacation?"

"Look, you're not my mother and I don't have to tell you anything. I'm on a road trip. The rest is my business."

"Why didn't you tell your family you were going on vacation? You could have saved a lot of people a lot of worry."

"You sure are nosy," she said.

"C'mon, Ruby. What's the scoop? You're an old lady. You know better than taking off without letting the kids know you're safe."

"I know a lot of things."

"Like?"

"Like my daughters want me in a nursing home or some kind of assisted living b.s. and I'm not ready. Like I'm still in charge of my life and I'm going to live it."

"Why do they want to lock you away?"

"Because it's easier than them waiting for me to fall and break a hip or have another stroke. Put me in a nice, safe place and they don't have to worry. And, 'Oohhhh, Mother, look how nice it is! Three square meals a day and all of these nice people! Isn't this staff fabulous?' I'm sick of them pushing it on me."

"Sounds bad, Ruby."

"You know that once you go to one of those places, you aren't coming out."

"Ruby, I'm starting to see why you're so pissed off."

"Pissed off isn't the half of it. You go in there and it is all downhill. I figure I've got a few good times left. I'm going to have them."

"Well, what can I do to help?"

"You can shut up!"

"Go Sister Ruby, go!" chimed Sister Liz.

"Okay, okay. I know I'm a brat. But I think we've got a few million people out there who can help you."

"That's nice. Actually, I'm doing fine on my own. I'm on this trip with my girlfriends."

"Where are you going?"

"M.Y.O.D.B. You know what that means? It means mind your own damned business."

"Ruby, you should watch your damned language. So, where are you going? The Liberace Museum in Vegas? Is that where you are going?"

"For such a know-it-all, you don't know so much. Anyhow, I'm going to get off the phone before you start being mean again. Tell everybody I'm okay and that they should worry about their own lives, not mine. Ruby Witherspoon is alive and well."

"Call me again, will you?"

"Behave yourself, young man."

"Thanks, sexy."

Ruby disconnected the cell phone, which was unfortunate, because she didn't hear when Steve Rosenthal, known world-over as a jerk, told the world, *"We gotta protect Ruby. I'm posting her picture on my* *website and the first person who leads me to her gets a $5,000 reward. How's that? Find me Ruby Witherspoon!"*

Chapter Nine

Thirty years after Mrs. Hobbs gave Joni a D in creative writing class and told her that she was stubborn, difficult, and lacking in talent, Joni filled a Super Big Gulp with Diet Coke, grabbed a bear claw, and got in the check-out line at a 7-11.

"Is that all?" the clerk asked.

Joni looked at her—really looked at her—then tried to figure out if who she thought she was seeing was who she was really seeing.

"Mrs. Hobbs?" Joni finally asked.

The seventy-year-old woman's eyebrows rose and she looked down her nose at Joni, hesitating to acknowledge what her expression most certainly gave away. Yes, it was Mrs. Hobbs.

"Long ago," the cashier admitted. "In another life."

"Goodness!" said Ruby from the candy aisle. "You actually ran into an old friend?"

No old friend. Joni'd always wondered whether Mrs. Hobbs remembered her, whether she felt great remorse over having discouraged a writer who so obviously *did* have talent, whether she knew just how successful her worst student had become. She knew it wasn't the most mentally healthy thing, looking back to a high school teacher who made her feel even more inadequate as she tried to navigate through puberty, but Joni still thought of her. She thought of all she'd done in spite of that woman.

"You were my creative writing teacher at Kennedy," Joni said. "I'm Joni Herrschwitz. You probably don't remember me…"

"I do," the woman said, still looking down her nose and giving off a chill, the same one she'd always given to Joni. "How could I forget?"

"I became a writer," Joni said. It bothered her that her tone seemed so vulnerable, like she was seeking approval, but it was hard to mute it.

"Oh yes, I know," said Mrs. Hobbs, or whatever her name was. "I recognized you on Oprah."

Elation! Mrs. Hobbs had seen the Oprah episode! Joni didn't have to rub it in because it was all right there. Joni was successful in spite of Mrs. Hobbs, and Mrs. Hobbs knew it and Mrs. Hobbs had seen her and… Why the hell did it matter after so many years? Joni wondered about that: why she would remember a compliment for two minutes and a criticism until she died.

"I am so proud I was able to help you become successful," she said.

Wait. No! Mrs. Hobbs was claiming credit for Joni's success? Was the woman that clueless or that rude?

"Are you married, honey?" asked Mrs. Hobbs.

Are.

You.

Married.

Honey?

Wait. No.

Mrs. Hobbs didn't.

She did.

She leveled the one dig for which Joni could not rebound. Ever. That bitch! Calling Joni out for being an unmarried woman in her forties! A spinster!

"Do you have children? You look good, Joni, not near as heavy as you did on television," Mrs. Hobbs said.

Okay, that was it. The crown trifecta of passive aggression, and it slapped Joni from nowhere. All Joni'd wanted was a Super Big Gulp and a bear claw, and this was what she'd gotten. She started paying Mrs. Hobbs—in pennies. Ruby came up behind her and dropped three dollar bills on the counter to help out.

"No, Ruby," Joni said forcefully. "I've got it."

Mrs. Hobbs just took the three bills and gave Ruby fifty-four cents in change.

"Good to see you again," Mrs. Hobbs said. "I wish I had one of your books for you to sign."

Joni perked up.

"I bet it would fetch me a pretty penny on eBay," Mrs. Hobbs said.

"I bet it would," Joni said, looking down her nose at Mrs. Hobbs. Her anger swelled. "If you are that desperate."

One for The Girl.

"For cripe's sake, I'm seventy years old and working at a 7-11," she said. "You think I'd be here if I weren't desperate?"

Joni looked at the woman's eyes, and now saw them as long-dead, and Joni suddenly felt the strangest emotion. Sympathy for Mrs. Hobbs. Joni didn't know what to say.

"Well?" Mrs. Hobbs said. "You want anything else?"

"No," Joni said. And she didn't. She didn't want an apology or acknowledgment or even praise. Mrs. Hobbs was bitter and unpleasant, but that had nothing to do with Joni and everything to do with Mrs. Hobbs.

"Good seeing you," Joni said.

"Good seeing you too," said Mrs. Hobbs.

Joni left the store and Mrs. Hobbs called every person she met in her life to tell them about seeing her famous friend. Her former student, the celebrity. "I taught her writing..." she said. "I was her mentor."

Chapter Ten

"You'll remember Ruby Witherspoon is the seventy-eight-year-old siren who ran away from home and scared the crap outta her daughters. I've already offered a $5,000 reward for leading me to her, and now our very own corporate pig boss has oinked. Yes, Mr. Generosity has upped the reward to $25,000, shameless sonofabitch that he is, he wants publicity. But if that will help us find Ruby, we'll take it. So Ruby, there's a bounty on you, babe. I just want to make sure you are all right."

"He sure has taken a liking to you," Maria said.

"Am I supposed to be flattered?" Ruby asked.

"Think so."

"Ruby, if you are listening, I want you to give me a call. I want a call every day if you can. Love you, girl. You make us all smile. And you boost our ratings. So, from the bottom of all our hearts, we're rooting for you to help us rake in those advertising dollars."

"I'm not going to call him," Ruby said, but she knew she would. So did Maria and Joni.

Ruby made the shock jock wait until eight a.m., then called from the North Carolina diner where they practically did face plants in their blueberry pancakes.

"I've got Ruby on the line. Where are you now, Ruby?" Rosenthal asked.

"Oh, Steve, you know I can't tell you that."

"Okay, are you within a day's drive of Gotham City?"

"We aren't driving a straight line. This is a pleasure trip."

"Gimme a hint, you sexpot."

"I am still in the United States."

"Tell me during the commercial break. I won't tell anybody."

"No, I don't trust you."

"Smart lady," said Sister Liz.

"All I want to do is come and meet up with you," he said. *"Just give you one big kiss on the lips. Don't deprive me. I am in my sexual prime."*

"Your sexual prime ended twenty years ago," Sister Liz said. *"Leave Ruby alone."*

"I'd ask what your mother thinks about how crude you are, but I think I know," Ruby said. *"Anyhow, why would I want to meet with you?"*

"I want to travel with you, Ruuuuuby!"

"Why would you want to come traipsing along with some old lady and her girlfriends on their road trip?"

"To go lawn bowling and play shuffleboard?"

"Oh, well that must be it."

"Besides, I know you are hot for me."

Joni groaned out loud. *"That guy is out of his mind."*

"Who's that?" he asked. *"Who's the babe with you? Wait a minute, you said you're with girlfriends. What girlfriends? They hot? That one sounded young. Is she blond? What do they look like? Are they single too? Big boobs?"*

"You wouldn't fit in with us. Your Sister Liz might. Not you."

"I'll go," Sister Liz said. *"Oh, lemme come with you, Sister Ruby. I'll be good! I'll bring the peanut M&Ms."*

"You keep outta this. You aren't going without me," Rosenthal said. *"Ruby's my girlfriend, not yours. What kinda group are ya traveling with, Ruby? Your mah-jongg partners?"*

"You are insulting us."

"You on a tour bus or something? Everybody stopping at the Piccadilly Cafeteria to get the early bird special? C'mon, Ruby. Let me come. Let me come with you. I want to run away."

"You can afford to take your own damned trip."

"Yeah, but if I go with you, my ratings will go up, I'll get media coverage, they'll renew my contract, I'll get a raise and be even richer. Then you'll be able to marry me for my money."

"You can't come on the trip, but I'll marry you for your money."

"I'll take it. I gotta say, I detect a definite degree of sexual tension in your voice, Miss Ruby. I know you are hot for me. You want me. I'll be the best lay you've ever had."

"Look, Sonny Boy, you need to show a little respect. And I assure you, you'll never be the best I ever had. Probably the worst."

"Verrry funny. Okay, I gotta go to commercial. I wanna woo you off the air, Ruby-Baby. So you hang on while all those people out in radioland listen to two minutes of delightful commercials for cheap auto insurance and expensive formulas to increase penis size."

He cut to break. While a commercial for the latest erectile dysfunction medication played in the background, the shock jock pleaded his case.

"Ruby?" he asked.

"Yeah?"

"I'm serious."

"Hey, look. I appreciate all your attention, but really, I need to do what I need to do."

"Just let me come along for the ride. I promise, it'll be more fun."

"No."

"Ruby, I won't tell anybody where you are. We'll transmit live, by phone. We can do this any way you want."

"We are doing quite nicely without you."

"You're wounding me, Ruby."

"Well, I don't mean to hurt your feelings, but this is a girl's trip."

"Lemme talk to the others. Let 'em take a vote."

Ruby looked at Maria and Joni, both of whom gave a thumbs down.

"Sorry, young man, it's three to zero, thumbs down. Not going to happen."

"When are you calling again?"

"Someday soon."

"Ruby, can you call tomorrow at 8:15?"

"No."

"Why not?"

"Because I'm not on your schedule. I'm on mine. I've got one place I've got to be, and everything else will happen when it happens."

"But it really helps when I can tease the listeners and tell them to stay tuned 'cuz you are calling. It helps my ratings."

"I am not on a schedule and I'm not on your payroll so I don't care about your ratings."

"I'll put you on my payroll. How much do you want? We'll pay for your trip. Get you a nice visit to that fat farm in Hilton Head. Just let me run away with you."

"I'll call again. Maybe tomorrow. But you aren't invited, so you need to give it up."

With that, she hung up.

Rosenthal came back from the commercial break dedicating "Wild Thing" to Ruby, then singing, *"WILD THING, I THINK I LOVE YOU."*

All twenty-five phone lines were lit with calls from Ruby fans. And that was when Rosenthal got the idea.

Billboards. Big ones, lining the interstates wherever he aired. Since Volcano Network Communications controlled more outdoor advertising than any other company, Rosenthal had free access to the world of billboards.

He marched into Sid Cole's office at Volcano headquarters and laid out the plan for the notoriously adventuresome CEO. Rosenthal wanted a billboard in Times Square. No, *two* billboards in Times Square. He needed an 800-number tip line, and someone answering phones 24/7. He needed access to helicopters on a minute's notice. He wanted hourly promos for the "Let's Find Ruby" campaign, and news coverage of the search.

In the broadcast industry, an opportunity like that would translate into millions of dollars in ad revenues—if played right. The news coverage would spread from Rosenthal's radio show to others at the station to other stations within the company to stations outside the network to the newspapers to the cable television stations to the networks. And they'd all be covering Steve Rosenthal and how he was helping the little old lady who was trying to escape the assisted living dungeon in which her mean daughters wished to lock her. The country would cheer for Ruby, and the masses would see Rosenthal as her savior.

"Cole, it's a winner," he said.

"Yeah, I think it's a winner," said Cole.

"I also want to up the reward to a hundred grand."

"Done," said Cole.

That's how the circus began. The billboards went up twenty-four hours later (Volcano owned six right there in Times Square) with a twenty-foot photo of Ruby next to the words "FIND RUBY NOW!" and a toll-free number straight to the Volcano Network Communications headquarters. By evening, ABC, CNN, NBC, MSNBC, and FOX News all beamed Ruby's face and story into American homes.

More than 900 people called with tips that first day. Ruby sightings were reported in twenty-two states, from Portland, Maine, to San Diego, California, to Seattle, Washington, to Charlotte, North Carolina, which was where Ruby actually was. Finding Ruby would be easy—there were hundreds of thousands of old ladies out there. They all looked alike.

"Ruby," Rosenthal coaxed from the airwaves. *"We need your help, babe. No insult, but you look like a lot of other old ladies out there and you're making it difficult for me to figure which of these leads is any good. You don't want to deprive one of my loyal listeners and your great fans of that $100,000 reward, do you? So call in, pronto."*

Joni pointed her cell phone camera at Ruby and took a picture. Then another. And another. Like she were one of the paparazzi on retainer for *Star Magazine* or something.

"What are you doing?" Ruby asked.

"Isn't it obvious?"

"Isn't *what* obvious?"

"I'm going to win that hundred grand!"

Chapter Eleven

The guilt piled up, so Ruby broke down. She checked her watch and did the time zone math. It was lunchtime on the East Coast, so nine in the morning on the West. She waited an extra twenty minutes to make sure, and once she felt confident Jackie, her bossiest daughter, was most certainly in full Type-A mode at work for another three hours, she called. Ruby planned to leave a nice voice mail telling Jackie not to worry, Mom was just on vacation and enjoying her life.

"Hello?" Jacqueline answered.

Unfortunate.

"Hi Jackie," Ruby finally said, her voice cracking between the "Jack" and the "eee." "Just checking in. How you and Julien getting along?"

Ruby heard rustling at the other end and figured Jacqueline was grabbing a pen and note paper so she could write down every single thing her mother told her, as though recording it for evidence.

"Just checking in? You can call some jackass at a radio station but you can't call me? Your daughter? Jesus, Ma."

Ruby listened as Jacqueline took deep breaths to calm herself. "You don't know what you've put us through. Or maybe you do. You obviously don't give a shit. Well, I'm pissed."

"Don't be…"

"Pissed, Ma. Can you tell?"

"I'm calling now, honey. I just want to let you know…"

"My co-workers all tell me to leave you alone. Ma, I am just trying to be a good daughter. You've made a fool outta me and a fool outta Nina."

"I haven't!"

"You made it like we are the bad guys in this. We've only been trying to do what is best for you…"

"I'm still in charge of determining what is best for me. Not you."

"And look at what a great job you are doing. You are God-knows-where doing God-knows-what with God-knows-who. You wait until I'm about to have a nervous breakdown to finally call me, and Mama, I know why you called at this time. Nine-twenty a.m., Jesus, Mom, you think I can't see through that? You thought you were going to get away with just leaving me a message. Right? You are…"

"Hello?" Ruby would get out of this call the best way she knew how.

"Mom, don't play that with me. I know what you're doing."

"Hello? You're…"

Jacqueline cut in and started mimicking her mother. "You're line is breaking up," she said in a perfect imitation of Ruby's voice. "Honey, I can't hear you,"

Ruby hesitated, but stayed on point.

"Honey, this line is crackling real loud. I can't hear you."

"Mom, don't do that! I know you can hear me perfectly!"

"Hello?" Ruby hung up. Jacqueline rang the cell phone right back, but Ruby sent it straight to voice mail. She felt a tad bad, but not really. She'd done her duty with her daughter by calling her, and if Jackie wanted to get all nasty and negative, then she could be nasty and negative to someone else. Plus, there wasn't time to waste. Ruby quickly dialed Nina's cell phone so Jackie wouldn't get to her first. If anyone was going to put the spin on that conversation, it would be Ruby.

"Ma, where the heck are you?" Nina asked as soon as she hit "talk." Ruby wondered how she knew who it was, then realized Nina must have seen her mother's cell number come up on her caller ID.

"Oh Nina, I'm out on the road and having the time of my life."

"So I've heard," Nina said sweetly. "So everybody on the planet has heard. Ma, where are you?"

"Don't ask for details."

"Ma, gimme details."

"I'm having too much fun to tell you."

"You're sure getting a lot of publicity," Nina said. "And I guess you can guess, Jackie's on the warpath. She's crazy worried and crazy mad. You'd better call her."

"Yeah, yeah, yeah. I just talked to her. We had a bad connection."

"C'mon, Ma. You always have a bad connection with her when you're up to your tricks. Speaking of that, did you turn off your cell phone for the whole world or just me and Jack? It would have been nice to be able to talk to you and make sure you were okay."

"I can't stand this cell phone thing," Ruby said. "I like being a free agent without it."

"Well, you made us crazy. I think you know that."

"I had no idea."

"When are you coming home?"

"How should I know?"

"How should you know? Ma, you should know! Where are you going?"

"Honey, I told you—no details!"

"This isn't funny. What if I'd have done something like this to you? Running away…"

"I seem to remember a few times when you disappeared without any notice," Ruby said. "And there's a difference. I'm of age. I'm legal. Remember?"

"Yeah, if you are of sound mind and body, but I'm starting to wonder. Anyhow, you've got a lot of people worryin' about you."

"Tell them not to worry. Your ma's fine."

"Yeah, I can tell," Nina said reluctantly. "Ma, they were talking about you on the Today show this morning."

"You're kidding? Shoot, I wish they'd called my cell phone. Can you give them my number?"

"Very funny. I about spit out my coffee. As much attention as you're getting, you need to get a publicist and an agent. I can just tell you're on your way to lucrative endorsements for Orajel and Metamucil."

"A whole new career!"

"Let me know if you need a lawyer."

Ruby smiled broadly. Nina could try and discipline her mother all she wanted, but deep down, Ruby felt sure her daughter enjoyed the commotion. Give her thirty years and she'd be doing the same thing.

"Okay, Ma, you know I love you and I am right behind you. But I'm worried. Jackie's worried. Sarah and Julien don't know what to do with us."

"I know you're all worried. But you don't have to be—"

"I am. So, here's the thing. I'm going to fly wherever you are and we can do the trip together. I'll go wherever you want to go…"

Years. It'd been years since Ruby gave up trying to get Nina and Jacqueline to come do something more exciting than visit New York to check on her and tell her what she was doing wrong. Now Nina would drop everything to come along for the ride? How amusing. It would have been so fun to add Nina to the mix. They hadn't done a road trip together since Walter died. Ruby thought about it for a moment.

"Let me join you," Nina said. "I just want to be there to make sure you're safe."

Make sure I'm safe? Again, the well-meaning but completely inappropriate nerve of one of her daughters. Ruby often wondered how her very gene pool could have created two daughters so completely clueless about their mother. But here was sweet Nina, willing to take off from her law practice—with no notice—to come on the road with her ma and be her—oh, Ruby couldn't stand to even think it—be her BABYSITTER. Her supervisor, bodyguard, attendant, assistant, chaperone, her governess. Forget it.

Why is it that grown children think they have permission to take charge of their parents? They don't even ask permission—and that really hurts—they just take it like they have all the authority in the world, and a duty to use it. She told herself, *Do not make this ugly. It does not need to get ugly— even though it is ugly.*

"Sweetheart, I love you," Ruby said. "But I will let you know when I am in need of a governess."

"Ma…"

"Really, Nina, I'm fine. I love you and miss you and appreciate everything you want to do for me.

"Wait…"

"But this is a time when you have got to let me do for me. I'm safe, I'm happy, and I'm still in charge. I love you, honey."

"Ma…"

"Say I love you back," Ruby said.

"I love you back," said Nina.

"Then leave me the hell alone, daughter! I know you love me, but leave me be!"

Silence.

Suddenly Ruby started laughing uproariously.

"Knock it off, Ma."

"What?"

"Ma, knock it off. You don't even listen to me. This is serious…"

"Hello? I can't hear you."

"Ma?"

"Hello? Nina? We must have a bad connection. The line is crackling…"

Chapter Twelve

"God, I love this stuff!" Maria shouted from the bathroom where she was drying her hair and reading Joni's book, *August Shade.* "'They collapsed in a frenzy of simultaneous explosions…'" Maria was impressed. She'd assumed that Joni was one of those starving authors, barely getting by. After that encounter with Mrs. Hobbs at the 7-11, she realized that her new friend was quite successful. Famous, even.

Joni scrunched her face in embarrassment when hearing her words read aloud. If she were honest, which she was, she had to admit she had no business writing such things. Think about it. Joni Herrschwitz, Diva of Desire? This was one of America's premier romance writers?

She'd had eight lovers in her life, but none of them—get that, *none* of them—gave her the "blood-rushing climax" that she wrote about, and in fact, she often fell way short of the "shattering release" that she'd so vividly described. Still, Joni remained in wait for a man's kiss to "capture her mouth with hungry urgency." Oh yes, she knew the lingo, she knew what sold, and she knew what she *wanted* from romance, but she did not know how to manifest it anywhere besides the pages of her predictable, formulaic, and hugely successful romance titles.

And why was that?

Too fat, she thought.

Too frumpy.

Too old.

Too boring.

Too unlucky.

Too whatever.

Her mind drifted. *The Power of Negative Thinking.* She should write that book. Yes, that would be the one she would know something about. How negative thinking made the Diva of Desire utterly undesirable.

"How'd you get into this?" Maria asked.

The question interrupted Joni's pessimistic self-talk tirade and took her back a moment to the serendipitous beginning of her career as an author. You don't go to college to become a romance writer because it's not like you can major in pap (at least not outright). But pap sells, and Joni was first introduced to the genre when working in the public relations office at New York University while a journalism student. One of the career employees there, Cheryl Ross, passed out copies of a book she'd written. Days later, she announced she was changing her name to Cassandra Kinnings and leaving her job to become a full-time romance novelist.

Cheryl's book was vapid and silly and Joni actually turned red-faced reading the sex parts because she couldn't help imagining frumpy, middle-aged Cheryl (er, Cassandra) sitting at her keyboard writing (or, God forbid, *doing*) such things. Yuck.

But two years later, Joni read in the *New York Post* that Cassandra Kinnings signed a $500,000, four-book deal and that gave Joni Herrschwitz an instant incentive to invoke the romance-writing formula Cheryl had laid out for her. It was all very, very simple. The book had to be set in an alluring and exotic locale. Joni'd need to build the plot around a loveable heroine, a manly hero, a situation that pushed the two of them together, then some horrible obstacle that they would have to overcome. Then, there would emerge some deep, dark situation that fools the reader into thinking the couple will not surmount the obstacle and that they will never make it together. Finally, she'd throw in a few more complications that they deal with and—poof!—love would conquer all and the whole thing would wrap up nicely with a happy ending where the handsome hero and beautiful heroine do, in fact, live happily ever after.

With such a roadmap, the writing and plotting challenge didn't seem so hard and she quickly learned that she could make a hearty living by trying to feed a practically insatiable romance novel market that didn't demand much in terms of quality. More than half the paperback books sold in the U.S. are romance novels, so Joni knew that once she was "in" the club, she was "in" for life.

She studied the lingo and before she knew it, it seemed obvious and natural to phrase a love scene in those nearly comedic terms. When describing her hero's body, she'd use phrases like "muscled chest," "lean muscular legs," "muscled flesh," "ripple of hard muscle" or "steely contours."

For the hero's penis, well, she could say "aching bulge," "erect manhood," "hot, bulging shaft," "stirring manhood," "torrid extension," "turgid shaft," and her own favorite—"virile masculinity."

Once she had her list of euphemisms and a generic plot blueprint (most writers would *never* cop to having such a formula, but c'mon), she was in business. Joni's first book, *Splendor's Fury*, took three months to write and brought her a $20,000 advance. She had agonized over trying to find the right words, plot twists, and new approaches, but her editor told her bluntly, "Don't try so hard next time. This isn't Tolstoy." The trick was quantity over quality, more books rather than fewer, so long as Joni could draw the reader in with some hot, pulsating verbiage. *The Devil's Secret* took just three weeks to write and brought in a $50,000 advance. Almost twenty years later, Joni's books commanded $150,000 advances—each— plus substantial royalties. She wrote three a year, so she wouldn't get too burned out or over-exposed.

"What I don't get," said Maria bluntly, "is why you and the other romance writers have to use all those silly 'throbbing manhood' expressions. Why can't you call a penis a dick or a prick?"

Ruby covered her eyes and shook her head.

"Because it isn't romantic to say, 'Ginger yanked his dick,' but it is romantic to say, 'Alicia slowly massaged Robert's swollen masculinity, and he had to restrain his wild, native response as he writhed from her burning touch. He exploded within her from bliss…"

"Oh, good God," Maria said.

"Mmmm hmmm," said Joni. "It's a good living."

"You make a lot doing that?" Ruby asked.

"Oh yeah."

"I should write one of those," Ruby said. "But I wouldn't know what to say about those sex scenes. Those days are long behind me."

"Don't give up, Ruby," Maria said. "You've still got time to get jiggy."

Joni may not have respected her genre, but she did respect the readers who faithfully bought her books and e-mailed her so many kind words. If she were going to do the road trip, she'd have to do a few book signings along the way, both to promote her work and reconnect with her fans. Actually, she loved the signings, unlike some authors who did anything short of feigning death to get out of them.

Ruby agreed to the deal with no objections, and Joni contacted her publicist to see what she could whip up on no notice at all. And what she whipped up wasn't bad. A signing at an independent bookstore in Richmond, Virginia, two advance calls in to radio shows and late-morning and noontime television interviews.

She stopped to buy a snappy plus-sized suit at Macy's, then showed up at the first television station at 11:15 a.m. with her entourage waiting in the taxi. The last thing Ruby needed to be doing was traipsing into some television newsroom while Steve Rosenthal summoned the country to find her.

"You're so famous and I never knew!" Ruby gushed as Joni left the cab.

Joni rolled her eyes. "I am sooooo famous," she mocked. "I'll be back in twenty minutes."

As usual, the interviewer had not read the book, press kit, or bio, so Joni guided the woman through the interview.

"Yes, it's my thirty-ninth book…Oh I love hearing from my fans. That is the greatest compliment any author can get…No, this wasn't what I planned for my career, but let me tell you that it is extremely fun and I know how lucky I am to be able to make a living this way…"

"Is it hard to write the steamy scenes?"

"No," said Joni. "Those are the fun parts."

Then the interviewer, a young thirties Barbie doll, dropped the question that made Joni die every single time. It was like the woman'd been consulting directly with Mrs. Hobbs.

"So, what about romance in your own life? Do you write from experience? Are you married?"

What was she supposed to say? That the longest relationship she'd ever had was two years, that she'd only slept with eight men and the sex was never all that great?

"I have to get the material for my books somewhere," Joni said coyly.

This time, Barbie the interviewer wouldn't drop it.

"Where? Who is he? Who's the hero? What kind of heroine are you? Tell us your *reeeeeeeeeal* romance story."

"Well, I am forced to keep that private," Joni said, her voice cracking a little as she shifted uncomfortably in her seat. "I'd never get any romance if I went on television and kissed and told."

As if she had any romance otherwise. Thank goodness Barbie finally ran out of time for more questions.

"Please come back and visit us again," she said.

Yeah, right, Joni thought as she unhooked the microphone from her suit lapel. Four seconds later, Barbie was on to her next story— about a Gerber baby food taste test that the company sponsored at the mall. Gotta love that daytime news programming.

Joni's interview at the next station went just about the same as the first, except the interviewer was a man who responded to Joni's vagaries about her love life by saying, "Well, if you are looking for a new stud to model your next epic on, we should have lunch after the show."

"I'll keep you in mind, Matthew." He nodded as though she were serious, which she wasn't.

"I can see my chest exposed on the cover," he said.

"Oh yeah," Joni said. "You really strike me as the next Fabio, right?"

After the interview, she unplugged her microphone and he slid her his business card.

"I'm serious," he said. "I'd like to take you out. I think you're fascinating."

She looked him over for a second time. Pancake make-up covered his face, but she couldn't ridicule a TV guy for that because he was just trying to do right for himself under the lights. Nor could she judge his stiff coiffed hair because she'd had days when she'd used half a can of Aqua Net too. The guy was at least six feet tall and, overall, not bad looking. An eight on a scale of one to ten. Joni couldn't believe she judged him in such a superficial way.

What the hell.

"Come to my signing," she said. "We'll go out afterwards."

Seventy people greeted Joni at the doors of Henderson's Book Drop when she arrived, and she hugged many. Her dependable fans always filled the stores for her, something she never took for granted because author friends in other genres didn't get that kind of devotion. Hardly. They were lucky to get a dozen people. Joni always got a full house of loyal devotees who didn't care how cornball or trite or predictable her plots actually were. She entertained them and they simply adored her. She exuded confidence and warmth and personality, so sure of herself. She wondered what they would think if they ever encountered the real Joni, the one who woke up every morning telling herself she was too fat and boring and undesirable. Such contradiction.

Ruby and Maria were impressed, watching Joni finesse the crowd. Riding in the taxi cab, Joni was the quiet one, the one who stayed more to the outside. In her element, she had star quality.

It was that attitude of Joni's that brought out the strangest twinge of—what was it, resentment?— in Maria because it reminded her of how cheap Joni had been regarding her "reward" at the casino. Maria had done all the work, got Joni all that cash, and Joni gave Maria just five hundred bucks. It was stingy.

But there was Joni, author superstar.

"Do you remember me? I was at your talk in New Jersey," one woman said.

Joni hugged her as though they were old friends, but she had no clue who the woman was. Joni loved the people who so loyally loved her every word, and she made sure every one of them had their moment with her. She looked around and saw that Matthew was one of two men who attended the signing.

She stood in front of the group and read from her latest book, *Summer Sky.*

"'Katherine arrived at the beach house a day before Édouard, wondering when he would arrive from Antibes and if he would dare to try to make love. Forgiveness wouldn't come easy—for either of them—but Katherine willed herself to keep an open mind...'"

As usual, Joni received a standing ovation after she finished the public reading. As usual, she wondered why. Why? It wasn't literature. It was crap! Joni knew that her writing was disposable and perishable. It was schlock. Her contribution to humanity was purely literary garbage and it did nothing to contribute to a more intelligent society. On the other hand, she did give her fans an escape from their problems, and that had to count for something. Maybe she didn't have hope for her own love life, but what she wrote gave them hope for theirs.

Book signing Q&A sessions always had four ritual questions:

"Where do you get your characters?"

"Are your stories based on real life?"

"How long does it take for you to write your books?"

"Are you married, honey?"

Why did they always—*always*—want to know about her? Like a woman wasn't valid if she didn't have some man's ring on her finger to mark her among the wanted. Her fans assumed there was something exotic, glamorous, and bigger than life about anyone who wrote such popular romantic stories and Joni wondered how they would react if she were honest for once and said, "Well, I just got dumped. I always am the one who gets dumped; in fact, I have never once had a relationship where I was the first to dump the other person. I have never had a relationship that lasted more than two years. I've been cheated on by just about every man I've ever loved. No, I no longer believe in love. I am a middle-aged frump who is in the midst of an identity crisis and I know my time has passed, if it ever existed at all…"

When had she gotten so dark and cynical? She'd sworn she wouldn't become a bitter old hag, but all her self-talks lately sure sounded like it. What she said out loud to her fans was completely different.

"I try not to go into the details of my own life so I can protect my privacy," she said. "My life is not as exciting as an episode of *Sex and the City*, but it has its moments."

As always, they bought it, and nodded appreciatively like she'd just shared an inside confidence.

Afterwards, Joni signed for her fans. Most of them bought the more expensive hardcover editions of her books because they wanted them as keepsakes or collector's items. Many bought four or more books—for themselves and their friends. She graciously posed for at least fifty photos with the pack of her fan paparazzi, although she never could understand why any of them would want a picture with her. Over the years, Joni had sold millions and millions of books but she never felt deserving of any special attention. That's why, when people lined up for her autograph, she made sure she wrote something personal for every one of them—to heck with writer's cramp.

TV anchor Matthew Cox, the last autograph seeker, looked at Joni with absolute fascination in his eyes, but she thought he looked a little goofy—especially since she'd doubted he would even show, and assumed if he did it would be just for giggles. But he handed her a long-stemmed rose, so he must have been serious about something.

"I'm very impressed," he said. "You really turn out a crowd and these people sure do love you."

"Well, I don't take them for granted for a single minute."

"You ready to see the best of Richmond?"

And that was that. Joni had a D.A.T.E. and Ruby and Maria ribbed each other about the whole thing, just like junior high school kids.

"Should we follow them?" Ruby asked.

Maria shook her head no and rolled her eyes at Ruby. "You are such a snoop."

Matthew gave Joni a moonlight tour of the azalea gardens at Bryan Park, looking especially pleased with himself for choosing it on a night when the orchestra's string quartet practiced for an upcoming outdoor concert.

"This looks like a scene for one of my books," Joni said.

"I'm angling for a part in the movie." He smiled, then pulled him to her and gave her a short, sweet kiss. "I needed to just go ahead and kiss you so I could get the awkward part behind me."

He was either a scarily smooth operator, or absolutely besotted with Joni. Being that she could not imagine anyone being captivated by her, Joni's suspicions automatically ratcheted up to high alert. She kissed him back, telling herself it was only to get some new material to write about. But the kiss was nice. Different. Wetter than most, not real forceful—but reeeeal sexy.

"Let's go to dinner," she said, killing the mood abruptly. She'd gone back to her dark place, where she realized she shouldn't even be hopeful about Matthew or anyone else.

Beauregard's Thai Room seemed far more metropolitan than one would expect from a city like Richmond, but it was exotic, exquisite, serene, and, best of all, the food was the *best*. Matthew requested an outside table and the night air was utterly intoxicating.

"You're amazing," he told Joni. "I'm so impressed."

She checked her watch.

"You in a hurry?" he asked.

She shrugged.

"Hmmm," he said. "Uhhh, you want to tell me a little more about yourself?"

"Why don't you tell me a little more about yourself," she said. She did not ask a single specific question.

"Hoookay. Uhhh, my father was in the Army, we spent my first five years living in Germany, then moved from place to place in this country until I was twelve…"

She actually checked her watch again, deliberately showing her agitation. Asshole. She could tell. She would not look him in the eyes. It bugged her, because she could sense he was trying to lure her into bed for a one-nighter, knowing full well she'd be gone in the morning. She was so sick of men sucking her in and spitting her out.

"…And when I was in college, I realized that I didn't have that drive to be a newspaper person. I liked the broadcast side of things better, so that's the path I chose…"

God, he wasn't going to shut up about himself now. She nodded politely, and he nodded back, but she could tell he fully understood he was conversing with himself.

"Look, you don't have to sit here with me anymore."

"What?" She sounded unconvincingly innocent.

"Really, if you aren't having a good time, we can just call it a night. But I'd like to know…I'd really like to know…what the hell happened to make you go so cold on me?"

Well, that was a loaded question. What the hell happened to Joni Herrschwitz to make her go so cold? Not just for him, but for all men? That's it. She was A Bitter Woman. An Angry, Bitter Middle-Aged Woman.

"I was really attracted to you," he said. "And I've never been treated so rudely on a date."

She checked her watch again, hoping he wouldn't see her tearing up.

"Sorry," she said. It was all she could manage.

"Did you kiss?" asked Ruby the second Joni opened the door to their motel room.

Joni hesitated, considered lying to them because she could tell them anything and they'd never know. Did it matter what happened? It was an off night. Big deal. Let it go.

Finally she told them. Whatever.

"Let's just say that he was the best date I've ever had and I was a total, unlikable, cold bitch. He was sweet and romantic and I was hostile and closed and I treated him like he was unworthy of my time." Joni flipped on the television in search of a change of subject.

They looked at her blank faced, but Joni could see plenty in their stares.

"You're kidding, right?" Maria asked.

"Believe me, I'm already tired of talking about it," Joni said. "I'm not feeling especially good about myself right now."

Ruby tried to hug Joni, but Joni stiffened and stepped out of it.

"I have to say that this side of you is not your most attractive side," Ruby said.

"Well, no kidding," Joni snapped back.

"So you weren't at your best tonight. We all have off nights."

Joni tried hard not to go to that dark place where she recounted every time she lost at love but, that list! Daniel, Warren, Al, Tyler, Nick, Ted, Bob, Doug. That put her at oh for eight. Her love life had always been *one* indignity followed by *another* humiliation:

Daniel. Cheapskate. Made her go dutch when dining with *his* parents.

Warren. Snob. Hamptons, Yale, Daddy runs KellerCo, can you spell trust fund?

Al. A very dumb man who thought he was smarter than she. A cheater.

Tyler. Finally told her he was gay. Which was too bad. He was the best looking and best acting of the bunch.

Nick. Mama's boy. Called every night before sleepytime.

Ted. Misogynist. Was there a name he *didn't* call Joni? And why did she let him? Another cheater.

Bob. Commitmentphobe. Fifty-five and never even got close. Cheater.

Doug. Oh yes, he was the reason for the current lifewreck, remember? Joni's relationships lasted an average of five months, with Doug—at twenty-six months—being the longest. Joni loved

Doug because he came to her just in time. A couple of months more and Joni would have officially given up on any hope of long-term love or marriage. She'd read that magazine story that said women who were still single by forty had a greater chance of being killed by terrorists than marrying. When she read the *Newsweek* article she was in her thirties, and had thought it funny. But once she hit forty, she felt certain it was fait accompli. Doug was her great last hope.

They didn't marry, but they talked about it plenty, mostly when Let's-Make-A-Baby-Doug brought it up. On Valentine's Day, he dropped to his knees and presented Joni with a one-carat diamond solitaire and told her he would marry her in Central Park—no, at the Eiffel Tower—no, at the Taj Mahal. The where kept changing, the when never got beyond "soon." Looking back on it, she realized the why was never really there.

So it flamed out with him and she knew it would flame out with anyone else she'd dare trust.

She tried to think positive. She'd seen exotic parts of the world with these men, had some memorable moments of passion (although nothing worth writing about), and learned a little something every time a relationship began or ended. But after Doug left, she wondered: "It all adds up to *this*?"

It hadn't been worth the bother.

So it was only natural that Joni would face an angry, bitter, middle-aged woman in the mirror, and she thought about that as she began her nightly skin care ritual with Ruby and Maria waiting for her mood to change. She couldn't wish or pray or order all her resentment and disappointment away—she'd tried, but she just couldn't. The embarrassment of so much rejection—of every single rejection—was always with her, nagging her that she did not have what she needed in order to be loved and that she attracted men who would betray her almost every time. Was it their fault that *she* made bad choices?

She thought about Matt and what a lousy date she'd been, and she considered writing a note of apology but then realized there wasn't much she could say. "Sorry I dumped on you. I've become a sorry, bitter bitch. You are far better off without me…" or, "Please understand. It was nothing personal. I am now this way with every man I date."

She looked at herself in the mirror again, the angry, bitter, middle-aged woman, and she realized she would be a lot less ugly if she'd just let that anger go.

If only she knew what to do with it.

Chapter Thirteen

"Look at that!" Ruby pointed to a truck stop with a Mack Truck hoisted on top of its billboard. "Let's stop here!"

And it was a damned good thing they did, because the music department of this very stale-smelling store sold a collection of CDs that made for beeeeautiful music for their road trip. They got everything from "40 Miles of Bad Road" to "How Fast Them Trucks Can Go" to "Looking at the World Thru a Windshield" to "Truck Stop Cutie." Oh, and of course, Willy Nelson's "On the Road Again," which they sang every morning, once Maria had her own, personal pot of coffee and became a human being again. Ruby, Maria, and Joni did everything families do in the car on road trips. They competed to see who could spot license plates from all fifty states first. They played "Roadside Bingo." They played alphabet games and color games. Joni never won at anything except trivia games because she knew things like every cast member's name from *Petticoat Junction* and the name of the surgeon who implanted the first artificial heart.

"Who cares about that crap?" Maria said every time, because she didn't know any trivia and, being the youngest of the three, had missed all those things anyway so she didn't care. "Why fill your brain with that when you can Google anything you will ever want to know?"

"Jealous, jealous, jealous," Joni laughed. "It is better to possess a wealth of knowledge than an empty brain."

The women immersed themselves in other important matters too, like shopping for tacky trinkets and curios at convenience and souvenir stores. Ruby snapped up things like Band-Aids that look like bacon strips, a ceramic smoking baby, a Jesus action figure, and a set of sixteen deluxe finger monsters. Maria pounced on a box of rubber affirmation bracelets that proclaimed things like "DESPAIR" and "APATHY" instead of uplifting or cliché statements like "LIVE STRONG." She also amassed a collection of lighters that included a slot machine, cell phone, and rocket ship. Joni grabbed a fez-wearing monkey bobble head and Pez dispensers depicting Joe Cool, Popeye, and Tom and Jerry. Simply amazing how a trunk can fill itself up on a road trip.

They treasured their sacred copies of *The National Enquirer* or *The Globe* or the *World Weekly News*, but Ruby did all the out loud reading because reading in a moving taxi made Joni carsick and since Maria was driving it was best that she not try. Ruby kept them laughing as she read articles headlined, "STAREOIDS! Growth Hormones Cause Bodybuilder's Eyes to Pop Out of His Head!" or, "HUMANS TURNING BACK INTO APES! Sports Fanatics & Politicians Most Susceptible!"

In Virginia, Ruby bought a fake instant lottery ticket and gave it to Maria as a gift. Maria scratched it off and leapt at least four feet in the air when she thought she'd won $100,000. Oooooooooh was she ticked off when she read the fine print that announced it was all a joke, and she came right out and called Ruby a loser.

As they drove in the mornings, the radio always tuned in on whatever radio affiliate blasted Steve Rosenthal to the world. Just about every morning, he'd try goading Ruby to call in by yelling, *"Calling Ruby, calling Ruby, come in Ruby, where are you?"* The more desperate he sounded, the less inclined Ruby felt to stop and make a call, but she clearly enjoyed sparring with him, so she usually obliged.

They tried not to drive more than four hours in a day. Get up early, get Maria and Joni their coffee, get some chow, hit the road, find a Days Inn, Super 8, or Motel 6, and settle in before heading out for whichever bizarre local attraction they'd been heading to.

Food? That was a problem. The best of intentions cannot carry any dieter on a road trip. You're not going to select fat-free yogurt when you can have Cheetos. It does not happen. You try getting in a car and driving for days and then see if you choose the banana at the convenience store when the alternative is a big, fat, salty hunk of beef jerky. You'll choose the beef jerky. If you're normal.

Or if you are chubby, chunky, dumpy, or frumpy, all of which Joni felt she was. She'd get pretzels or pork rinds, corn dogs or nachos. Dieting, schmieting. She felt guilty and she felt bloated, but one morning, as she walked past the full-length door mirror in the Comfort Inn, she caught a glimpse of herself. She stopped, turned, and took a good look. She sighed and groaned in the same breath.

"What is wrong with you?" Ruby asked.

"I'm fat. I hate looking in that mirror and every other mirror. I hate that fat woman who looks back at me."

"I don't see a fat woman when I look at you."

Joni rolled her eyes.

"You beat yourself up for how your body looks instead of embracing your body for how it works. You take everything for granted. Your body—*all* of your *beautiful* body—works. You can walk and run and swim and dance. You can climb steps and get down on your knees. Your health is perfect. Do you think that is going to last forever? It's not."

Joni felt a little ridiculous. She did need to lose some serious weight, but her body did work. She wondered how she would ever shut off that inner voice that told her she was fat all day long, 365 days a year, and then she decided to start small. What if she stopped putting herself down and just accepted—and dare she try *love*—herself "as is" until the trip was over? She should be able to do that. She should shut that voice off for a little while. Just make a conscious decision to be grateful she had a body that worked. The fact that it worked made it beautiful.

As everyone knows, Ruby's own weight and food issues caused her a great deal of consternation, but only because she was heading to Weeki Wachee. She honored her Slim-Fast vow, but did consume a DQ Blizzard a day, as well as a little KFC and other junk that no self-respecting mermaid would eat the week before a performance.

Did it really matter?

She hadn't been this happy in twenty years. Twenty-five. And even if she wasn't the slim mermaid she'd always been, she could still swim with grace.

But she needed some wardrobe work. They all did, because none of them had packed for their extended expedition.

"I'm sick of these clothes and I am sick of stinking," Maria proclaimed.

"Okay then, today we shop," said Ruby.

They were the first people in the doors of Ross Dress for Less, and they went through that store on a spending spree that looked like one of those 1970s game shows where they send people into a grocery store and see who can spend the most, the fastest. They went, shopped, conquered, and loaded up with brand new underwear, bras, shorts, socks, slacks, jeans, sandals, and other essentials they figured they would need for ten more days of travel. Maria had a knack for dressing Joni with the right tops and the right bottoms to slim her appearance.

Then they each bought wheeled suitcases in which to keep their stuff. At checkout, Maria spent $370, Joni, $427, and Ruby $200.

"Don't make any assumptions about who got the best wardrobe by who spent the most," Ruby lectured on the way back to the car. "I won. You know I did."

Of course she did. Dresses, slacks, coordinated outfits, jewelry, a new purse, sunglasses—the woman knew style and knew how to buy.

After the shopping bonanza, Joni went into their motel room's bathroom and did a little accounting with the money she kept hidden in her purse in the cab's trunk. She'd left the house with $50 and left Atlantic City with $26,250 after-tax dollars, she gave Maria that $500 finder's fee for helping her in the casino, so she should have had $25,373 after shopping.

"Twenty-four thousand, seven hundred and seventy-two…"

Joni felt her stomach drop. There was only one bill left, and it was a one-dollar bill, not a six-hundred-dollar bill. At twenty-four thousand, six hundred and seventy-three, she was exactly six hundred dollars short.

She counted again, and a third time, just to be sure.

She knew she didn't spend it, she knew she didn't lose it, she knew no one had mugged her, and she now knew she was missing six hundred dollars. Joni was not the type to shrug off the loss of six hundred dollars or six. Money meant a lot to her because she'd grown up with so little.

The thief had to be one of two people.

Ruby or Maria.

Obviously, it wasn't Ruby.

"That bitch," she said to herself. She knew it was Maria. That bitch.

Joni knew she was stupid for riding around with that kind of cash in her purse—even before the theft. How many Bank of Americas did they drive past? At least a couple of hundred, but she didn't want to hand an out-of-state bank branch a bunch of cash because the idea made her feel like she would be depositing her winnings into a black hole. She thought about it many times. She could give them the money and then never see it again. She even thought about depositing half of it, just so she could at least preserve the other half. But, she never got around to doing it, and now she paid for her poor judgment. She could have lost everything. Losing just $600 was probably a blessing.

Joni knew she wouldn't have had any of those gambling winnings without Maria. Joni knew she *should* have given Maria a little more than $500 from her proceeds without Maria having to ask for it (much less steal it), but Joni figured that Maria was a cab driver and a $500 tip was one hell of a big bonus. Joni liked having all of her "found money." She would never begrudge Maria's reward, but for Maria to reach in Joni's purse and *take* it from her? Would she do that? Why? Weren't they friends? Joni asked herself those questions dozens of times. Maybe Maria resented that Joni hadn't automatically split the winnings with her. Or she thought Joni had money because of her success as an author. Should she have split it fifty-fifty? Maybe. But, then again, why should she split it in half with someone who was ultimately a thief? Five hundred dollars was plenty. And now Maria proved she didn't even deserve that.

Joni'd been having such a good time too, but she couldn't get the theft out of her mind because it only reinforced her belief that just about everybody in the world operates with a secret agenda and will betray you the minute it is to his or her benefit. So she should not be surprised about Maria.

Bitch. Never trust a New York cab driver.

Joni thought about Maria, trying to figure her out, trying to see through her. That cab driver sure acted chummy, so Joni and Ruby both were too trusting. They thought she was a friend, but what did they really know about her? She drove a cab and carried a gun. That was it.

Joni started obsessing about it, and the issue wasn't the money— it was the betrayal. She counted the money again. Still missing. Maybe Maria figured she needed that cash more than Joni, which was true, but this was America and that was not how things should work. You don't just *take* someone's money because you need it more. You either borrow some or make your own money. Joni kept fixating on how Maria must have assumed she deserved something for helping her win it in the first place, and how Maria was probably seething because Joni didn't come through.

Joni wondered, why six hundred dollars? Why hadn't Maria taken more or less or some uneven amount? Why had she taken it so early in the trip? Maybe she'd swiped it before she knew they'd be gone so long. And where had she put it? Well, Maria spent about $350 that day, and Joni had to wonder where she got the cash. Ruby hadn't paid her or advanced her anything.

Ruby and Maria were napping when Joni rejoined them in the room. She fantasized about waking them, handcuffing Maria, and making a spectacular citizen's arrest. But she didn't.

She just didn't. Joni said nothing. She pretended nothing was wrong. She sure kept watch over Maria, but did she have the guts to say, "Pardon me, but did you happen to steal six hundred bucks out of my purse?"

No.

Unassertive Joni Herrschwitz would much prefer seething in silence, letting the resentment build inside until it had no more room and exploded outward.

Maria felt she was being watched. But by now, she was used to that feeling.

Chapter Fourteen

You don't stop playing because you get old, you get old because you stop playing.

That's what senior mermaids say.

But tell that to your arthritic joints and the joints will just laugh. Ruby knew the underwater ballet moves would come back to her—they had to. She was on deadline, and she would not make a fool of herself in front of the fans—or, more importantly, the other mermaids.

"Y'all don't bother me. I'll be in the pool perfecting my art," she joked as she wrapped a towel around her legs so nobody would notice her flab bouncing around on her way to the pool. She committed to a full hour of synchronized swimming practice in the pool of the Super 8.

What you'd expect in a made for television version of this would be:

1.   Old lady gets in water and is completely a mess.

2.   She begins training.

3.   With help from supportive friends, she gets better at it, but her progress is slow—probably way too slow to make it pretty by the time the curtains rise in the underwater theater. At the last minute, her friends find a

way to bring her tired old bones back to life in a massive training session, and all is well in the last second when it's showtime.

However, this was not some senior citizen trying to pick up the clarinet or do a back dive after sixty years. This was a mermaid. Once a mermaid, *always* a mermaid. That's what they say, and it's the truth.

The mermaid jumped in the water, and it felt cool and invigorating and familiar. The mermaid splashed around like a mermaid.

Front layout. Back layout. Easy.

Dolphin. Chin back, back arched, head, shoulders, and back all arched backwards to the extreme as the body propelled itself in a full, graceful circle, all the way, all the way, all the way around until the head came back up straight at the surface. It went well, so well that Ruby did it twice. Ha! Everything was coming right back. Once a mermaid…

Ballet leg. Ruby floated on her back, kept her left leg extended on the surface, then drew her right leg in and up so it was perpendicular to the surface. As she lowered it, she brought her bent knee to her chest, then completely lowered it back to the surface. It was not exactly pretty. But she did it, and there was time to make it better.

Front tuck, front pike—these were somersaults—back tuck, back pike. Not ready for prime time, but look at Ruby go! She may have been rusty, but her bones knew the drill and in that water, she might not have been eighteen years old, but she sure as hell didn't feel seventy-eight.

She'd save the "oyster," the "tub," the "log roll," the "porpoise," the "swordfish," and all the others for the next torture installment. But Ruby had to smile. And laugh. Girl's still got it, she thought.

When she climbed out of the pool, she saw Maria heading toward her. Looking to show off a little, Ruby spun back around so she could dive back in. Unfortunately, Ruby couldn't spin like she used to. The turn shifted her weight too quickly and she fell hard on the cement.

"RUBY!" Maria yelled as Ruby first grabbed for her ankle, then tried to roll onto her knees so she could push herself up.

"Don't move, Ruby!" Maria yelled again.

"Aw, crap!" shouted Ruby. Getting old can really suck. Turn around too fast and your butt lands on the cement, your ankle swells, and your friends start screaming about how they're going to get you to the damned hospital. Maria didn't understand that things like this happen to seniors, and that she needn't react until it was time to react. Having watched at least six friends lose their mobility and independence because of broken hips, Ruby took careful steps and always tried to protect herself.

Ruby slowly tried to bend the ankle. It moved.

"Don't move it!"

"You're not the boss of me!" Ruby yelled back, then moved it again and tried to rotate it in a circle. It hurt, but the ankle moved and rotated, so Ruby figured she should try standing again.

"No, Ruby!"

"I'm seventy-eight, not seven hundred and eighty," Ruby snapped. "Lemme be."

She stood up, wobbled a little, steadied herself, then proclaimed, "No worse for the wear."

"Right," Maria said. "Ruby, sit down."

"No. Watch me." Ruby turned toward the pool—far more carefully than she moved the last time, took three steps, and gracefully jumped in. Ballet leg, front layout, back layout, dolphin. The ankle throbbed as she pushed it through the water—actually, it hurt like hell—but she focused intently on her moves.

Maria clapped from the pool deck, very impressed with the performance but hoping to coax Ruby out of the pool. That just encouraged the contrary Ruby, and she folded her body into the "flamingo" position, pulling one leg to her chest while stretching the other perpendicular to the surface of the water. Ruby thought her maneuver looked sloppy, but Maria clapped once again, so it couldn't have been all that bad. At that point, Joni wandered up to the other side of the pool and clapped as well, even though she only got to see the flamingo.

"Our mermaid took a spill," Maria alerted Joni from across the pool.

"She looks okay now," Joni said, making a supreme effort not to glare at Maria.

"Mmmm hmmm. Makes me wonder how often this stuff happens when nobody's watching," Maria said.

"MYOB!" Ruby shouted.

Ruby carefully lifted herself up the pool ladder and back onto the deck, casually glancing at her foot, now swelled to twice its normal appearance, then trying to walk back to the motel room with a little dignity. She did not turn when Maria once again hollered, "We need to get that ankle looked at by a doctor."

Ruby just rolled her eyes then threw her legs up in a dozen mini-can-can kicks as she sang out, "On the road again, Just can't wait to get on the road again, The life I love is makin' music with my friends, And I can't wait to get on the road again…"

Chapter Fifteen

Forget the sore ankle, Ruby had to go. She jumped from the cab and made an urgent dash for the bathroom the second Maria pulled into the gas line at the Lumberton, North Carolina, Stuckey's. If there were ever any doubts about her ability to function physically, one need just see Ruby Witherspoon when she really had to use the can.

And oooooh, Ruby really had to go. Unfortunately, when she got to the door of the ladies room she saw that it was blocked by a row of fluorescent-orange traffic cones and a sign that announced "RESTROOM CLOSED FOR SERVICING." She peered past the door and saw three plumbers ripping the place apart. Without hesitation, Ruby turned to the men's room, took a breath, opened the door, and covered her eyes.

"Cover up, boys!" she said. "A girl's gotta go when a girl's gotta go!" She made sure she didn't see anything she shouldn't see, but she did notice there were two men at urinals. She raced straight to one of two open stalls and apologized several times saying, "I'm so sorry!" When she finished she flushed, walked to the sink, and announced, "I'm not looking!" then washed her hands with eyes closed. She rushed out, still not believing she'd actually done it. At least she left the seat back up for them when she was done.

She wondered if Walter'd seen her from above, and figured he had.

Maria was shopping inside the store, so the cab was most definitely locked. Stuck in the Stuckey's and hoping the men who'd seen her in the bathroom wouldn't say anything to her, Ruby took two boxes of pecan divinity to the very long line at the register.

"Feel better?" the man in line behind her asked.

How tasteless, Ruby thought. How absolutely rude and insensitive and utterly tasteless. She didn't say a word; she didn't turn around.

"Where ya headed?" he tried again.

She ignored him.

"You need to turn up the volume!" he said.

Huh? Ruby turned and faced a handsome man about her age. "Pardon me?" she asked.

"Your hearing aid," he said, smiling warmly. "It's not working!"

"You're very rude," she snapped, then turned her back to him again. "I have no hearing aid," she muttered. Jerk. Ruby paid the cashier $6.77 for the divinity.

"Used to be free," the man behind her said.

"What?" Ruby said, totally annoyed.

"That candy used to be free with a fill-up. Remember? They'd give you the box of pecan divinity just so you'd stop and your kids would make you spend a fortune on souvenirs and other assorted junk."

The memory did make her smile, but the obnoxious man certainly didn't.

"My name's Milt," he tried again, not oblivious to Ruby's cold shoulders. "I'm on a long trip and I guess I'm a little lonely for the voice of another human being."

She said nothing.

"Lady, you're makin' me feel like an idiot. I'm tryin' here, okay?"

She thawed.

"Sorry," she said. "I guess too many miles in the back seat of a cab are making me a crabby old gal."

"Where ya headed?"

"South."

"South?"

"Florida."

"Oh, me too," said Milt, who on second glance looked far more attractive than most guys his age. "I'm taking my RV down there for three weeks. A week in the Keys, five days on the beach at Fort DeSoto, four days at Ginnie Springs, and the rest of the time at Gulf Islands in Apalachicola."

"Wow," said Ruby. "That's very ambitious."

"Well, I saved all my life so my wife and I could live like this when we finally retired," he said. "I just didn't figure I'd be doing it all by myself."

"I know," Ruby said. "Life is full of those kinds of surprises."

"Again, my name is Milt Flynt. I'm from Skokie, Illinois. How 'bout you?"

"Ruby Witherspoon," she acquiesced. "Of New York City." She shook his hand.

"My pleasure," he said, then kissed her hand. The gesture was cornball, but the well-built guy made Ruby smile.

"Sorry to interrupt." Joni stepped into the conversation. "But Maria's ready to go. You coming?"

"Joni, this is Milt," Ruby said, motioning to him. "Milt is also heading to Florida. He's in a motor home."

Joni nodded a "that's nice" smile.

"Maybe I'll see you all along the way," Milt said.

"Race you to the next Stuckey's?" Ruby laughed.

Joni shook her head like a bemused parent, then headed out to the cab.

The next Stuckey's was only about ninety miles away in Kenly, North Carolina, but Ruby insisted they stop, just in case Milt had taken her seriously.

"Do we have a crush on him?" Joni asked.

"Do *we*? Well, I don't know about you, but I thought he was nice," Ruby said. "For a friend."

"Mmmm hmmm," Maria said. "That's what I have to look forward to in life? Picking up old farts at Stuckey's? There's got to be a country and western song in that somewhere."

"Quiet," Ruby said while re-applying her lipstick and running a comb through her hair. "Besides, he doesn't look like the typical old fart. He's got blue eyes and muscles. He also has hair."

They stopped at the Stuckey's, waited ten minutes, and just when Maria was going to suggest they move on, in came one of those mondo-RVs that barely fits in a single lane on the highway. Behind the wheel sat blue-eyed Milt, obviously as smitten with Ruby as she was with him.

And that is how the caravan began, really. With Milt Flynt and his RV. Stopping at every Stuckey's in North Carolina until late in the day he and Ruby finally decided it best that Milt follow the big yellow taxi wherever it would lead.

Before Ruby sneaked out the next morning, she did two things. First, she took Maria's gun into the bathroom and expertly removed all of the bullets—again, then put it back in Maria's suitcase. She knew how to do that, and how to fire a gun, because her neighbor insisted on teaching her all the gun basics after Walter died, even though she would never keep a gun for herself.

The bullet situation had become a running battle, if not a joke. Ruby would take them out, Maria would reload. Ruby would tell Maria how bad guns were, Maria would tell Ruby to mind her own concerns.

Ruby grabbed a pen and scribbled a quick note to Joni and Maria, telling them she'd be busy until lunchtime, because she was going to practice in the pool and "get the kinks out of my tail" at the Sunshine Kamp, where Milt was staying in his RV.

Milt stood in front of his RV in the motel parking lot, waiting for her. The aroma of breakfast wafted out the door of the camper, making Ruby far more hungry than she'd been. He played Benny Goodman on the CD player, and that made her smile because here was a guy who not only knew the big bands, he also lived through the same things she'd lived through: The War, The Bomb, segregation, world's fairs, the polio crisis, the space race, the introduction of the TV dinner, and Elvis.

A good man. With hair! Indeed. He didn't need a woman twenty or thirty or forty years younger to prove he still had a pulse.

"Hope you like a Western omelet," he said as he drove her a mile away to his campsite, where he'd prepared a picnic table with a classic red checkered tablecloth and paper plates. To set the mood, he burned a Christmas candle, the only one he could find in the camper.

"A Santa candle?"

"More romantic than no candle at all, Ruby."

"Well, you're right about that," she said. "I love it."

She was so glad that Maria wasn't there because Maria would most certainly mock them as Milt hand-fed warm croissants to Ruby by the light of the Santa candle. Anyone would, because the two seniors were acting like high school juniors.

"Ruby, you fascinate me."

She imagined what cynical Maria would have said.

"I'm not so fascinating," she said. "Just a little old bluehair out for the day."

"You're one of a kind, taking such a huge road trip—in a cab. That's kinda fascinating. Or nuts."

"It's nuts. But it made sense to me. My travel buddies are dead, so I hailed a cab and made some new friends. Now I've got two new travel buddies, and they're good ones."

"Three," he corrected.

"Three," she agreed.

Milt reached over to her face and wiped some grape jam off the side of her lips.

She smiled. She couldn't believe she was having such a gooey moment after so many years alone. Flustered, she stood up and said, "Mermaid's got to go to work. Coming?" She walked over to the pool, limping from yesterday's sprain but ignoring the pain and trying to seem feminine and graceful. She confidently sailed into the pool with a swan dive into the deep end.

Milt stood there, charmed. He'd known the woman for a day, but his heart was a goner.

Ruby trained by doing the oyster, porpoise, and swordfish moves and felt much lighter in the water, far more comfortable than before. Still, pool practice is nothing like the challenge of performing at Weeki Wachee where success depends as much on a mermaid's mastery of physics as her physical conditioning. Ruby practiced controlling her buoyancy, even though the real test would be in the spring when she had the actual air hose. At Weeki Wachee, spectators watch the mermaids from an underwater theater sixteen feet below the surface. The mermaids swim in a spring that goes down to forty-five feet. Ruby would once again have to use her breath to become a human elevator, raising and lowering herself so she is right where she is supposed to be in the formation with the other mermaids. It's all a matter of taking a sip of air or letting it out at the right time. To make the elevator go up, the mermaid needs to put air into her lungs. To go down, she needs to let it out. There is no practicing that kind of athletics in a five-foot-deep campground pool, but Ruby was becoming much more confident and adept with the moves she'd be expected to perform. She'd never forgotten them. As far as the buoyancy techniques, she figured they had to be like riding a bicycle, right? They would all come back. Especially with a little practice, once she got to the spring.

Milt rested poolside as he watched and drank a Coke. He stared at her like a fascinated puppy. Finally, he dove in to join her, and raised and lowered his legs with her as though he were some sort of merman. She did a dolphin, he did a dolphin. She did a pike, he did a pike. Hers were professional and graceful, his were klutzy and endearing.

"What the hell do you think you're doing?" Ruby finally inquired as she treaded water in the far end.

"Training," he said simply, then swam to her and gave her a hug. It was the first time their bodies touched. In fact, it was the first time she'd felt a man's skin against her body since Walter died. It felt soft, and warm. Electric.

Erotic.

What the hell was happening? She swam to the shallow end and he followed her.

He kissed Ruby's cheek, then kissed the side of her lips. She kissed him back—on the cheek. Milt held her face in his hands, then kissed her lips and held the kiss there for a long moment.

She thought about saying something stupid to break the intensity, and, as if sensing as much he kissed her again. She kissed him again. They kissed each other again and she realized how very much she liked kissing him.

"You make me twenty years old again," he said. "I'm melting inside."

"That sounds like a bad line some old person would say in some dumb movie," Ruby said, then kissed him because she didn't want him to think she was being a bitch. The difficulty of late-in-life romance for Ruby was that she felt clumsy at romance and had grown too cynical to fall into a cliché "senior citizen finds love" tale that could run on the seniors page in the local paper. But this *was* late in life, which made everything a little more special. Who'd have thought seventy-eight-year-old Ruby Witherspoon still had another romance left in her?

And think of it. Here was an older gentleman—someone who remembered Roosevelt and the Sputnik and *Truth or Consequences*—and he was not only open to dating a woman his own age, *he was turned on by her.*

Okay, that was a big deal in itself. But most amazing of all: Ruby was turned on by *him*.

Chapter Sixteen

The missing money had to be in one of two places: on Maria or in her cab. It wasn't in her jeans—Joni checked those pockets at night when Maria was sleeping, not knowing that Maria watched her the whole time. The next morning, Joni was bent on scouring that cab for her money.

"Hey, lemme have the keys to the cab. I left my hairspray in there," Joni said.

"I'll go with you," Maria said, sounding helpful.

"No need," Joni said.

"No bother," Maria responded, pulling the keys from her pocket and jumping up to be of service.

Right, Joni thought. Just come on down and keep an eye on ol' Joni so I can't find the cash you swiped. Mmmm hmmm. The cash was in the cab—Joni could feel it, and all she needed was a few minutes of alone time to get her hands on it.

They walked down the motel corridor and Joni knew there was no hairspray to be searching for in the cab. She could pretend to start looking, then find the money and say to Maria, "A-ha! What are you doing with my money in your hubcaps!" But then Joni started thinking about Maria being armed and it didn't seem like the best plan in the world. Actually, it sounded a little stupid.

"Y'know what?" Joni said. "I think I left that hairspray up in my suitcase."

Maria just shrugged and turned around.

Joni kept her passive aggression in check and did everything possible to forget the missing six hundred dollars.

Worry about it later, she told herself. No big deal. Don't spoil the trip.

But, oh, it ate at her. Why, with all that money missing, why didn't she confront the obvious thief? Call the cops? Do *something?* She could have at least told Ruby, but Ruby was busy with Milt, and Joni didn't want to drag her in and ruin any part of her trip.

Two days passed, and Joni tried hard to put it out of her mind.

It ate at her as she tried to search for clues about this Maria woman, who Joni realized she knew absolutely nothing about, save the fact that Maria drove a cab and stole. Maria didn't talk about friends or family, or where she was raised or how. She never said whether she had a boyfriend, husband, girlfriend, or children. Whether she'd graduated high school or had a PhD. How did she wind up in that cab? Did she have any friends on this earth?

Joni didn't say a word about the missing money, because Joni had a big issue with speaking up. When it came to a professional matter, she did what she had to do. When it came to something personal—especially if it involved personal confrontation—she was a complete marshmallow. As always, she kept waiting for the right moment to say something, and because that never seemed to happen, her anxiety mounted.

The way Maria kept ingratiating herself to Ruby annoyed the hell out of Joni. "Ruby, I'll get your things," Maria would say, and Joni would think, "I just bet you will." Maria would say, "You look hot. Let me get you something to drink," and Joni would think, "Yeah, ass kisser." Maria would say, "Ruby, you need some rest," and Joni would think, "Yeah, so you can swipe *her* ATM card and start making the rounds to make withdrawals." Almost every kind gesture by Maria caused Joni to eye her with even more suspicion.

Each day, Joni counted again, as though the money would have been put back by the thief.

For two days, nothing. But on the third day, another $700 was missing.

That made $1,300.

Not chump change. Thirteen. Hundred. Dollars. Total.

Joni's stash had now dwindled to $24,073. If she could just wait another coupla days, maybe the whole wad would be gone.

This time it was her own damned fault. Joni felt like the biggest schmuck on earth. Why, with $600 already missing, hadn't she deposited her money somewhere? Why had she kept it in exactly the same place in the same purse, exactly where it was the first time money was stolen? Was she fool enough to wait for Maria to just put the stolen cash back?

"Gosh, I'm missing some money," she finally said after Maria came back from dropping Ruby off at Milt's.

"Really? How much?" Like she didn't know. "I wonder where it is."

Way too cavalier, Joni thought.

"How much?"

You tell me, Joni thought. "Never mind," was all she said.

She knew better than to try direct confrontation in a situation like that, and worried she'd given Maria time to come up with a good lie. Joni couldn't stand to even look at her.

"What do you want to do about lunch?" Maria asked.

"I don't care," Joni said.

Later, Ruby, noticing the tension between Joni and Maria, finally cornered Joni at a bathroom break at McDonald's.

"You don't seem too happy with Maria," she said.

Joni considered (again, for the eighty-seventh time) telling Ruby about the missing money, but she couldn't do it. It would spoil Ruby's absolute bliss over the road trip, and Ruby would probably do something stupid and blab right back to Maria. It didn't seem as pressing as it would have been had the stolen money been "real" money that Joni had taken from her bank account. This was "found" money from the casino.

"Oh, I'm just a little grumpy today," Joni said. "Maria's fine." But she was thinking, *Ruby, if you only knew.*

Chapter Seventeen

Smells like piss.

Of all the indignities facing the residents of the Sunrise Center, none could be more overt than the heavy odor of urine that overwhelms visitors the second they enter the nursing home. After Maria and Joni dropped her off at the Wilmington, North Carolina, nursing home, Ruby walked through those doors, smelled the odor, and her heart palpitated, her chest tightened, and she felt so dizzy she braced herself against the wall so she wouldn't fall. She'd felt this anxiety only once before—at Walter's funeral.

She looked inside the Sunrise Center with great trepidation because she feared she was staring into her future. Ruby took inventory of every wheelchair and walker, every smell, and every sound. The people there seemed so willing to submit to the humiliation of aging as they moved so slowly down the carpeted institutional hallways of their "home." What was "home" about it? The photos the residents were allowed to put on the bulletin board in their rooms? The warm colored paint and the cozy little lounges for family visits that usually went unused because so few families actually visited? The televisions set at volumes deafening to people still functioning in the real world? It wasn't a home, it was a hospital—without the staff needed to change diapers and feed the residents at mealtime. A place where you wait to die and die as you wait. Where you can ring your buzzer a hundred times but the overworked and exhausted attendant won't come until time allows, which isn't often.

Ruby looked into the faces of all those left-to-die seniors and wondered who they'd been when they were at their best. No doubt, the residents included brilliant doctors and successful businessmen and women, engineers and lawyers, good mothers, good fathers, good people whose identities now blended together into the sad final label of "residents." So many fading people.

Cousin Camille had moved to the Sunrise Center six months earlier when her husband Earl died at age eighty-six. The end of Earl was essentially the end of Camille because, with him gone, she didn't have anywhere to go. Severe osteoarthritis made it impossible for her to tend to her hygiene and nutritional needs, her mind wasn't as sharp as it was back in her day, and since her daughter Elizabeth didn't volunteer (and ignored every subtle and not-subtle hint that Camille dropped with all the tact of a land mine), there was no one left to change her Depends.

That's the sad truth of it. Come all this way in life—educate yourself, make a successful and remarkable career, raise your children to be successful and decent, and still, in the end, your diaper is full and there is no one to change you because you are alone. Period. Alone. With no one. Damn Elizabeth.

Camille had visited the Sunrise Center for its free breakfast and tour, and since it was rated higher than any other nursing facilities in the county, she got on the waiting list. Her next-door neighbor helped her have a mammoth garage sale and winnowed Camille's belongings down to two trunks worth of mementos and necessities. Saying farewell to her ten-year-old cocker spaniel, Mitzi, was the most defeated moment of her life—worse than losing her son in Viet Nam and her husband to old age. There it was—the realization that Camille, one of the nation's first female oncologists, couldn't even take care of a cocker spaniel. And she couldn't keep her cocker spaniel around to take care of her.

Ruby imagined how it must have felt to leave a vibrant life behind in exchange for this world. She thought about it a lot because it could be her—and probably would be one day. What would that day be like, checking into a nursing home, knowing you will never check out until you leave this earth? How could anyone consciously make that choice? How could anyone make that choice for anyone else that they care about? From the time they check in until the minute they die, every day is the same. Life becomes scheduled. Lights on at seven in the morning, lights off at eight at night. Breakfast at eight, lunch at eleven-thirty, dinner at five. All that time to just wait for the next meal or the next bedtime.

"Hello," Ruby said to a very genteel-looking eighty-something man who had a very nice moustache and even wore a tie around the Sunrise Center. "How are you today?"

"I just shit my pants," he said. "Change my diaper, will you?"

Ruby Witherspoon, speechless.

He let his response sink in. "I didn't shit my pants. But what an idiotic question, lady. How am I today? Why would you ask that here?"

He was right, of course. She was just making small talk, but at this point, small talk reduces the already diminished to even less significance. To be stuffed away in a place like this, so short-staffed that the minimum wage certified nurse's assistant has to worry about so many residents that she can't remember a single one of their names? People live in a place like that and pay seven grand a month? The food tastes like nothing at all and smells like prison slop. Diapers go without changing for hours because that poor CNA keeps reminding everybody she only has two arms and two legs.

"Well, hi!" Camille brightened the minute she saw Ruby, the cousin who had lived in the house next door from the time they were both three until they graduated high school together, side by side. The girls were born six days apart. "I didn't know you were coming!"

Actually, she knew. Ruby called a week earlier, a day earlier, and the day of. Three times in all, not that manners matter when showing up at Sunrise Center. The residents don't care when you come over, so long as you do. Forget the formalities. The cliché about old lonely people in nursing homes? True! Camille got three or four visits a month—only from church friends—and an occasional special visit like Ruby's, or the ones Elizabeth made to assuage her guilt. Put in perspective, a month has almost 750 hours in it. Visits made up five hours of that 750—at best.

"Rube, you did call me, didn't you? I'm forgetting everything these days. What is wrong with me?"

"I have to admit, I'm not much better."

"Think it's Alzheimer's? I worry about that. Some days, I can't even remember who's president."

"Some days, it is best to forget who is president," Ruby said. "And I don't think we have Alzheimer's. I asked the doctor. He told me that if I forget something and I know I forgot it, that's aging. If I forget something and I don't know I forgot it, that's Alzheimer's."

"Wonderful. I'm still among the with-it."

Camille used the walker to go to the lunchroom because she was too embarrassed for Ruby to see her in a wheelchair, even though she used one nine days out of ten. Camille sat in her assigned seat, the same chair where she sat every day, three times. Ruby kept thinking, "Is this what's ahead for me?"

"How do you like it here?" Ruby asked.

"I love it."

"You love it?"

"I do. I feel safe."

Ruby checked out the daily activity schedule, on display in the middle of the table. Camille could go to bingo, singing, movies, finger painting, a cookie party, or a current events class.

"Do you do a lot of these things?"

"No, never."

"Why never?"

"I don't know."

Oh. Never? Just sit there? Granted, bingo and finger painting did seem a little silly for someone so smart, but the alternative—nothing at all—was worse than silliness. Ruby silently vowed that, if she wound up in a place like Sunrise Center, she would go to bingo and finger painting and the sing-a-longs every single day. She'd paint plaster of paris clowns and papier-mâché a balloon and learn to foxtrot in a wheelchair, if it would help define the days. If she wound up in a place like that, she'd find a way to do something with her time, something more than just sit there. For a long moment, Ruby sat there thinking about the possibility that she'd end up in a home like that, hoping it wasn't an inevitability, but swearing that, if the time came, she'd face it with finesse.

"How is life treating you, Rube?"

"Pretty good. Remember Weeki Wachee? Remember how I used to be a mermaid there?" Her tone came out unintentionally sing-song, like she was talking to a five-year-old.

"Ruby, of course I remember." Camille's knock-off-the-kiddy-talk tone made its point. Then she lightened up. "You were the star of the family."

Ruby smiled at the memory, thinking back to performing in that underwater theater, swimming up to the windows and peeking through to see which members of her clan were watching her. It was like they were watching her swim in a goldfish bowl, and she was the goldfish.

"Well, the park is having a sixtieth reunion for all us old mermaids. I'm traveling down there with a few friends and we're having some crazy fun. Stopping at every single tourist trap we can find."

"Sounds like fun. Just like something you'd do!"

Then Ruby got a faaaaabulous idea. Sign Camille out—she still had that right to be in charge of her own self—get Joni to bring the cab around front, then whisk her cousin off to join the Originals on the big adventure. It wouldn't be that hard to take care of her, not with so many people to help her get around. A great last hurrah kind of thing. Camille could ride in the back seat of the cab with her and, God, it would be so good to have her around again!

"Camille, why don't you come with us? Just take a little vacation from the Sunrise Center."

Camille thought for a moment as she tapped her hand on the lunch table, quite agitated.

"Leave here? I won't do that."

"Why not? Think of the fun we'll have. We'll just be gone for a little while—maybe a week. We'll take good care of you. You can go to Weeki Wachee again."

"I don't want to go to Weeki Wachee again. I've been there."

"I *promise,* we'll take care of you. You won't have to worry about anything."

What happened to Camille, who used to do somersaults off the high dive or swing from the oaks over the Rainbow River to see how far she could fly before landing in the water? What happened to the woman who graduated second in her class from the Johns Hopkins med school and grew so prominent in her field that she was featured for her prostate cancer treatment in both *Life* and *Look* magazines? Who was this old lady?

"Camille, you've got to do this! Once we get you out of here, you'll be your old self again."

"This *is* my old self," Camille shot back. "I like it here. I don't want to go anywhere."

"Camille, you are dying in here."

Camille scowled at Ruby. "I am as alive as I ever was."

"Well, of course. But…"

"But nothing," Camille said, standing to move Ruby out to the patio for a little sunshine. "I know what you think of this place, but you are wrong."

"It's just…"

"These people take good care of me, and they do the best they can. No, I don't do their silly finger painting classes, but I still enjoy my life. I still live my life. I don't want to die. I just don't want—or need—to live like you. There is nothing wrong with that."

She was wrong to judge her cousin—or anyone—like that. But Ruby couldn't decide whether Camille's attitude suggested empowerment or surrender. Did she choose that road or was she on it because it was the last one? How would she cope if it were her in a nursing home?

"I'm trying to understand," Ruby said. "But I'm afraid, Cammy. I don't know if I could adjust to this. I don't think I'd be as strong as you."

"You have no choice when the time comes."

Ruby hated those words, "when the time comes," because that kind of future had loomed dark over her ever since her stroke.

"Stop assuming it is so bad," Camille said. "There is still a lot of living here. It is just different. If you interviewed every one of us at the Sunrise Center, you'd only find a handful who want to die."

"You're kidding me."

"No. If we wanted to die, we would have done something about it before now."

"So how do you deal with living like this?"

"How do you deal with anything? How did you deal with Walter dying so young?"

"I just did. I didn't have a choice."

"Exactly. You just do what you have to. My body gave out on me, so I'm here. But my mind is in a happy place. I am here, counting my blessings, again and again. I've lived a wonderful life. Now I have time to remember it. I go to Earl and talk to him or have lunch with him. I travel to France and Australia and Africa, I swim in the Caribbean and dance on the Mexican Riviera. I do whatever the hell I want."

"Your mind does all that?"

"Free of charge. I'm sure you could find some psychiatrist to say I am nuts, but I'm having a great time. Is there any sin in that?"

Maybe there is peace when one idles the engine. Ruby considered the possibility, but couldn't imagine it.

The time hadn't come.

Chapter Eighteen

Ruby had read all about it in *Modern Maturity:* Of the seniors aged sixty to seventy-four who had partners, one in four women had sex once a week and seventy percent had it at least once or twice a month. That seemed like a lot to Ruby, but of course, that wasn't the kind of thing she or any woman her age would ever talk about.

She wrestled with the idea of intimacy, because she was convinced that every moment from here until death was a now or never moment. Living her life—really living it—meant exploring everything, and that meant being a woman again, not a widow. No disrespect to Walter or all that he meant to her (and he still meant *everything*), Ruby knew time was a finite commodity that was running out. When you are twenty or thirty years old, time is infinite and you can do every careless, stupid thing, including waste it. By the time you are forty, it hits you that some things on your body aren't working as well as they used to, and there is no denying that you are, at best, middle-aged. By fifty, you claim to be empowered by menopause, by sixty you say you're loving retirement and by seventy you have to face reality. In the best of all possible worlds, you've got twenty good years left, but really, you might only have two or three. Better live them. Or, as Ruby decided, better *live* them.

She hadn't even *kissed* a man in twenty-five years, much less made love. And the notion of that (sex!) really scared her because the only man she'd ever been with at all was Walter.

What was she supposed to do? This was a mechanical question, as much as an emotional one. She didn't want to seem forward, or like she'd planned any of it in advance because premeditated sex was still downright promiscuous and that was still unacceptable, regardless of how times had changed or how old she was getting. But how did all of this work? So much had changed, she knew that from just reading the newspaper. Should she ask him to put on a condom? It seemed silly, but that article she read said she shouldn't make any assumptions that any man was clean just because he was old, and Ruby didn't want to have to report to the doctor with any kind of sexually transmitted disease—she would rather die. Not to mention that they now say that sex can kill if you aren't careful, so she wondered just how careful someone her age (and Milt's) needed to be.

The article said thirty-five percent of the women her age said they would be "quite happy" if they never had sex again. Ruby realized she would have answered that question the same way, until she really thought about it. It wasn't so much that she missed having intercourse or especially wanted to have intercourse, but she hadn't had it in a really long time and it seemed kind of silly to shut off the possibility just because you are being loyal to someone who has been dead for decades.

Rain poured down from the sky, turning the Sunshine Kamp in Wilmington into a muddy mess. Maria made two passes through the park trying to find Milt's motor home in a campground where every RV stood chock-a-block in rows where they all looked just alike.

"You sure you trust this guy?" Maria asked as Ruby tightened a rain bonnet on her head and collected her coat and overnight bag in the cab.

"I'm sure," Ruby said.

"Well, I am going to park right over there by the bath house and I'm going to stay there for an hour. And you've got my cell number, right?"

"Oh, good grief," Ruby said. "Don't sit out there in this rain!"

"You've got the cell, right?"

"Right," Ruby said.

"I just don't want to leave you there with him without a backup."

"Okay, let me have him move his little camper next to our hotel room," Ruby said. "We'll consummate our relationship and then we'll come in and watch television with you."

Maria widened her eyes, pretending she loved the idea.

"Okay, old lady, get the hell out of here!" Maria laughed. She leaned over, hugged Ruby, and felt like she'd just learned how she'd feel if she were a mother dropping her child off at the first day of school.

Ruby stood out from the cab and confidently took one step away, then turned right back around and lunged herself back in the front seat.

"What am I doing?" she asked.

"Don't scare yourself to death. Just go in there. Stop asking these questions," Maria said.

"I don't even know what to do anymore! C'mon, let's go. Let's drive around."

"You're kidding me," Maria said as the rain pounded down even louder.

"Go! Now!"

They left and Maria began doing laps around the Sunshine Kamp.

Ruby thought about the e-mail her friend Rose once copied her that was a sex manual for senior citizens: "1. Put bifocals on. Double check that you're with the right partner. 2. Set alarm on your clock for two minutes...in case you doze off in the middle. 3. Create the mood with lighting. Turn all the lights OFF! 4. Make sure you put 911 on your speed dial before you begin...just in case! 5. Write partner's name on your hand in case you can't remember what to scream out at the end." Whoever wrote it sure knew the score.

"What do I do?" Ruby asked Maria.

"What do you mean, what do you do?" Maria said.

"What am I supposed to do? Physically. I think I forgot."

"You didn't forget."

"I did."

"Just do what feels good. *Only* do what feels comfortable to you. Remember, it is your body and you are in charge of your body."

"Oh, I know *that*," Ruby said. "I haven't done anything like this since Walter, and that was twenty-five years ago and…"

"And what?"

"I don't know what to do!"

"I don't think it has changed much, old lady."

"Well, I know that, but Walter was the only one," she said.

"Okay, what exactly do you want me to tell you?"

"What. Do. I. Do?"

"Just relax. Let him take the lead, but the minute you feel like you are doing something that you don't want to do, you stop him. You are in charge. If it feels right, go with it."

"But what do I *do?*"

"Sweetheart, you will know what to do," Maria said. "I promise. And if you don't, tell him you need a break to run and check one of those sex manuals Joni writes."

Ruby chuckled.

The next time they passed Milt's RV, she motioned for Maria to stop, then she stepped out of the car tentatively, walked to the camper, and rapped on the door. She waved bye to Maria, who mouthed the words "good luck!" and shot her a thumbs up.

"Let's have a drink," Milt said as he took Ruby's raincoat and draped it over the front recliner. "Not that I'm a big drinker, but Ruby, I'll admit I'm a little nervous."

"Me too," she said. "It's been awhile."

"Me too. What'll you have?"

"Something strong." She let out a little laugh—it was quite nervous.

Milt picked up a corkscrew and was about to open a bottle of Peruvian merlot when she said, "Milt, ya got any whiskey?" He smiled, then reached in the cupboard for a fifth. He poured a shot for her and one for him. Ruby noticed his hands shaking as he poured, and the sweetness of it all touched her. Her mind drifted to the memory of her wedding night when Walter tried to make love to her so delicately while she tried to figure out what she was supposed to do.

Ruby and Milt threw back their shots and then downed one more before they went back to the bedroom. The whiskey made everything so much better. Milt put his arm around her and drew her in, going in for the kiss. He kissed her like a man would kiss a woman, not like an old man would kiss an old woman. She liked that.

She'd forgotten how good it felt to kiss and be kissed.

Milt blew lightly into her ear, which caused an immediate outbreak of goose pimples on both her legs and arms.

"Mmmmmm," Ruby said.

He kissed her again, even more physically, and in that moment their bodies proved Maria one hundred percent right. They knew precisely what to do, as long as they didn't stop to think about what they were doing. There is no real romantic way to get a woman into bed in a thirty-three-foot motor home. You can't carry her (Milt's back wouldn't have carried her under any circumstance), you can't walk side by side, you can't dance your way back there. What Milt chose to do was take Ruby's hand, kiss it, and lead her to the queen-sized bed in the back. He tried to unbutton her blouse, but his fingers weren't as agile as they used to be, so she had to help while he kissed her.

If it were left to romance-writing Joni to describe what happened, it would have gone something like this: "Milt passionately captured Ruby's lips with his hungry urgency, so intensely probing her soul with his mouth."

But what really happened was this: Milt kissed Ruby and it was quickly apparent that his body was very turned on. That turned Ruby on, and she kissed him back just as hot as he kissed her. Since she'd only been with one other person, one might expect a degree of shyness or hesitance from Ruby, but she skipped formalities and boldly reached for Milt's zipper. The two humped away like fifty-year-olds.

This is the kind of life event that *nobody* talks about. Not with elders! If it is *ever* discussed, elder sex is talked about like it is just sweet lovemaking or cute and comical, but it is never, ever described as a hot roll in the hay. But guess what? That's what it was for Milt and Ruby, because those two got lucky. All their equipment still worked, and so did they.

Chapter Ninteen

Maria opened her eyes and his hand covered her mouth.

"Shhhhh," he whispered, then lowered his mouth to her forehead and began kissing her lovingly. "I am going to remove my hand from your mouth and I am going to trust you, honey, because I think you want this too. Stay silent, okay? You know what to do, baby. Shhhh."

Her eyes moved left, to Joni, who slept soundly in the same queen bed. How could Joni not feel this? How could she sleep through this? Wake up! Joni, wake the hell up!

He lifted his hand from Maria's mouth and put his mouth on hers, kissing her hard, invading her, assaulting her. She squirmed, hoping the movement would wake Joni, but it didn't. He pulled away. "Shhhhh," he warned again in a stern whisper. "Don't worry about her. She won't hear us." He climbed in, on top of Maria.

"NO!" she screamed. "NO!"

Joni heard Maria's night screams, but did nothing. Just let her suffer through whatever her subconscious wanted to do to her.

Chapter Twenty

It was a dark and stormy night. No, not really. It was sunny and time for breakfast.

Joni and Maria waited for the elevator, even though three flights of stairs never killed anybody. They weren't in the mood.

Pity, because the motel elevator announced its arrival with a screech and a lurch and, even though the coughing jalopy gave them adequate forewarning, the two women boarded. The door shut, the boxcar plunged downward in a terrifying jolt.

It died. Somewhere between the second and third floors. And there they were, stuck.

Joni reached for the emergency phone, which automatically dialed and connected her to a computer recording of a woman who so cheerfully told her, "The number you have reached is temporarily out of service." She closed her eyes and hung up, then tried again, to the same result. And again. And again, before slamming the damned thing down.

"Out of fucking order," Joni relayed, then began obsessively punching the elevator alarm until, in a burst of rage, she stepped back, kicked a hard, defiant kick right at the button, then tried it again as it squealed its final, fading cry. She was trapped. With Maria. This could not be.

Maria tried prying the doors open with her fingers, figuring she and Joni could either push themselves up to the third floor or drop down to the second, but the doors wouldn't budge. "Shit, shit, shit, shit."

Both tried their cell phones; neither had reception.

"Gimme a boost," Maria said, eying the false ceiling. Joni bent her knee and Maria stood on it, steadying herself with Joni's shoulders. She popped out the ceiling tiles, then evaluated whether there was a way past the solid steel roof. Fortunately, the designers chose to include a trap door; unfortunately, some moron padlocked it.

Nobody heard them screaming, either because the elevator company built its cars like soundproof tombs, or because the few people who stayed at the motel were smart enough to take the stairs.

Ruby had skipped off to do whatever with Milt in the RV, so Maria and Joni were stranded.

"We are so screwed," Maria said.

"WE'RE STUCK!" Joni shouted, pounding on the doors. Nobody responded. She checked her watch. And again. And again. Maria checked hers too, and it was merciless how slowly time passed.

Finally, they sat down on the floor of the elevator and gave up.

Maria lost no time in testing Joni's nerves, chomping her gum like a cud-chewing cow. Of all the people with whom to be trapped.

"Spit out your damned gum!" Joni shouted.

Maria wanted to snap back, "Go fuck yourself!" but bit down on her lip as she counted to ten in hopes of calming the intensity of the moment.

"I'm sorry," Maria finally said with great restraint. "I'll be glad to." She took a wrapper out of her purse and stuck the gum in it. Joni let out an intolerant sigh.

"You've been really cold to me lately, and I'm trying to figure out if I did something to offend you," Maria said.

Joni took a deep breath and exhaled nice and slow. Be calm, girl. This is no place to start talking issues. Minimize, deny, change the subject, don't go there, Joni, just don't.

"No," Joni answered.

The "no" hung there like the big, fat lie that it was.

"No?"

"No."

"Because I think something is wrong here. I've been barked at, ignored, ridiculed, and you have even ditched me a couple of times. We used to be playing on the same team, but we aren't anymore."

Whatever, Joni thought, but instead of addressing it, she again slapped the elevator door and yelled "HELLLLLP!" She checked her watch, waited a minute, then checked again.

Use it or lose it.

As studies show, once a senior citizen stops having sex, it becomes all the easier to stop having sex. Having stopped, then resumed, Ruby felt unprepared for the challenges in front of her. She now remembered the basics of what went where, and she even started relaxing and letting herself be right there in the moment. But Milt approached lovemaking as a highly athletic activity—something Walter hadn't done. Walter was considerate and practiced in bed, but Milt was a wildman. Not kinky, but he certainly didn't hold back. Ruby had always wondered what the deal was with the "G-spot," and now she knew. Ohhhhh yes, she knew what the G-spot was, and now she knew a lot of other things too.

On this particular morning—the fateful morning when Maria and Joni were trapped in that elevator—Ruby boldly knocked on Milt's RV door once, then opened it, walked in, and locked it.

"Good morning, beautiful!" he gushed.

Ruby pushed her index finger into his chest, backing Milt into the bedroom, where he surrendered by falling on his back onto the bed. Ooooooh, baby.

"What are you staring at?" Joni asked.

"I'm not staring at anything, Joni," Maria said.

"Right."

"Stop being paranoid."

"You're staring at me."

"There's nothing to look at in here," said Maria. "You want me to sit here with my eyes closed for four more hours?"

"That'd be nice."

"What is your problem?"

"What do you think?" Joni asked, looking her thief straight in the eyes.

"What do I think? I don't know what to think," Maria said.

"You can't think of anything that might upset me a little?"

"I don't know. Why don't you tell me what put that bug up your ass?"

Joni rolled her eyes, then crossed her arms.

"Joni," Maria said. "I have no idea."

"I don't think we should talk about it here."

"Whatever."

"I want pancakes," Ruby whispered in the ear of her love. "You cookin' or buyin'?"

"Cookin'," Milt said as he kissed her forehead. He sat up, pulled on some boxers, then bounded out of bed to the RV's galley.

Ruby rolled over and coasted off to sleep.

Hour five.

"Y'know, since we're stuck in here and can't go to the bathroom and can't get out, maybe we *should* have a little talk," Joni said.

"Fine. What the hell has been eating you?"

"What do you think?"

"If I knew what to think, I wouldn't keep asking."

"Well, I'm missing something," Joni said. "And I don't think I need to say any more."

"You're missing something? Hmmm. You're missing your right mind?"

"Funny."

"What are you talking about?"

Joni rolled her eyes and knew now there'd be little to gain by going any further, but there was no stopping.

"Maria, I can count."

"And?"

Joni shook her head. This charade was absurd.

"I want my money back."

Maria looked back at her quizzically. Joni let out a loud, exasperated gasp.

"I am missing a lot of cash from my winnings at Atlantic City."

"You're kidding."

"Maybe you figured you deserved more than I gave you, but that was for me to give, not for you to take." Joni watched Maria's body language to catch any telltale signs of guilt, but Maria just sat there on the elevator floor feigning surprise and insult.

"How much cash is missing?"

"Thirteen hundred dollars."

"And you think I stole it from you."

"Well, it certainly wasn't Ruby," Joni said.

"Well, it certainly wasn't me," Maria shot back forcefully.

Joni said nothing. Not a damned thing.

"First of all, why would I steal from you?" Maria asked.

"I have no idea. Maybe you figured I wouldn't notice. You just reached in my knapsack and stole a few hundred here and a few hundred there. But I count. I count my money. I know when something's up."

"Congratulations on your mathematical prowess, but I have my own money. I don't need your money and I didn't need that pathetic tip you stuck in my pocket after I got twenty-six grand for you in the first place. Believe me."

"Right. I'm sure you socked away quite a fortune driving that yellow cab. You're probably just living off the residuals from your many investments and the royalties of that screenplay you wrote that Steven Spielberg just optioned."

"You know nothing about me," Maria said.

"I know you steal."

"I don't steal, and I'm not going to get into it with some psychoneurotic lunatic woman who blames everyone else for whatever it is that doesn't work inside of her. I'm not your problem. You need help." Maria shrugged.

"Thank you for your valuable professional analysis. I bet you learned all those big words in your GED class."

Maria said, *"Vive del cuento,"* the Cuban saying for "lives on lies" to herself.

"You're not going to bring me down to your level. I would not take the money you are too selfish to share," Maria said. She stood up, pounded on the elevator door, and again tried pushing the floor numbers so she could turn away and Joni wouldn't see tears in her eyes. She pushed those buttons again and again, like a lab rat in a psych experiment who goes insane as it tries repeatedly to achieve a different result by doing what it's tried unsuccessfully a thousand times.

But this time...

The elevator lurched downward with a sudden jolt, then slowly and noisily cruised down to the first floor. The doors opened.

There stood Ruby.

"Oh, hi girls! Where are you two going?"

Maria angrily marched past Ruby, ran down the hall to the stairs, and went directly up to the room where she sobbed, nonstop, through a forty-minute steaming hot shower. She made up her mind that she'd drive Ruby to Weeki Wachee—straight to Florida with no more sightseeing or goofing around. All business. These were not her friends, they were her passengers—customers—and if they wanted her to be their lowly driver, then that was all she would be.

"What do you mean, no more stops?" Ruby asked.

"I committed to taking you to Florida," Maria said. "If this doesn't meet with your approval, you need to hail another cab or catch a bus or ride with your boyfriend. I'm over this."

Cold.

"What happened today?" Ruby asked calmly as Maria threw on a pair of shorts and a tank top.

Maria just shook her head.

"Maria?"

"Joni accused me of stealing money from her," Maria said. "She said I went right into her backpack and stole thirteen hundred dollars."

"You're kidding."

"And I didn't steal anything."

"Of course you didn't," Ruby said.

"Ruby, I'm serious. I didn't touch her things."

"I know you didn't," Ruby said, grabbing Maria's wrist. "Come with me."

"I'm not taking the elevator."

Joni approached them, carrying two completely full bags from the Target across the street, as Maria and Ruby walked toward the cab.

"Where're you going?" she asked.

"Come with us," Ruby said.

Maria unlocked the cab and Ruby climbed in the back seat. Joni got up front in the passenger seat, per usual. Maria sat behind the wheel.

"I understand the two of you have had words," Ruby said.

Joni nodded.

"Before you go accusing anybody, Joni, you need to know what you're talking about," Ruby said. "You need to get your facts straight. You need to get rid of that 'whole world hates Joni' attitude. The whole world is not against you."

"But I did get my facts straight," Joni said.

"Really?" Ruby reached into the fold of the back seat cushion and extracted a wad of cash, which she tossed to Joni. She probed into the side pocket near the door handle and extracted another wad. She bent over and pulled out a third wad from under the front seat. "The rest is in the trunk with the flat tire."

Joni raised her eyebrows as she sighed, embarrassed.

"Why did you take it?" she asked.

"Why did you leave your money out in the open so somebody *could* take it? You had that backpack sitting wide open in the car when we went to a convenience store in Delaware and the doors weren't even locked. What were *you* thinking?"

"I wasn't…"

"I had two teenage girls who used to leave their purses out in the open. How do you think I taught them this lesson?"

Joni held up her right hand, trying to halt the discussion. She looked like an idiot and she looked like she felt like an idiot, so did they need to go further down this line? Yes. Ruby had great respect for the value of a dollar, even though she spent her money in ways that drove her girls and her accountants nuts. She knew exactly how much she had and where she spent it. Why on earth would Joni carry that fat stash of cash and leave it in the open? Crazy.

"If you'd have asked about the money the first day it was stolen, you'd have had your answer. Instead, you didn't say anything to any of us…" Ruby said.

"I didn't want to ruin your trip."

"Oh, bull," Ruby said.

"Maria, I'm so sorry," Joni said. "I suck."

"Yeah," Maria said. "You really do."

Chapter Twenty-one

There wasn't much talk in the taxi until Ruby saw the billboard summoning travelers to stop to see the yodeling hostess at the Cracker Barrel.

"Maria, we've got to stop."

"No extra stops, Ruby."

"Maria, knock off this bull. We are stopping. The exit is right here…"

Maria kept driving, went right past it; didn't even look.

"I'm serious. No unnecessary stops."

"That was a *necessary* stop. Please turn around."

"I am not turning around."

"Maria, you are ruining everything. Everything!"

"I'm not the bad guy. I'm just the driver."

"Maria, could you pull over?" Ruby asked.

Maria looked at her through the rearview mirror.

"What do you mean?"

"Pull over," Ruby said. "Side of the road."

"Is that a necessary stop?"

"Yes, I believe it is."

Maria pulled over and Ruby motioned for all of them to get out of the taxi. Milt pulled the RV over behind them, but Ruby held up her right hand to him in a halting motion, warning him not to join them.

"I have just missed a yodeling hostess because of you two," she lectured Joni and Maria. "That might not mean much to you, but it means something to me. I have never seen one and now I likely never will. No telling what I might miss next."

"Ruby, you don't have to take a taxi and you don't have to take this taxi, but under the circumstances…"

"Get over it, Maria," Joni said. "I said I was sorry. I said I was sorry a hundred times, maybe more. And I said that I was wrong and embarrassed and all the things I thought I could and should say to make things better. But you carry a grudge. You want that chip on your shoulder, fine. I'm done apologizing. There comes a time when you have to just make peace."

Ruby sent an approving look toward Joni, and then held up her right finger toward Maria in a scolding fashion. "Enough of this. Enough, all right? This is ridiculous."

Stubborn, stubborn Maria. Here she was, feeling twelve years old again, driving her mother and her sister crazy because she wouldn't back down or give up fighting long after the time had come to be done with the conflict. When someone hurt her, it was hard for her to forgive it. She knew that Joni reacted to the missing money the way most other people would have reacted: by blaming the hired help. What was the big deal? But the insult stung Maria especially deep because this unexpected odyssey into the working class was not of her making. She hadn't signed up for life as a taxi driver because she wanted a new career. The stalker made her do it. *He* forced her to give up the work she loved. When she stopped to think about it, she resented dropping down those few notches on the class scale, as though that were something so bad. She was just as classist and judgmental as Joni. She knew that. She knew that Joni wasn't to blame for everything she was feeling or even most of it.

But she didn't know how to back down now. It wasn't in her. She wasn't good at making or accepting apologies. She hated admitting she'd gone too far with it, that now it was she who was wrong.

"Just shake hands and make up," Ruby instructed. "Let's get back to business."

Joni extended her arm toward Maria.

Maria extended hers back. They shook.

Joni hugged Maria.

Maria did not hug back.

But they were back in business. Maria turned around to take Ruby to the Cracker Barrel.

Chapter Twenty-two

Charleston woman killed Friday by longtime stalker

By Sandra Kallens
of the Tribune Staff

A young Charleston woman was found dead in her apartment Friday after being bludgeoned to death by a man who had been stalking her for more than two years, police said.

Neighbors reported hearing screaming shortly after 1 a.m. in the Meadowwood Apartments. Police arrived shortly after the first 911 call and found the body Terri McAlister, 29, in her kitchen.

Police arrested 20-year-old Rex Baard at the scene. Baard is a former history student of McAlister's at Lincoln High School.

Chief Ray Park said McAlister contacted police more than two years ago because she'd been receiving threatening, anonymous letters.

"She felt she was being stalked and the department did everything it could to ascertain who was bothering her, but there were no fingerprints and we had no leads. Unfortunately, you can't arrest someone when you have no evidence or clues. It could have been anyone. We can't arrest the whole city."

Neighbors said McAlister had told them about the letters and asked them to watch out for any intruders.

Park said that, despite police urging, McAlister did not have a gun to protect herself...

Maria ripped the story off the front page and bolted out to the cab without even excusing herself from the breakfast table.

"What's the matter with her now?" Joni asked.

Milt shook his head to Ruby to signal to leave Maria alone.

Maria popped the trunk and pulled out a zippered leather case that she'd hidden with the spare tire. In it were all the letters, all her police reports, and a copy of her will. Everything was in perfect order, culminating with a letter that summarized everything that had happened—with dates—and gave directions of who to contact if there were an emergency.

Since the stalking began, nearly every moment felt like an emergency to Maria, even when she was just reading the newspaper and eating her waffles at Denny's. Her hands shook as she reread the article and thought of how well Terri McAlister must have known her same feeling of always, always being watched. Maria wondered what would happen when her turn came to defend herself. She'd done everything she could to prevent a newspaper article like that, but it's so hard protecting yourself when every person you meet could be the one who wants to hurt you.

Maria reached under her seat in the cab and pulled out her revolver. She checked it and it was loaded, as it should have been. She and Ruby had gone back and forth on the gun for so long that Maria had to check it every day to make sure her bullets were back. Ruby acted like it was a joke, but it wasn't.

"Hey."

It seemed odd that it was Joni—not Ruby—who'd gone to check on her.

"You still hatin' me?"

"No," Maria said. "But I'm not lovin' you, either."

"Well, that's better than nothing, especially since you are armed."

Maria barely smiled.

"Why're you cradling that gun? It makes me nervous."

"Sometimes, guns are our friends," Maria said, looking toward the "Let us make your day!" sign in the restaurant window.

"You are so secretive…"

"You are so nosy…"

Joni shrugged. "Just trying to be helpful."

Right.

"You know just about everything there is to know about me," Joni said.

"Mmmm hmmm. You're shallow, cold. and judgmental."

"Keep it up, sister. Anyhow, you know about me and you know just about everything there is to know about Ruby."

"My hero."

"We know nothing about you. We know you drive a cab. Your hair is brown. You drink way too much coffee and way too much Diet Coke. That is all we know."

"And from that, you've presumed a lot. That I am uneducated, that I have no money, and that I can't be trusted. That I am of a lower class than you and am somehow less worthy."

"Thanks. Keep it up. Don't let anything go."

"That's me."

"Well, you taught me that lesson already. I don't need it again." Joni stood up to head back into the restaurant. There comes a point when you stop trying to apologize or make nice. If Maria wanted to be that way, she could be that way by herself. Joni didn't have to stand there and let Maria slap her around. As she turned to walk back to the restaurant, she heard Maria again checking the bullets in the cylinder.

"Don't shoot me!" she yelled, pretty sure she was joking.

Maria squinted her eyes as though she were considering it, then smiled weakly.

What the hell is it?" Joni asked. "Did you rob a bank or something?"

"I didn't do anything," Maria said. "But if you are so damned curious, read this. Whatever. You want to know my world, here is my world." Maria handed Joni the letter that explained everything, put her gun in her fanny pack, then headed back into the restaurant.

> *"If you are reading this letter, my fears have probably been realized, and my stalker has found me again and that I have been harmed in some way. My name is Maria Muñoz, my parents are Reuben and Anna Muñoz of Atlanta, Ga., and I have been stalked for the past two years by someone who I can't identify because I don't know who he is. He may have been a client in the image consulting business I had to abandon in order to hide myself and protect my safety. He has sent numerous letters suggesting sexual violence and has broken into my home on at least two occasions. When the police told me there was nothing they could do to protect me, I moved to New York and started a new life.*
>
> *"This all began with a note mailed to my studio that quoted from Romeo and Juliet. I never had a secret admirer before and was flattered. The next letter came with a gold puzzle necklace that said, "LOVE YOU." The card asked me to meet for a*

casual lunch at Downie's restaurant in downtown Atlanta if I was interested in meeting my secret admirer. Of course I didn't go. It felt creepy and I didn't know why he wouldn't just ask if he wanted a date. A day later, I found a dozen dead roses in a black vase on the stoop in front of my studio. I tossed them out and figured I'd been right about skipping the lunch. The next note said, "You think you are better than everybody else? You're not. Cunt." I called the cops, and an officer showed up, took a lot of notes, but admitted he had nothing to work with. He told me we couldn't even get a restraining order when we didn't know who to restrain. Then he told me, "This kind of thing happens all the time."

Joni read the news article about Terri McAlister.

Happens all the time.

No wonder Maria had nightmares.

"Why didn't you tell us?" Joni asked when she came back into the restaurant. Ruby and Milt were in the bathroom.

"I don't talk about it. It makes it real. It gives it way more power."

"But we could protect you…"

"Nobody can protect me."

"It's too much to keep in," Joni said.

"Do not tell Ruby," Maria said. "I'm serious. She doesn't need any reality in this fantasy trip."

Two hours later, Ruby rehearsed her routine as Maria fell into a deep sleep at poolside.

"You know what to do, baby," the voice said.

Maria squinted toward the sun and saw him, headless again.

"I don't," she said. "I don't know what to do. I don't know what you want. What will it take to get you to leave me alone? To go away?"

"You know what to do! Do it. Do it, baby."

"What do you want?"

"You know what I want."

She looked for Ruby and Milt, for Joni, for anybody, but it was just her and the headless man under the flaming sun. Her body felt burned, really burned, and her throat parched and she could barely move because she'd so overexposed herself to the sun that it depleted her of everything, but she had the gun, she always has the gun, and she knew it was right there underneath her towel, next to her lounge chair.

"Other people can see us," she said.

"No they can't."

"You need to go."

"You need to shut your fucking mouth."

"Please. Please go."

"Not until you do it, baby."

He closed in on her, reaching for his zipper and…

SPLASH! Milt flew from the deck into the pool with an aerodynamically spectacular belly-flop that covered half of the pool deck with cold water and woke Maria in an instant.

A blessed instant.

Chapter Twenty-three

You can't *not* stop at South of the Border, even if you know better.

Ruby asked a dozen times, and Maria kept saying no. But as they passed a billboard that said, "KEEP YELLING, KIDS, THEY'LL STOP!" Ruby and Joni both yelled, "STOPPPP!" and Maria finally gave in. They'd seen about 400 billboards trying to entice them to visit, each one tackier than the next. "YOU NEVER SAUSAGE A PLACE," said a hot dog on one sign. A weather forecast read, "CHILI TODAY, HOT TAMALE." But South of the Border's neon sombrero, glowing some 200 feet in the sky, hypnotically pulled Ruby and Milt and almost every person on the road into its magnetic force field. Again. You can't go from North Carolina to South without stopping. Or South Carolina to North.

On some level, there is disappointment in what is found at the base of the sombrero—rubber snakes, souvenir shot glasses, leather whips, t-shirts, blankets, "anteeks," and sombreros—but there is a definite charm about the gaudiness of the place.

Ruby handed her cell phone to a stranger and asked that the woman use its digital camera to photograph her with Joni, Maria, and Milt next to a thirty-foot gorilla statue.

"Say cheese!" the woman shouted.

"Cheeeeeeese!" they replied.

"Ruby, take another one. My flab was hanging out," Joni said.

"Do you mind?" Ruby asked the woman. "Her flab was hanging out."

The woman stared suspiciously at Ruby. Took a real long look. Nodded her head.

"No problem," she said. "Do you mind if I take a picture of your group with my camera too?"

"Not at all," said Ruby.

The woman didn't even bother with Ruby's cell phone camera, but instead started taking pictures with her own digital camera, click, click, click, lots of pictures, as though she'd stumbled onto Paris Hilton or Lindsay Lohan. "Say cheese!" the woman shouted.

"Cheeeeeeese!" they replied.

Click. Click. Click. Click. Click. Click. Click. Click. Click.

"Uh, don't you think you have enough?" Maria asked.

Click. Click. Click. Click. Click. Click. Click. Click. Click.

"Lady, what the hell are you doing?" Milt demanded. "Use Ruby's phone, like she asked."

"Oh, these are such great pictures!" the lady said. "I'll take another with your cell phone, but why don't you sign this napkin with your name and address and I promise I'll send you a copy. The quality will be way better than what you'll get with that cell phone."

"That's so nice of you," said Ruby.

The woman took out a pen and paper and handed it to Ruby, who wrote down her name and address and passed it back.

"Ruby Witherspoon?" the woman said.

"Yes," said Ruby.

"Pleasure to meet you. I'll send you the picture. Where are you all headed?"

"South," Ruby said.

The worst of South of the Border—or the best, depending on your appreciation for all that is tacky in the world—is the Eiffel Tower of the South. Oh, it is awful. But for a dollar apiece, visitors travel in a glass elevator to the top of the 200-foot neon sombrero to get a one-of-a-kind view of not-a-damned-thing. That's right.

Except for the neon absurdity of South of the Border below, there is nothing worth seeing no matter how many times you look.

But Ruby led her gang to the top of the tower, and their "fan" from the gorilla statue followed right behind them into the elevator, taking pictures as they went up the elevator and then out on the observation deck.

"You're getting on our nerves," Milt told her. "Why are you doing this?"

Click. Click. Click. Click. Click. Click. Click. Click. Click.

"I'm over this place," Joni announced.

"Me too," said Ruby. "Stupid."

Unfortunately, the place was not over them. In one unexpected moment, the entire world seemed to know that Ruby Witherspoon had arrived. Once the sombrero elevator took them back to the ground and its doors opened, South of the Border tourists acting as paparazzi blinded Ruby & Co. with nonstop flashes, apparently figuring that if they each had hundreds of empty kilobytes on their camera memory cards, they'd better fill them up. "Crazy" minimizes the scene. These people pushed and shoved and hollered and one guy even spit. It was quite insane.

"GO FUCK YOURSELF!" a woman yelled at Ruby, just to get her to look.

A man pushed right into Joni and knocked her to the ground, just to get them to stop.

"Ruby, just stop and pose for us so nobody gets hurt!" somebody yelled, pleading for reason, not issuing a threat.

"What the hell is going on?" demanded Maria.

No one would answer. They just kept flashing their cameras and taking pictures. Finally, Milt led them to the cab so they could leave the madness behind. As if that were possible.

The paparazzi citizens took pictures of the women, of the cab, of Ruby telling Milt good-bye with a quick kiss, of the women in the cab, of the license plate on the cab, of the cab racing back to the interstate.

"We're being followed," Maria said.

In her rearview mirror, she could see four cars—at least four cars—lined up behind her whether she accelerated to ninety miles an hour or dropped back to forty-five.

Ruby called Milt on his cell phone.

"We're being followed," she said.

"I see that," he said. "Want me to block 'em?"

Maria shook her head no. She turned on her right blinker and slowly pulled into the emergency lane. Every one of the cars pulled over too. Drivers emerged from three of the cars. Two stayed put.

She reached for her gun, not planning to use it in any way, but to have it if necessary.

"No," Ruby said firmly. "Absolutely not."

Maria looked at her and considered Ruby's resolve. She put the gun back in the side panel of the door, then got out and marched toward the tailgaters with immense confidence, puffing up her chest as she confronted the South of the Border wackos.

"I have just called the State Patrol. You can hang around if you want, but I suggest you get moving, real quick. But don't speed. I wouldn't want you to get a ticket."

"We're not hurting anybody," said a man with a Mr. Spock haircut.

"We just want the reward," said a woman.

"What reward?"

"From Steve Rosenthal."

"Well, we aren't interested in any of that," Maria said. "You need to go now. The cops are coming."

And just like that, the pursuers left. Maria thought it was because she'd been forceful and strategic. Actually, it was because they realized they had enough pictures and needed to get to a computer immediately to claim their reward.

Steve Rosenthal would be so pleased.

Chapter Twenty-four

"This is it, everybody. All those fake Ruby sightings and now we have got the real thing, Ruby in the flesh with her friends at South of the Border. Go to my web page at SteveRosenthalsucks.com and see our friend with her friends. I'm not sure how to split this reward money because we had ten people e-mail photos to us. Ruby actually gave her name and address—actually signed it—for the third person who sent a picture in, so my guess is that she should win the most because she's the one who has authenticated it with us. But we're getting all these people on the air with us, so tune in at 7:30 for our first interview and we'll start debriefing them on what they saw."

Seven-thirty finally arrived, and Ruby & Co. nervously waited in Milt's RV to hear the reports from those idiot spies Rosenthal had unleashed on them.

"First up, Tammy Hardman, our third place winner. Tammy, what'd you see?"

"Well, I got to see Ruby and her friends real good. Ruby looked good, so she's not suffering or anything. One of her friends is a real pretty Mexican-looking girl and one is a little chunky, but she has a nice smile. And there is a real old man with them."

Maria glared off into the distance, angry. This media exposure may be "cute" for Ruby and that sorry-ass disc jockey, but for her, it was risky and frightening. She kept telling herself not to be paranoid, but it didn't feel good, being out of control like that.

"Ruby was very nice to me. She said she had to go, but personally invited me to visit her when she gets back in New York. I really liked her…"

Joni turned around in the cab and shot Ruby a quizzical look. "You made a new friend?"

She just shrugged.

"Really?" Rosenthal said. "Tammy, that is very interesting. Glad to know that Ruby is making friends and is so kind to our listeners. As our third prize winner, you will receive one week in the Westin Hotel of your choice, and that's a great treat because, as all of my listeners know, Westin has its famous Heavenly Bed®. Now, you all at home, stand by and at eight a.m. we're going to have an interview with our second place winner."

"Well, that's just great," Ruby said.

"Now what?" asked Joni.

"I'm calling that bastard," Ruby said.

She speed dialed him from her cell phone.

"I've been waiting for you, my lovely," he said. "Hang on a second. I'm going to put on a song. What's your favorite song?"

"Rosenthal, I am not in the mood," she said.

"Oh, good. Glenn Miller, 'In the Mood.' We'll play that so we can boost our over-ninety audience. Hang on a second." He switched his microphone on. *"I'm going to play this oldie for our good friend Ruby Witherspoon, because she likes it so much and we like her so much…"* He came back to the phone.

"Hi sweetheart."

"Don't b.s. me," she said. "I'm not doing this to entertain you or your listeners."

"Ruby, have a sense of humor."

"Look, I do have a sense of humor! That's why I am on this trip. But I can't have you hounding me. What are you going to get out of this?"

"My listeners love you and your story."

"Your stupid listeners swore at us, spit at us, tripped one of my friends, chased us, and then followed us in their cars. That's a real nice way to show love. Drop it. I don't want you talking about me any more."

"Ruby, I have to remind you that this all started because you didn't tell your daughters what you were doing. You're big news now. We can't drop it."

"You have turned my last big adventure into a big national joke."

"It's not a joke," he said. "And it is not just national. It is international. And I'm sure it is not your last big adventure. But it's news, so you might as well enjoy your fame."

"I have no need to be famous," she said.

"One of my spies sent me pictures of you traveling in a yellow cab. What's that all about?"

"I'm not confirming or denying anything for you, you jackass. You've already caused enough trouble."

"But why are you in a cab? Isn't that a little expensive and a little silly?"

"Steve, when I have finished what I need to finish, I'll tell you the details. Until then, *please* do not tell the world I am in a yellow cab."

"Too late, Ruby. It's on my website."

Ruby looked at Maria. "He put it on his website."

For that moment, Maria saw the world in slow motion. She was hiding out in her cab, the cab was her safe haven, and now her safe haven was a media spectacle.

"C'mon, Ruby. Go with this," Rosenthal said. "It's a party. Let us all join in. Use it to show the rest of the world that you don't stop living once your hair turns blue. Hang on…" He switched on his microphone. *"I hate to do this to you folks, but Ruby and I are arguing on the other line, so I've got to turn you over to my favorite song by Coldplay. Hold tight."* From Glenn Miller to Coldplay. What a morning.

"I've pissed you off," Rosenthal said.

"What do you think?" said Ruby.

"I can't unring the bell, Ruby."

"I know."

"So let the world come with you."

She hung up.

"Ruby, he's putting me at risk," Maria said.

"What are you talking about?"

Maria glanced at Joni who mouthed the words, *"Tell her."*

She shook her head no.

"Well?" Ruby asked. "What's going on here?"

"Ruby, it's no big deal. I used to have someone kinda following me and I just don't want him to know where I am."

"Who?" Ruby asked.

"It's a long story that I really don't want to go into. But it is the reason I keep the gun. I don't want to minimize it, but I don't want to dwell on it. Okay?"

"But…"

"That's all I am going to say about it."

"Well, honey, we're all watching out for you. People are going to be looking for the crazy old lady, so blend into the background."

Like that would be possible now.

Nearly fifty thousand people checked out the pictures of Ruby and her friends within thirty minutes of them being posted at www.rosenthalsucks.com. Within a day, more than 750,000 people took a look-see. The more the media covered the story, the more it grew. It wasn't long before the site was drawing a million people *a day*. The webmaster posted an interactive map so fans could plot where Ruby started, where she was last seen, and where she was possibly headed. The last category was absolute fiction, with arrows sending her everywhere from Walt Disney World to Las Vegas to Yosemite National Park. Again, plenty of false reports were called into the hotline, and when the callers could send photos, Rosenthal posted a full six pages of the faux Ruby Witherspoons. But the interactive map showed that Georgia was red hot, because people called in all kinds of reports that Ruby and her friends were on this road or that. One Georgia television station dispatched its news chopper to search for Ruby, and when the pilot spotted a yellow cab with New York plates, the station went live, and E! and CNN joined in for the Ruby Witherspoon version of the O.J. Simpson Ford Bronco chase. The chopper flew low over the cab as it moved south along Interstate 75 about an hour from Atlanta. When the driver finally pulled over at a truck stop, the chopper landed in a field next to the station and the cameraman ran to film the passengers as they disembarked. Meet Al and Rena Schmitt, and their daughters Katie and Wendy. Al and Rena owned their cab and saw nothing wrong with using it for their family vacation. "What the hell is the big deal?" Al growled before he realized he liked the idea of being on television and started smiling. "Hello to all of my friends in New York!" he said as a quite chagrined television anchor announced they'd immediately return to their regularly scheduled program.

The real cab was quite far from the Schmitts' cab. Ruby wanted to see Rock City, not Atlanta, so they took the back roads that edged them toward Lookout Mountain, Georgia, right near Chattanooga, home of the Rock City. Yes, *that* Rock City, as in "See Rock City," as in the attraction that once advertised itself on nearly a thousand barn roofs off highways from Michigan to Texas, as in the place at least half of our parents promised they'd take us, but never did. It also was home to the beautiful Ruby Falls, which Ruby Witherspoon had to see—if just to get the Ruby t-shirt.

Rock City was quite cool in a 1950s sort of way. If you want Disney or Universal, the Fairyland Cavern, the Mother Goose Village, and the little enclaves of illuminated dwarfs and elves won't do it for you. But the naturally formed streets that pass through the rock formations lead to a view that goes from the top of the mountain to forever. You can see seven states from the vista at the top—not that they looked all that different—but on this particular day, you could also see Ruby Witherspoon kissing her boyfriend Milt.

That's what Betsy Gannon saw as she passed through the "Grand Corridor" and saw Ruby and Milt, sitting by a tree, k-i-s-s-i-n-g.

"You're Ruby!" she said as she pointed her cell phone camcorder at the couple and started recording.

Ruby thought for a moment how odd it was that, at the age of seventy-eight, she was secretly enjoying this late brush with fame. But she relished it. Although she pretended to want her privacy so she could be left alone to enjoy her big adventure, being recognized by some stranger on top of a mountain was an absolutely spectacular thrill.

"Ruby, wave to the people at home!" Betsy yelled.

Ruby waved. "Hi, people at home!"

"Where are you headed?" Betsy asked, as if she were a reporter or something.

"Oh, that's top secret," Ruby said.

"Who's your boyfriend?"

"You from *The National Enquirer?*"

"Well, I do have an 'enquiring mind!'"

Ruby laughed. "This is my prince."

Betsy Gannon zoomed in. "Give him a kiss!" she said, and Ruby obliged.

Not even an hour later, the video was on www.rosenthalsucks.com, and people hurried to the mountains to get a live look at Ruby and her man. The website's interactive map had a big star right over Rock City and announced "LATEST SIGHTING! SEE RUBY AT ROCK CITY!"

As Ruby & Co. headed down the mountain, Rosenthal's fans headed up. They spotted the taxi, found a turn-around, started a line right behind Milt, and the convoy was born. Hard to believe, but true.

Chapter Twenty-five

An hour outside Rock City, Milt called Ruby on his cell phone.

"Hey, darlin'."

Ruby turned around and Milt waved at her from the RV.

"Hi sweet pea."

"I don't want to make you all nervous, but we're being followed again."

"By whom?"

"Don't know. But there are three cars, one pickup, and a semi that have been on my rear for the last forty-five minutes. They've turned with us twice. Oh, look. Someone else just did a U-turn in the middle of the road and got in the line."

She held the phone away from her ear.

"Milt says we've got people following us. Can you make a quick turn so we can check if he's right?"

"No problem, Mama," Maria said, smiling at Ruby in the rearview mirror and waving back to Milt.

"Get ready, Uncle Milty," Ruby said into her phone.

Without signaling, Maria exited and Milt followed. So did the next car and the next and all the others. In a repeat performance of the last time the citizen paparazzi followed in pursuit, she pulled over onto a wide, gravel emergency lane next to a foul-smelling field filled with pigs and pig dung. All the others followed. Maria opened her door to get out, but Ruby insisted, "I'm handling this."

Ruby stepped from the taxi, took one whiff of the pig stench, and switched to mouth breathing as she first stretched her legs, then motioned for Milt to join her as she moved toward the delighted members of her caravan who hurried up to her, snapping away with their cameras.

"What the hell are you folks doing?" Ruby asked.

"Ruby watching!" answered a tubby fifty-something man wearing a dirty Dallas Cowboy's t-shirt and a scary comb-over. "Saw you on the map on the Internet and we figured we'd come along for the ride. We love you, Ruby!"

The others clapped, then shouted, "We love Ruby! We love Ruby! We love Ruby!"

Another car did a U-turn and pulled over behind the caravan.

"Y'all are acting like a bunch of fools," Ruby said. "Now I am trying to take a vacation with some of my friends. I can't see cause to get rid of you because joining some sort of convoy like this is something I might do myself. But since I don't recall asking any of you to join us on this little trip, I have to count on you to respect our privacy as much as possible. Keep a little distance."

The longer she stood still, the more people arrived.

"You said there is a map of my trip on the Internet?" she asked.

"Yeah, at Steve Rosenthal's website," said the comb-over. "It tells everywhere you have been spotted, and projects your travel path."

"Really?" asked Ruby. "Where does Mr. Rosenthal think I am going?"

"Oh, it doesn't matter what he thinks. The odds-makers in Vegas have you going to Orlando two to one, to Key West ten to one, to Albuquerque 200 to one. You know, people will bet on anything."

"Maybe we should get in on this action," Ruby said.

"I don't think that's legal," said Milt.

"By the way, my friends call me 'Coach,'" the comb-over said.

"You're a coach?" Milt asked, shocked.

Coach patted his pot belly. "I coach from the couch."

"You needed to get out of the house," Milt concluded.

"Yeah. My wife left a couple months ago and I haven't had much t'do since. Figured you all wouldn't mind."

Ruby nodded. "You figured."

"You don't mind, right?"

She just shrugged. "Guess not."

The truck driver stepped forward and extended her hand, "I'm Shane, Shane Sykes, Shane Sykes of Arcadia, Florida, and all cities between," said the very butch middle-aged woman who came with a red Peterbilt Model 379 semi. "I was just on a run to Raleigh-Durham and heard all 'bout you and decided this sounded like too a good time for old Shane to miss. I don't have to be down to Tampa for another week, so I thought I'd hang with Ruby to give her a little support and protection."

Anyone looking at Shane knew not to mess with this mulleted he-woman. Only about five-foot four, she sported wide shoulders and walked with a mean "back off" sheriff's kind of saunter. She wore her keys on a ring on her already loaded-down belt, which also carried her pocket knife and cell phone.

"Li'l filly," she said to Maria. "You need a li'l air in your back right tire. I've got an electric pump with me."

Maria smiled her great approval of Shane Sykes as another woman stepped forward and announced, "My name is Loretta Wheatley, and I guess I'm here because I don't have anywhere else to go." Loretta was an extremely attractive black woman who had to be Joni's age. "I finally fired my boss and am free at last. This sounded like exactly the kind of thing I needed to do with my temporary retirement."

"What kind of work did you do?" Joni asked.

"Senior V.P. at SNY Insurance."

If all the lonely people in this world got together, would they still be lonely people? Ruby wondered.

Milt must not have been thinking when he referred to Ruby's followers as the "crazies," because Ruby took great offense and told him so. Instead, she dubbed the convoy "The Originals," and within forty-eight hours, there were twenty of them blindly following to points unknown to all but Ruby, Maria, Joni, and Milt: an H&R Block tax consultant, a Roman Catholic priest, a Goth guy who asked to be called "Lucid Nightmare," a Winnebago lady riding with her nine cats, a Tarot-reader, an emergency room physician, a PTA president, a former Georgia state representative, and a few others of whom Ruby lost track.

"Calling Ruby, calling Ruby, where are you, Ruby Witherspoon?" Rosenthal summoned during his eight o'clock drive time block. *"I'm hearing all kinds of gossip, Miss Ruby. You got a boyfriend? You cheatin' on me? Call me, baby. Tell me about this geezer you've been banging."*

Ruby tsk'd out loud, but called right in.

"You are very disrespectful," she scolded the second Rosenthal answered the hotline in the studio.

"Yeah, but at least I'm rich."

"I'm glad you have deep pockets. I'm going to have to take you to court one of these days for all the chaos you've unleashed in my life."

"You love it, Ruby. So tell me what's going on."

"Well, at last count, I've got about thirty of your listeners who are followin' me," she said. *"They're nice people and all, but this wasn't what I was after when I left New York."*

"I'm coming too!" he said.

"That's all I need," she said.

"Where are you going, Ruby love?"

"If I tell you that, I'll have 400 more of your people followin' me. Enough's enough."

"But really, I want to come with you," he said.

"I'll tell you when it's time. It's not time yet."

"So, about this boyfriend of yours."

"Yes, Steve?"

"Where'd you pick him up?"

"Stuckey's," she said.

"I bet he couldn't wait to show you his pecan log."

"You disgust me."

"You love me."

"I don't love you."

"Is your boyfriend good in bed?"

Ruby thought about how or if she should answer.

"Yes," she finally said, going into her most private life if only to show the world that old people aren't dead. *"We've found my G-spot, Steve."*

For the first time in radio history, Steve Rosenthal's big mouth wouldn't move.

There was nothing to say.

Chapter Twenty-six

"I've been acting out again…"

His mind worked itself into another loop, like a computer trying to solve an unsolvable equation. There had to be an answer, but what? Maria didn't want him.

No, she really wanted him. Deep down. Ever since they paired up on a microeconomics project in their sophomore year of high school. He asked her to a movie and she went, but they didn't make out and then he moved when school ended and he never did get the nerve to call her up after that, but he felt sure she liked him, and he was that age where he thought about her day and night and it had a memorable effect on his body. He tried to forget her, and for the most part he did until he took his fiancé to The Season's on his twenty-second birthday and saw Maria eating three tables over. He stopped by to say hello, and she was gracious and pretended to remember him. His face seemed familiar, but she couldn't place it. He ended his relationship with his fiancé the next night because it just didn't feel right to him. He knew he would do better with Maria. Knew it.

Still, all these years later, things had not progressed much, if at all. Maria didn't know she wanted him, didn't know how much he loved her, how happy he would make her.

Where the hell was she now anyhow? Was she running from him? Why? Didn't she get it? He loved her. He wouldn't hurt her.

He *loved* her. She thought *he* was dangerous? It wasn't danger, it was infatuation, it was love, it was passion, it was attraction, it was electric.

"I did some E. It calmed me down. Made me feel worthy for a whole goddamn day."

"What caused the slip?" asked Dr. Cavender, his counselor.

He would marry Maria if he could find her. Get down on his hands and knees and propose. If only, if only, if only he hadn't bungled everything so badly. Okay granted, even he would admit he'd gone too far in the past. He couldn't help himself! He'd never been obsessed before. He liked Maria. A lot. Loved her. Madly. Wildly. Beautiful, beautiful Maria. Warm. He had to be with her. He would win her over. He knew it.

"What's the matter?"

"Oh. I'm anxious. I don't know where my girlfriend is. It's freakin' me out."

Why did she get rid of her old cell phone? That was his greatest coup, but it was now useless. When she was still in Atlanta, he broke in her house at night, took her cell phone, registered it on a website that tracked her movements to precise addresses, and then he returned the phone with her never knowing it had been taken, never knowing she was sending out a beacon that told him exactly where she was at all times. She never knew, and as long as Maria kept that cell phone on, he knew precisely where she was. He would log into that website, tell it to locate that phone, and a map would pop up with the street address. He could even have the website plot her movements every half hour.

"I thought you said it was your ex-girlfriend."

Well, if he was going to tell the truth, she really wasn't his girlfriend at all, but he never told Dr. Cavender the whole truth about anything. Why should he? He was better at analyzing people than Cavender, but the court order from the DUI mandated the substance abuse counseling. Did it make any difference that he called Maria his girlfriend or his ex? One day he'd call her his wife.

What a knockout. The first time he saw her, she took his breath. Gorgeous. Those brown eyes. Her lips. Hands. Breasts. That waist. Her ass.

"So you are doing this because your former girlfriend won't see you?"

"Right." He cleared his throat. *"I'm having trouble getting over it."*

"So the relationship ended because she moved to New York for career reasons. Why didn't you go with her?"

"Well…"

What could he say? She went to New York to run away from him because she thought he might kill her? That he had to hire a detective to track his lover down? How absolutely absurd. Someone of his education and accomplishment!

Some nights, he'd sit in front of the computer for hours, tracking whatever scraps of details about her life that he possibly could, piecing together a psychiatric profile of her from her background and what he'd seen in her house. He knew who her parents were, what they owned, when they immigrated to the U.S. from Cuba, how her dad made his fortune, where Maria went to school, the location of her first, second, third, fourth, and fifth apartments. He knew she'd been on the debate team in high school and in the Anchor Club. And, in college, she lived for just one year in a dorm and was photographed by the Associated Press at a pro abortion rights rally in D.C. There is so much in the public record. He could go to Google Earth to get an aerial view of her home, he could go to the property appraiser's records to see the floor plan, he could check the public record to re-learn that she was a good Democrat who had voted in every election (including primaries and runoffs) since she turned eighteen. He knew her house cost $360,000 when she bought it, and that she put down $200,000 in cash and financed the rest through Wells Fargo. The list went on and on, because the Internet is a stalker's best friend. Oh, and don't call him a stalker. He hates that word.

"Why not go up and surprise her?"

Oh, that'd be great, considering.

Considering that there had already been more than enough surprises. Breaking into her place back in Atlanta, well that went a little far. He knew that. He knew it was inappropriate and illegal, but he wanted to see where and how she lived. He wanted to see the books she kept on her nightstand, the pictures on her refrigerator, the art on her walls. He wanted to smell her home, her clothes, everything. Breaking in through the back was surprisingly easy for someone with no burglary experience, so he went there several times before he ever mentioned it in one of his notes.

He knew he shouldn't go in there while she was home, but the vision of her peacefully sleeping called him and, this is not a lie, he really didn't go there to scare her, although he knew that it would. He went there to be with her, not scare her into leaving him forever.

"Maybe she's waiting for you to come for her. It is romantic in its own way."

Maybe that was it. Maybe. He imagined being her husband, the candlelit dinners she would make for him, the mornings when she would awaken him by making love to his sleeping body…

He knew that some of the things he did and some of the things he wrote could have been misinterpreted, but he really meant well. And at least Maria did not know him as her stalker.

"She left me and I haven't felt whole since. I am empty. Dead."

"She never called you after she left?"

The decision to hire a private detective came after great deliberation because, if it were noticed, it could lead authorities straight to him. Benny Haikem was known to be good and fast and trustworthy, and since he wasn't having luck finding Maria, he knew Haikem would. It took two days. Haikem even let himself in her apartment. He found paperwork for her insurance as a cab driver. A cab driver! He couldn't believe it when Haikem told him that one.

He figured he'd plan a reunion trip to New York in a few weeks and just accidentally cross her path. Wouldn't that surprise her if he wound up in her taxi!

In the meantime, he waited.

In the meantime, like half of the U.S., he found his way to www.rosenthalsucks.com and clicked on the "Save Ruby" link. And he clicked on the link to "Photos of Ruby's Traveling Caravan."

Maria.

Those brown eyes. Her lips. Hands. Breasts. That waist. Her ass.

Maria. All his.

Chapter Twenty-seven

The Fat Dixie Grill House off Georgia 27 is busy anyhow. It's busy anyhow because it is the best home style, old South fixins' in Georgia and if you are heading south on 27, you have to stop there and if you're not heading that way, you always get there just because. Fried green tomatoes—a half-inch thick, fried chicken livers and gizzards, mashed potatoes, onion rings, fried okra, peach cobbler, and biscuits as big as your head. You walk in and waddle out.

"Fat Dixie Grill House!" Joni shouted to Maria, who didn't hesitate to steer the cab into its already full lot. Milt followed, with all of Ruby's Originals. Shane parked her semi in the emergency lane out front, and when another semi pulled in right behind her, it became clear that a second long-haul trucker had joined the convoy. It was getting ridiculous.

In all, nearly fifty Originals crowded into the Fat Dixie Grill with no warning whatsoever. Not that the restaurant couldn't handle getting slammed, because getting slammed was the routine at the Fat Dixie Grill, but all the pink-uniformed servers and most of the already seated patrons had to stop and take a gander at all these one-of-a-kinds who looked like circus folk, only cleaner.

By this point, it was clear that meal stops were all about back-slapping and hand-shaking and loudly making friends and chowing down. Ruby gave these misfits a family where, for once, they all belonged.

"I can't believe these people," Maria said to Joni. "Who in the hell drops everything to join some stranger on some strange caravan?"

"Yeah. Don't they have lives?" Joni said. Then she realized how judgmental she was being, especially since she'd done that very thing, so she had to shut up. Even though she was an "insider," she was also an Original. But one of the original Originals, so that gave her status. While Ruby and Milt would mingle with every new arrival to meet, greet, and eat, Joni kept to her core group. Maria, too, until the day at the Fat Dixie Grill when a fine-looking hunk of man-flesh walked in and said to Shane, "I'm looking for Ruby's Originals."

"Ya found 'em!" Shane said, "Why don't you sit your tall, dark, and handsome self down and have some lunch."

"How'd he get so damned fine?" Joni said to Maria, who looked the golden guy over, taking in his tanned skin, tight black t-shirt, and sexy blue jeans.

Joni fanned her face for effect. "That guy looks like Peter Callahan."

"That must be it. I've been in love with Peter Callahan since he was in *Tempest.*" Actually, everybody in the world fell in love with the tanned, muscled superstar from *Tempest*, so his look-alike walked with great confidence—like a man bound to score.

A second later, a CBS News satellite truck parked behind the trucks in the emergency lane in front of the restaurant and a male reporter (who couldn't have been any older than twenty-five and deliberately rolled up the sleeves to his starched shirt) loudly proclaimed, "We're here for Ruby Witherspoon."

Nobody pointed her out or even acknowledged him, even though he obviously thought everybody's world should melt into a simultaneous climax with the appearance of a network camera and newsman.

"Excuse me?" He walked up to the oldest woman in the restaurant, who just happened to be Clara Sue Higgins, who lunched at the Fat Dixie twice a week. "You're Ruby Witherspoon? I'm Dex Stevens from CBS and we're here to join your little caravan for the day." He motioned to his cameraman to start rolling. Clara Sue looked over to Ruby, who winked the go-ahead for her.

Maria slipped outside to avoid the media intrusion. Dex turned to the camera and spoke into the microphone. "I'm here with America's most celebrated senior citizen at the Fat Dixie Grill in Hayfield, Georgia. Ruby Witherspoon, we finally found you! Tell us a little about your big adventure…" He dropped the microphone in front of Clara Sue's mouth.

She looked at him, then at the camera, then back at him.

"Young man, you're an idiot," Clara Sue said, as the Originals clapped and cheered in the background. Dex Stevens squirmed uncomfortably as she lit into him: "You think all old ladies look alike. Well, they don't. I'm not Ruby Witherspoon. And before I tell you which old bag is the right old bag, you'd better learn a few things about old bags. We are damned easy to piss off!"

With that, Ruby and two other senior women—all about the same age but no two looking remotely alike—circled and high-fived a triumphant Clara Sue Higgins. But that young man wasn't as clueless as he'd seemed. He picked up the microphone, turned to the camera, and said, "Folks, I *am* an idiot. And I think what you just saw proves the whole point Ruby Witherspoon has been trying to make on her much ballyhooed journey into the heart of America." He turned to the women. "Now, which of you sirens is Ruby Witherspoon?"

Ruby stepped forward and shook his hand for the camera.

"Good to meet you," Dex said. "You certainly have amassed quite a collection of fans to join you on your road trip."

"They're my Originals," Ruby said. "Thanks to that crazy Steve Rosenthal, I've lost my privacy but gained a whole world of friends."

He turned to the camera. "For those of you who haven't heard of Ruby—and it's hard to imagine that you haven't—this seventy-eight-year-old lady has raised holy hell with her daughters, who want to stick her in assisted living." He turned to Ruby: "You don't look like you deserve that fate. I hope your girls will stop being so cruel."

"Well, wait a second. Everybody assumes that my girls are being mean to me. They are not. I've got the best daughters a mother could want, but they are overprotective and I don't need that."

"So you are trying to teach them a lesson?"

"No, I'm not trying to teach anyone a lesson. I'm trying to live my life. And if they learn a lesson by seeing that, then that's a bonus. Just because a person gets older and encounters a few obstacles, it doesn't mean they have to be put away and sheltered from any and all harm. I could be safe in a home or I could be here at the Fat Dixie Grill with all my friends. Which is a better place for a seventy-eight-year-old? I just wish my girls were with me to enjoy this."

Thousands of miles away, Nina picked up the phone and dialed Jacqueline.

"You watching?" Jacqueline asked.

"Mmmm hmmm."

"What do you think?"

Nina thought for a moment. "If this were anyone else's mother saying and doing all that, I'd think that she was the coolest chick on planet earth."

That night, Ruby and her gang joined the Originals for a bonfire at the KOA, where Milt and some of the others camped. The night was gorgeous and humid, a lush southern night, complete with lightning bugs and a cricket choir. Shane got out her guitar and started plucking away, really bad C&W music that was perfect for the occasion, songs like Roy Rogers' *Happy Trails* and Gene Autry's *The Yellow Rose of Texas*.

"Let me get you a beer, darlin," Paul Preston, a skinny psychiatrist who'd joined the Originals offered to Maria.

"I'm fine," she said.

"No, I wanna buy you a drink," he slurred, putting his hands on her shoulders.

"I'm fine." She jerked away coldly.

"Uppity woman." He shrugged as she moved on. "But I think I love you!"

She pretended to ignore him and joined the others singing "Back in the Saddle Again."

"I'm back in the saddle again.." she sang, and all the others joined in. *"Out where a friend is a friend, Where the longhorn cattle feed, On the lowly gypsum weed, Back in the saddle again."*

"EVERYBODY!" Shane ordered. The chorus of Originals was now huge. There had to be at least a hundred people—black, white, Hispanic, Asian. The youngest was a baby and the oldest was…wait, Ruby hated when people kept tabs on that.

"Ridin' the range once more!" they sang. *"Totin' my old .44, Where you sleep out every night, And the only law is right, Back in the saddle again…"*

All those Originals singing, hooking arms, and toasting their beers in honor of good friends. What a night.

"Whoopi-ty-aye-oh, Rockin' to and fro, Back in the saddle again…" the Peter Callahan look-alike crooned as Maria walked past. He'd caught her attention all right.

"Whoopi-ty-aye-yay, I go my way, Back in the saddle again," she sang back to him.

Milt came up behind Maria, tapped her on the shoulder, and asked her to dance, and Joni, feigning jealousy, made him dance as a trio. Curly Watson, a seventy-year-old insurance salesman who refused to retire, brought out his fiddle and started playing "Sweet Betsy from Pike," and Ruby took center stage, singing along with him, *"Oh don't you remember sweet Betsy from Pike, Who crossed the wide prairie with her lover Ike, With two yoke of oxen, a big yellow dog, A tall Shanghai rooster, and one spotted hog…"*

Maria had been so suspicious of these strangers joining their posse, but they were so much fun, such good people just wanting to connect and let loose.

All Ruby's fault.

Chapter Twenty-eight

Maria looked like hell.

Like hell! One long, realistic stare in the mirror and there was no pretending. This was not the vibrant, exotic-looking woman she'd been in her old life, not at all. *What happened to me? Where did I go?* Maria wondered. Lord. If you took before and after photos of her pre- and post-stalker, you'd have documented proof of how stress wears a person down to nothing.

The cops couldn't fix it. Shrinks couldn't fix it. Escaping to New York couldn't fix it. And neither could the road to Weeki Wachee. That stalker was right with her, wherever she went. She checked the bullets in her gun and rechecked them. She wrestled with her decision not to tell Ruby about the stalker, because if Ruby knew, she might stop messing with the gun but she'd never stop worrying. Maria bolstered herself with affirmations like, "I am safe and secure and am capable of protecting myself," just like her old therapist told her to do, but affirmations can't kill off a stalker, or the fear.

She'd let herself go.

And that sallow reflection in the mirror was all that was left.

Maria phoned her mom and dad from outside the Fat Dixie Grill.

"I miss you, daughter," her father told her.

"I miss you, Daddy," she answered. "I know you're busy, but I'm not far away. Any way you could meet me tomorrow morning? And bring Mom and Nadia?"

They would drop everything to see her, without question or hesitation. So as directed, they headed for her room at the Birdsall Motel near Barnesville, Georgia. Her father didn't even ask why she was there or how long she'd be there. He hadn't seen her in six months, and as much as she worried for herself, he worried tenfold. At least. They'd be there. They always were there.

As she prepared for their arrival, she washed her hair twice, shaved her legs, did her nails, and then carefully painted on her make-up because the most important thing she had to do was convince her mother, father, and sister that she was doing just fine, fine, absolutely fine, and all their worry was overblown. She smiled at herself when she finished revitalizing her image. Now the reflection in the mirror was familiar and attractive and someone she knew—and loved.

Girl, ya still got it, she thought.

"Oh my God, are you beautiful!" Joni gasped when Maria finally emerged from the bathroom.

"I must be on a roll. That's the second time someone's told me that in twelve hours."

"Dish. Who else is calling you beautiful?" Joni asked.

"Well…"

"I know!" Ruby interjected. "It's that young man with the movie star eyes and the Olympic muscles. Hell, I'd go for him if only I were only about fifty years younger…"

"He's pretty hot," said Joni.

"I know, but he's not hot on me. No, my admirer—the man so enchanted by my charm and beauty—was none other than Coach. Mmm hmmm. That's the best I can do for now."

Ruby chuckled. "Keep on that make-up. You'll get your movie star."

This cleaned-up version of Maria looked nothing like the cab driver version. It would be possible to know the cab driver and walk right past the made-up woman, or know the beautiful version of Maria and walk right past the cab driver. But only an expert would ever see any similarity between the two, because there was none. The beauty was confident and strong and she had an edge about her that almost dared others to engage. The cabby was diffident, wary and very, very defensive. Made-up, she exuded her old confidence.

Maria blew Ruby and Joni kisses as they left, and minutes later, Maria's father knocked on the motel room door with the same rap he'd always used to wake her when she was a kid, oversleeping for school. "Be cool, girl. Be cool," Maria told herself. "Don't cry. Be strong. Be strong. Be strong…"

But one look at Mom, Dad, and Nadia, and Maria completely shattered inside. All of them were in tears the minute they saw her and she kept telling herself, "Buck up, buck up! Buck the fuck up!" But she cried anyhow, she cried a lot, and she really hated herself for it—with good reason, because these days, her family worried more than she did, and that made her worry even more. She knew that, if she could just give the right impression of self-confidence, happiness, and calm, they'd realize she was doing okay on her own. Crying like that—so vulnerable—meant they would worry even more.

Stalker bastard. Of all the things he'd done to her, tearing her from her family was the worst. She'd lost too much time with her parents and sister already, and what time she had for these next-to-never visits and occasional phone calls was always colored by fear. She used to see her family at least once a week, but now it felt like never. Even with Ruby and Joni in her life, the world was empty without her family because her family had always been the center of her life. For now, there was no way around it. After so much fear, Maria still couldn't tell how much of the stalker threat was still real and how much was her own paranoia, and she did not want to put the people around her in danger, so she insisted on minimizing contact with her family until she felt certain the stalker had lost interest in her. That meant calls from pay phones outside restaurants and meetings like this—in generic motels in Nowheresville, Georgia.

"Honey, you look great."

Dad. What a gentle man. Her inspiration. When she was growing up, he used to say, "When the sun rises, it rises for everyone," and, "In America, anything is possible." He was proof of the American dream, as she would be—and he made sure of it. She couldn't remember a day when she didn't hear him prod, "*¡Arranca!*" (Get going!) or "*¡Dale a todo meter!*" (Give it all you got!"). He drove her— he drove both of his kids—but with great confidence and love that taught them to grab hold of the possibility of living, rather than letting life just play out.

He wrapped his arms around his oldest baby. "We love you and care about you," he told Maria, and it made her smile because he said it that very way every single time, in person, on the phone, in voice mail, and in e-mail. "We worry about you."

As much as she hated the burden she'd forced upon her parents, there are times when it is good to be worried about. Maria hated that her life brought such grief to her parents, but knowing they were there like that made her feel less alone. And loved. Very, very loved.

"Don't worry about me, Dad. I'm on a harebrained adventure in my yellow cab. When I get done, they'll make a movie about this."

"A movie!" he laughed.

"Like *Thelma and Louise!*" her sister, Nadia, said.

"We could do without the movie. We want our daughter home."

Nadia threw a pillow at him. "C'mon, Pop! You promised you wouldn't get all sad and serious. You're turning this into a soap opera."

"Yeah, Pop!" Maria shouted as she threw a pillow too. Her dad fended the girls off as they started a pillow fight like they did when they were kids. He hoisted Maria up by the waist and tossed her on the bed, then growled at Nadia like a bear. But he quickly turned serious again. "I worry about my daughter. I haven't seen her in more than six months," he said to Nadia, a little out of breath.

"We all worry about your daughter," she shot back. "But you aren't helping things getting all boo-boo faced, Pop."

He got one of those smitten Dad smiles he always got when one of his daughters made him blush. Maria kissed his cheek.

"This change of scenery was the best thing I ever did," she told him, doing her right-best to sound convincing. "I'm having a blast. You shouldn't worry, because I don't."

They knew she was lying.

"I don't believe you," Reuben Muñoz said, thumbing his daughter's chin. "I think you say that because you want me to sleep better. The only way I'm going to sleep better is for you to be home with us." He kissed her forehead.

"It's my big adventure, Pop."

It surprised her that, considering the inconvenience and the sacrifices, what she'd found in her new life was actually good for her. Just months ago, she lived a truly comfortable and somewhat glamorous life, mingling with celebrities and living in an extraordinary home in Atlanta's best neighborhood. Now she drove a cab. She used to pull in at least six grand a week, and now, she was lucky to have a hundred bucks in her pocket after expenses. Back when, if a Tarot reader would have told her that this was the life ahead of her, she would have left, certain that the reader was a fraud and the Tarot was a fraud. It was way too bizarre and unrealistic, but sometimes, that is what life is. Way too bizarre and unrealistic.

"Have you heard any more from that man?" Mom asked.

"Naw," Maria said. She thought about the break-in at her apartment but didn't say a damned thing about it.

"How long do you think you need to keep doing this?"

"I have no idea."

"Not forever, though."

"Not forever."

"Thank God. But how long?"

How long?

Nadia pulled Maria into the bathroom and whispered, "We got a letter just this week. Mom and Dad weren't going to say anything."

Maria froze. "From him?"

"Yeah. All it said was, 'Tell Maria I'll wait for her. I'm a patient man.' "

Maria let out a defeated sigh. She wondered how many years she could stand this. When she moved to New York, she'd hoped the change would be so temporary that she could move home in a few months and resume her life.

"Do you think you were followed here?"

"No way," Nadia said. "Not the way Pop was acting. I had to go to a Krispy Kreme restaurant where they picked me up in a rental car. It was his James Bond double-oh-seven moment."

Maria wanted to laugh, but she couldn't.

"Who is doing this to me? Son of a fucking bitch! Why doesn't he just die or go obsess on somebody else?" She often felt the urge to kill the son of a bitch. Just blow his fucking head off. She felt guilty for thinking it, much less speaking it, but she wanted him to let go or vanish—she didn't care how.

"Maria, I want to move up to New York and stay with you for a few months. I've already talked to H.R. about a leave of absence."

Oh for God's sake.

"No."

"Oh, shut up for a minute, will you? I want to do it. It would be fun to spend some time living my old acting dream and going to auditions and seeing if I can get anything. Dad says he'll pay, and I miss you a lot. It'd be fun for me."

"I miss you too, sis," Maria said. "Every day. But I need to get through this myself. If you were there, I'd have to worry for two people—not one. I need to do this my way."

Nadia hugged her sister. "Your way isn't working, sister. You're all alone in the big city. I'm going to come."

"No, you're not."

"Yes, I am."

"No…"

"For once, let me be the good sister, okay?"

"The good sister would…"

"The good sister would be up there with you, and I am going, like it or not. You're not in this alone anymore."

"I want to be alone."

"If you don't let me move in, I'll rent an apartment in the same building. You aren't stopping me. I'm coming."

Maria shrugged. She thought about her sister living in that tiny apartment with her and she knew they would kill each other. Probably within five minutes. Nadia was such a slob. She watched too much television. Her cooking sucked. She talked on the phone nonstop.

"It won't work."

"It will."

"I love you, but I don't want to live with you."

"Well, if I can deal with your obsessive-compulsive cleaning disorder, you can deal with my obsessive-compulsive slob disorder."

Maria suppressed a laugh.

"And what if my rat-bastard psycho stalker comes by when you are there alone?"

"Then I will feel sorry for him," she said with an air of absolute confidence. "Because he won't get out of there with his balls. Either of them."

It was such a Nadia remark. But the idea of Nadia moving in really would amplify Maria's stress. Nadia might have thought the gesture would help, but it would just make Maria wonder if her sister was okay, what she was doing, and if the door was locked. Imagine the stalker harming the wrong prey.

"You can't come. I don't want you there. I only want to worry about myself. I can take care of myself."

"Two worriers are better than one."

"No, they aren't. But I love you," Maria said.

"Love you right back. But get ready: You are about to host the houseguest from hell. I'm coming and I'm bringing my curlers. You know how good I look with curlers and all my skin care creams on my face."

"You're not coming."

"I'm coming. Debate over."

They hugged, Maria's way of formally submitting to her sister's insistence like she always did. Nadia was eighteen months younger, but always got her way, something that used to bug the hell out of Maria when she was young. Now it was endearing. And, whatever. Maybe it'd be good to have the girl around.

"When will we see you again?" their mother asked when Maria and Nadia rejoined them. Anna Muñoz took Maria's hand and squeezed a Saint Christopher medal in it. "I worry about you every minute. Every single minute. Every single second of every single minute."

Maria bit her tongue hard because she did not want to completely lose it, but she dissolved into tears again. Soft, full, child tears, the kind she used to cry when she was a kid, when Mom could fix everything.

"Mama, don't worry about me!" Maria cried out.

"Mamas worry about their babies." She wrapped her arms around her daughter.

Babies need their mamas. Even when they swear they are strong enough to take care of themselves, they need their mamas. Maria looked at her mother and rested her head on her chest. Her mother kissed her hair and squeezed her baby tight.

It was the safest Maria'd felt since she'd left Atlanta.

Chapter Twenty-nine

There is every reason in the world to come to Dublin, Georgia, especially if you like 103-degree, high-humidity heat or you care to observe a game of Redneck Horseshoes, where the Billies (hillbillies) toss toilet seats instead of horseshoes or other events like the Mudpit Belly Flop or the Butt Crack Competition. Dublin, Georgia, is just spittin' distance off the track and well worth the visit if a trip coincides with the annual Redneck Games. Damned lucky for Maria, Joni, Milt, and about three hundred Originals, Ruby's trip to Weeki Wachee coincided with opening day of the games.

A radio station hatched the games as a South Georgia rival to the '96 Atlanta Olympics, but after the first competition, the rednecks wouldn't wait four years to hold another. These Olympics happen every summer. Instead of an Olympic torch, some clodhopping hillbilly who calls himself "L'Bow" runs into Buckeye Park with a propane torch and lights a ceremonial grill to uproarious hoots and hollers, surrounded by almost 20,000 hicks and bumpkins and rubes and rebels.

Some rednecks are real rednecks, and those rednecks take the business of rednecking very seriously. The best of it was the laughter. The worst was the sight of Confederate flags that were everywhere, sometimes with stickers that said, "HERITAGE NOT HATE."

If they were looking for the opportunity to remind the world that they are "Redneck by the grace of God," the flags certainly proved it.

Ruby's gang arrived just in time for the "Bobbin' for Pig's Feet" competition, where the bold and the brave dunk head and shoulders in huge plastic bins filled with water and icky, raw pig's feet. Ten crazed competitors plunged in with exuberance, biting down on the revolting pig's feet that still had the bones and hooves. Shane was one of them, of course, and she wore a t-shirt with a map of the state of Arkansas and the slogan "Lit'racy ain't all thet impo'tant." The gold medal winner retrieved seven pig's feet in under twenty seconds. Shane only retrieved four.

"Care for a Moon Pie?" asked the Peter Callahan look-alike, who wore a green shirt with a white drawing of a trailer, with the word "TRASH" underneath it. He held out a chocolate Moon Pie for Maria.

"Oh baby…"

"I'm Ethan. Figured I should finally introduce myself formally."

"Maria."

And that was it. Paired up for the Olympics at a festival where the pickins were pretty slim—unless you were in search of a pot-bellied hillbilly with a greasy mullet.

A pregnant woman in her late thirties, wearing a Confederate-flag bikini, cheered from the sidelines, smoking Camels. "Don be so ignert, Billy! Git them pigs foots!" In black marker, her belly declared "FUTURE REDNECK."

That was nothing. An hour later, right there on center stage, Joni realized she was about to witness the nadir of the fine arts, a rather astounding symphonic performance unlike anything she'd ever even imagined in her life.

An arm-farting competition.

"Mah name is Buck Rabbitt," a seventy-something emcee announced. "I'd like to welcome you to this year's famous arm-farting serenade. In this here competition, you'll see the most talented among us compete for a two hundred dollar gift card from the ACE Hardware by serenading us with their favorite tunes. This takes a great deal of practice and concentration, so we hope you know what an honor it is to welcome our famous arm farters. Okay, Jug, you're up first. Please welcome Jug Walker, who is a-gonna play 'I've Been Workin' on the Railroad' for us."

There is indeed an art to cupping one's left hand in the air pocket in the right underarm, then flapping that right wing down with enough force to create a majestic fart note that may be a B-flat or an A-minor, depending on what the song happened to be.

First Jug played, then came Cletis doing "Clementine," then came Imogene with "Yankee Doodle," then Cooter did "She'll Be Comin' Around the Mountain." A man called Skeeter arm-farted his way through the "Star Spangled Banner," and that proved controversial because the true arm-fart aficionados knew how hard it was to hit the high notes, but the red-blooded patriots found it un-American to arm-fart the national anthem. Some in the crowd actually held their right hand to their hearts as Skeeter played.

The competition's finale came when Buck Rabbitt took the microphone and said, "Finally, let's welcome Buster Rollins, the son of our own Dwayne and Raylene, who will perform 'Old Folks at Home,' or as most of us old folks know it as, 'Way Down Upon the Suwannee River.' "

The crowd broke into riotous applause and yelling, and Buster Rollins took the stage.

It was *that* Buster.

It was that very Buster from the Polkamotion, the guy who gave Joni the note that she'd read a million times, the note that said "I'll never see you again, so I think you should know that you are a very beautiful woman. Best, Buster."

And here he was, seated like a concert violinist preparing to perform for his hundreds of frenzied fans, arm-farting his way through Stephen Foster's "Suwannee River" before segueing into a truly inspired version of "Camptown Races." The crowd went insane when he got to the "doo-da, doo-da" parts—not that they weren't insane already.

Barefoot Buster, dressed in Lee jeans with a red "INSTANT REDNECK (Just Add Beer)" t-shirt, passionately arm-farted his way through the medley. He stood from his chair, took a bow, and leapt off the stage into a throng of back-slapping Billys. Joni waited and waited and waited for his admirers to disperse and head off to evaluate butt cracks. Finally, Buster's eyes connected with hers. He instantly recognized her, and his pleasure at their reunion was evident in his broad smile.

"JOOOOON-EEE!" he shouted to her.

"Bust-ah!" she shouted back playfully.

He skipped toward her, wrapped his arms around her, and swung her in a circle.

"What the heck are you doing here?"

"Ruby steers the taxi, and this is where it stopped."

He nodded knowingly.

"You and your friends are all over the media. Can't believe I was hitting on such a famous celebrity."

"Yeah right. I thought I'd never see you again."

"Y'know, the minute you all drove off I realized I was the biggest chicken-shit dork on earth. Didn't get your phone number or even your e-mail address."

"Maybe we should swap info right this minute so we don't lose each other."

Buster said that seemed like a good idea, considering he'd already let her slip away once. He pulled out his wallet, extracted a business card, and handed it to her. It had his name, cell number, and e-mail address. His job title was listed as "Recovered Exec in Transition."

"I told my folks I'd meet 'em here," he said. "Y'gotta meet them. They're right serious about all this rednecking."

He escorted her across the park, past the toilet seat horseshoe toss to a picnic area next to the Oconee River.

His barefoot dad wore overalls with no shirt underneath, a brown, floppy hillbilly hat, and he sported a ten-inch matted-fuzz beard and jagged yellow teeth.

"He really went all-out for this!" Joni laughed, and when Buster didn't say anything, she realized his dad wasn't in costume.

Dwayne Rollins slapped his son on the back and smiled at Joni.

"You're worse than a pet coon. Dayum! You can't keep your hands off of anything!" Dwayne said to Buster, then turned toward Joni. "Hey little darlin'."

"Nice to meet you. I'm Joni."

"I met her up at that polka festival," said Buster, just as they were approached by a Budweiser-toting woman who weighed at least 215 and had a gut the size of an Igloo cooler.

"Join us for lunch," said Raylene Rollins as she cordially extended her hand to Joni, then said to her son, "She's prettier than a spotted heifer in a pansy patch."

Joni looked to Buster and shrugged helplessly, in need of interpretation.

"Ma thinks you're lovely," he said.

"Well?" asked Raylene.

"Ahsposo," said Buster.

"Well butter my butt and call me biscuit," said Raylene.

Shoulda been there. Shoulda seen that look on Joni's face. My God. The family from Redneck Mars landed in South Jawjuh and begat its only son, a normal-looking white boy with white teeth and nare a stubble of beard. And Redneck Raylene and Redneck Dwayne thought long and hard about their only son and named him Buster Ralph Rollins. This was a gene pool to be feared.

"Hot today, isn't it?" Raylene muttered to Dwayne. "Pass me that there beer, please." To Raylene, "beer" was pronounced "bare."

Dwayne tossed her a Bud, which she opened, chugged, then crumpled with her hand and banged against her head before tossing it on the ground.

Joni's eyes widened, horrified.

"Y'ain't used to good country folk?" Raylene asked her.

What was she supposed to say?

But then Raylene started laughing, and Dwayne sneaked up behind his wife and gave her a big smooch on the neck, then pretended to bite her like a vampire. Joni cringed at the site of those disgusting teeth chomping on real skin, but then he looked at Joni, started laughing extra hard, and extracted a full set of Billy Bob teeth from his mouth. Underneath the novelty teeth was a perfect set of pearly whites. Raylene pulled hers out too. Dwayne even peeled the side of his beard off so she could see it was a good fake.

"'Just putting you on, pumpkin," he said. "It's all in fun."

Joni stepped forward and hugged Raylene. "I'm so relieved."

Buster smiled. "Yeah, they're game for anything. Pop's a mechanical engineer and Ma's a chemist."

"We're boring," said Raylene.

"So we like to act out," said Dwayne.

That was the moment when Joni not only fell for Buster, but also his bloodline.

Time came for another signature event. The Originals scooted over to the swarm around the Hubcap Hurl, which most obviously is like the discus throw, except that this was South Jawjuh and there ain't no discuses in the region, just old hubcaps. The spectators chugged their swill as the athletes flung their hubcaps as far as they could.

Dwayne wound himself up, turned away from the path of his hurl, then spun around a couple of times to gain momentum before letting it go. It floated through the air a good sixty feet before it dropped straight down to the ground, dead.

Buster followed, practicing the same professional winding, turning, spinning, and casting motions, but his hubcap made it 120 feet, which didn't put him in the running for a medal but was nothing to sniff at.

Coach made his own weak attempt, but they didn't even bother to measure it because the result would have been too humiliating.

Joni saw Ruby entering the ring, and felt a sense of pride seeing a member of her own "fambly" in the competition. She also noticed that psychiatrist, Paul, watching Maria's every turn.

Ruby focused. Spun around a few times, then hurled that hubcap to the sky with the pride and confidence of an Olympian. Twenty feet in the air it stopped cold and dropped.

But the crowd cheered wildly for Ruby, more than for any of the previous redneck competitors.

Standing proud in front of her hushed fans, Ruby spoke to her people.

"That's the fine thing about getting old! Fry mah hide! Varmints are impressed by ennythin' you do! Fry mah hide!" she yelled.

"Ruuuubee! Ruuuuuubeee! Ruuuuubeeee!" they cheered, That crazy hayseed Ruby was even presented with a key to the city and invited to come back the next year, which she vowed she would do.

Ruby knew how to work a crowd, and at the Redneck Games, she owned it. She was so damned cool, and Joni felt proud to be in her inner circle. She also noticed a little action off to the side, too, because Maria—yes, Maria—was getting a hubcap hurling lesson from Ethan, and she was obviously liking it. He stood right behind her, wrapped his arms around her on both sides, and taught her the proper grip. Like she really needed a lesson on how to hurl a hubcap. It was just like a Frisbee, for Pete's sake. But Maria, so obviously besotted, melted into that he-man's arms.

"Your friend seems to have made a friend," Buster said.

"Oh yeah," Joni said.

"Ready for yer belly flop?" Buster urged, grabbing her hand and leading her to the central attraction at the games.

One at a time, she saw big rednecks and little rednecks, male and female, stand at the side of a huge, muddy pool, then leap into the air for a spectacular flop into the soupy mud pit. Buster kept nudging her with his elbow, then motioning with his head toward the pit, goading her on.

There really wasn't much to think about, because when you think about doing something that seems silly or uncomfortable or childish, you don't do it. You hesitate, and Joni is the North American Queen of Hesitation. It's impossible for her to let go. Can't be done. Can't.

But then again, maybe she could.

Joni signaled to Raylene to toss her a Budweiser and she gulped it without pausing for air. This Joni stood at the side of the mudpit, lifted her arms above her head, bent her knees, and hurled herself into the air as she shouted, "SHEEEEE-IIIIIT" and flopped magnificently into the pit below.

Gross was not the word for the mud pit, because *gross* sounds too clean for what Joni landed in. Mud filled her pockets, her bra, her hair, her nostrils, her ears. She climbed out of the pit, looking like a caramelized version of her old self, but underneath all that mud was a woman suddenly cleansed of all angst who was laughing—out loud—unrestrained. Even as she wiped the mud out of her eyes, she looked at the crew hollering around her and realized for the first time in years that she was really right there in that moment—alive.

She felt, well, she felt beautiful. In her skin, alive and beautiful.

Mud Monster Joni trekked over to the river and took a nice, cool dip, trying to wash off as much mud as possible, not caring that it likely would take weeks before she felt clean again.

"OUTTA THE WAY!" a muddy Maria shouted as she gave herself a running start to leaping into the river a dozen yards up. She caught sight of Joni and swam to her.

"Ah reckon ah foun' mahse'f a fellafriend, but he's th' son of two pow'ful serious rednecks," Joni giggled.

"Huh?" said Maria.

"Fry mah hide!"

"What the hell is wrong with you?" asked Maria. "Did you eat something rotten?"

Then Maria caught sight of Buster, just a few feet away. "Oh, helloooo," she said. She winked at Joni. "The dude from the polka fest, right?"

"Right," he said. "And you're starring in the upcoming production of Driving Miss Mermaid, right?"

"Right. God, I can't believe how hot it is here."

"I know," Joni said. "I feel like I am cooking in this water."

"You're *real* hot, lady," Buster said coyly. He then reared up and splashed a wave right at her, launching a battle royal on the high seas of the Oconee.

You ain't seen nuthin' like a splash fest in 103-plus South Georgia heat. Hundreds—get that, *hundreds*—of mud- and sweat-covered rednecks responded to the call and leapt into the water like pigs being called to the mess.

"Yeeeeah haaaaww!" hollered the first flying hillbilly.

"Yeeeeah haaaaww!" yelled the next.

And the next and the next and the next. The hootin' and hollerin' from all those yippy-yappy hillbillies splashin' around was quite a spectacle.

Nobody even noticed when the ambulance pulled up to collect Ruby.

Chapter Thirty

One thing that sucks about getting old (and truthfully, it is just one of many things) is that you have to take so darned many pills. Something for arthritis, something for blood pressure, something for clotting, some sort of diuretic, something to loosen up those ol' bowels, something to lower cholesterol, one of those calcium pills because of osteoporosis and oh—the list just keeps growing so long that it will leave you completely depressed (and broke) if you think about it.

And what is so deceiving about it is that the situation creeps up. There's that first pill separator that one buys as a matter of convenience so that thyroid pill isn't missed. There comes a point when that is replaced by a pill sorter that has three compartments for morning, afternoon, and evening. Then the granddaddy pill sorter, which has, like, ten compartments for each day. And when you use them you realize how much of a crock aging is because it is almost a full-time job to sort out all of those damned pills and make sure the right one gets in the right compartment. It's downright challenging, especially when it is so hard to read the small lettering on the labels on the prescriptions.

When Ruby left New York, she left confidently with a perfectly sorted and stocked pill sorter. She hadn't thought through one big problem, being that she was going to be gone for more than seven days, which would mean she was going to run out of medicine.

She felt so darned good that she didn't see how it would matter much, and often wondered if her life would be better, worse, or just the same if she stopped taking pills altogether. But she didn't want to mess with the status quo too much before the Weeki Wachee reunion, so she came up with a brilliant Ruby idea, born of a woman who came of age during the World War II years.

Rationing.

If the U.S. government could ration for sugar and butter for hundreds of millions of people, Ruby Witherspoon could ration a few pills for herself.

So, there's Ruby, and she's standing right over that silly mud pit and calculating the possibilities. Her biggest concern about playing in the mud was that she somehow would not be able to get all the mud out of her hair when she got to Weeki Wachee and would show up for the reunion like a Pigpen version of a voluptuous senior mermaid. But then she figured Maria and Joni would help her clean up. When would she ever have another opportunity to dive into a soupy hot mud pit? She thought about her back for a moment—something every senior considers before doing something stupid—but then decided it wouldn't get hurt if she minimized the belly flop and did it more gracefully than the professional redneck mud pit divers. Mere mortals only get one back and once it goes, life is forever different and less fun. You can't be a mermaid with a bad back.

She stood on the edge of the pit.

"Ruuuu-bee! Ruuuu-bee! Ruuuu-bee!" shouted the crowd.

She faced her audience and bowed to her people, then turned to the pit and did a gentle splash into the mud. The crowd went c-r-a-z-y for Ruby, who stood right up, spit some mud out of her mouth, wiped some dirt out of her eyes, and then bowed again. She stood straight up and the world started slowly spinning, slowly spinning, slowly…

She didn't remember any more than that, and it's best that way because it might have scared her from doing other Ruby Things in the future.

But Milt jumped into the mud pit and rescued his dearest darling, laid her on the grass next to the muddy mess and listened for breathing, which he could not hear. He tipped her head back, cleaned out her mouth (and there was still plenty of mud there), and gallantly began mouth-to-mouth resuscitation.

"Ruby, can you smile?" Milt asked. "Ruby?"

"Stop bein' sech a dumb shit! He'p her!" someone yelled.

In his head, Milt went though the list he'd memorized so long ago to determine whether someone had a stroke. *"Get her to smile. Get her to raise both arms. Get her to speak a simple sentence,"* he silently instructed himself. *"If she can do those three things, she hasn't had a stroke."*

But Milt couldn't get Ruby to do any of those things, because Ruby wasn't there.

From the back seat of the cab, Joni called to Ruby: "Your husband called. He said to meet him at your bench."

Ruby nodded, blinked her eyes closed, and when she opened them, she sat next to her handsome Walter on a park bench facing the Atlantic Ocean. Walter sitting there in khaki pants and a blue Polo shirt like it was no big deal. He winked at her, then scooted closer as he pulled his handkerchief from his pant pocket and gently and easily rubbed her clean of mud. She looked at her clean hand, which was no longer wrinkled, she felt for the wattle on her neck, but it wasn't there. She felt her hair and it was long and blonde—not its natural color, but the one that had been natural enough to her from the time she was seventeen until the gray won the battle when she was in her fifties.

She knew what was happening: Either she was dreaming, or she was dead. In the event she was dreaming, she turned up and kissed her beloved Walter, kissed him, kissed him a hundred times so she could get as much of him as she could before waking up. He tenderly kissed her back.

"Missed you," he said.

"Missed you more," she said.

They didn't speak for a long while. They just held each other and it felt so good to be together. All those years, and all she'd needed was this moment. His warmth, his way. That safe feeling.

"I've been waiting for this," she whispered in his ear.

"For what?"

"For our time to be together."

He nodded.

"We're always together," he said.

She looked at him and tried hard to memorize what she saw. He appeared younger than he was when he died, but his hair was whiter. He smelled good— so good. She smiled, because he'd finally gotten the after-shave thing right, having graduated from Hai Karate to Brut 33 to Old Spice and Paco Rabanne. She wondered if he still had to shave, then wondered why she was wasting time thinking about it. She breathed him in, so deep.

"Do I get to stay?" she asked.

He shook his head no.

His eyes and hers welled with tears. He bumped his hand to her chin and gave her a "buck up" nod.

"You've got a nice boyfriend," he said.

"Oh, no," Ruby said, embarrassed. "He's not my boyfriend, not like you. He's just..."

"Ruby, it's okay. It's good. I'm still here for you, but this isn't our time."

"He's not..."

"He is."

"Walter, I miss you so much!" she told him, crying even harder.

"Our day is coming, Ruby, but this is your time. Enjoy it. Enjoy him. Our day is coming. I'm so proud of you."

"Love you," she whispered.

She felt his warm kiss on her lips.

"Love you back," Milt answered.

Ruby opened her eyes and saw muddy Milt's face about six inches above hers, and two paramedics messing with her arms and strapping an oxygen mask around her face. By the time they rushed her into the emergency department at Laurens County Medical Center (some thirty miles from the games), a half-inch-thick layer of mud was caked on every inch of her, except her mouth and nostrils, which they'd cleaned for her. She'd shed so much mud all over the floor, seats, and door handles of the ambulance that they had to go straight to a car wash and then back to home base to sanitize the inside. Mud soaked all the way through the sheets on the stretcher through the mattress. The medics were happy to wheel Ruby into the emergency department and unload her.

"Good-bye to you and your muddy old boyfriend too," one paramedic said to the other once they were out of hearing range.

"Cute couple," said the other.

And Milt and Ruby really were. Especially because the mud made them look more like chocolate covered bunnies than mud-encrusted rednecks.

Of course, the people who kept the emergency room as sparkling and sterile as the state required cringed when Ruby and Milt came in the doors, but what else could be said? Head nurse Becky Rass called for a special janitor and assigned him exclusively to Mrs. Witherspoon and her fella.

Buster rode in the cab with Joni, while Maria and Ethan followed behind in his Dodge Ram to the hospital. Some hospital. The whole emergency room had just eight beds. The triage nurse looked thrilled to see more muddy people traipsing through her emergency room. There was a rule that patients can't have more than two people with them there, but Nurse Rass didn't want those muddy fools tracking all over the place, so she put them in the only actual "room" in the emergency department, one of two that had walls instead of curtains.

"Y'all can stay here with Mrs. Witherspoon," said Nurse Rass. "But you can't leave. You can't walk around. You want something to eat? We'll call for a pizza delivery. You want to use th' bathroom? You just have to hold it. Get what I'm saying? Don't leave this room unless you are leavin' the hospital for good."

They all nodded, obedient.

They passed the time by letting Milt tell and retell the story of what happened. They also took bets on what their backwoods doc would be named, and Ethan offered all the "b" possibilities: "Bingo, Bogey, Bosco, Biggum, or Buck." Eventually, a meticulous and well-starched doctor introduced himself.

"I'm Dr. Westfield," he said.

"First name?" asked Ruby.

"Stephen."

"CRAP!" everybody said in unison.

"Loser," Ethan whispered to Buster. Buster nodded.

The doctor looked at the muddy bunch, rather astonished, but he had learned long ago not to pass judgment on those who wound up in this particular emergency room. He wasn't in Connecticut anymore, but the pay was good and he figured he'd get rich one day when he finished writing a screenplay about the middle-aged preppy doc who moved to the heart of the Confederacy in search of a little peace and quiet.

"Mrs. Witherspoon," he said, then took a long look at his muddied patient. "Mrs. Ruby Witherspoon?" he asked.

"Yes," she said.

He squinted closer.

"*The* Mrs. Ruby Witherspoon? From the nightly news?"

"Yes," she said proudly.

"Well then, the pleasure is all mine."

The doctor reviewed Ruby's blood work and had her recite every single medication on her usual list, and that was a challenge that got the best of her because she could only refer to them as "the pill for my blood pressure" or "that yellow one I take three times a day."

"Have you missed any of your pills?"

Ruby explained the situation as simply as possible. She took her pills, but not quite in the quantity or order that she usually did because she had to resort to rationing or else she would completely run out. She figured it would be better to make her supply stretch over the two weeks of her trip, rather than run out altogether. If she was supposed to take something once a day, she switched to every other day. If it was to be twice a day, it went to once a day. She arranged her pill schedule according to her supply, with absolutely no consideration of what the pill was or how desperately she needed to take it. At some point, she'd built a relationship with her meds where she did not see them as her caretakers, but rather "that blue one" or "the yellow one" that interrupted her normal schedule. Since her normal schedule was now absolutely abnormal, Ruby was taking a little of this and a little of that and just hoping for the best. And that's something you can't do once you have one of the giant pill separators.

"Ruby, you gotta be kidding," Joni said.

"Mrs. Witherspoon," the doctor said in a stern, lecturing voice. "You have to know that it doesn't work that way. You have to know that you put yourself at great risk. Self-medicating like that can be fatal."

But the truth was, Ruby didn't know that. She did what she did because it did make sense—at least it did to her.

"Your blood pressure is way up because of the change in dosage, but your internal homeostasis was altered because you have been traveling and not getting the fluids you need."

"Blah, blah, blah," she said, trying for humor. "To be honest, I don't want to drink too much water because I don't want to be going to the bathroom every ten minutes. I'm in a cab and the meter's running."

"Well, you've got to drink the water, even if it means you stop the cab to go to the bathroom every ten minutes. This is serious, Mrs. Witherspoon. My business would go down ten percent of my senior patients if they would just drink the water they are supposed to drink. Problem is, as we age, we lose our ability to know when we are really thirsty. Drink *before* you get thirsty. It's critical."

Ruby rolled her eyes to Maria, but the doctor caught it.

"You think I'm kidding? Half of the people hospitalized for dehydration die within a year."

She looked at him with sudden reverence.

"Doc, can I have a glass of water?"

Outside the room, Joni huddled with the doctor.

"Should she really be that scared?" Joni asked.

"Well, she's not going to die if she pays attention," he said, then smiled at Joni.

Nice smile.

"Want to get a cup of coffee after you take a bath? Get a bite to eat?" he asked, looking at her as if Joni was the best-looking woman he'd seen in South Georgia in eons.

There was no mistaking his interest, and Joni wondered what the hell was going on with her. She never attracted this kind of attention from men. *I must be giving off some kinda pheromones or something,* she told herself. She couldn't figure it out. Granted, she wasn't quite as mud-caked as Ruby, but she was a mess. And Dr. Stud wanted a date? The same day she was getting cozy with Buster? The same week as that TV anchorman took her out? What had changed?

Buster stuck his head out the door of Ruby's room.

"We'd love to join you for dinner, Doctor," Buster told Westfield, "but we have plans."

Chapter Thirty-one

In the backwoods of South Georgia, there aren't a lot of restaurants, so just about everybody who wants a good meal winds up at Jack's. You've been there—we all have. For $8.95, you can get a rib-eye steak, tossed salad, baked potato, and scoop of sherbet. The walls are painted bright yellow and the booths are lime green. The food is just a smidgen above average, but it beats going to another Cracker Barrel, so by comparison it is most delicious and the atmosphere utterly charming.

But not exactly the kind of place where you'd expect the kind of conversation that would involve the kind of life change that Milt envisioned. He visualized his future with Ruby in great detail.

Meeting her marked a huge moment for him. Cancer had taken his beloved Alice after forty-eight years of marriage, and his method of coping with his loss entailed quickly marrying local actress Samantha Basset, thirty years his junior, a woman who told him he was "the most captivating man I've ever met," a woman his kids couldn't stand. Two months after the nuptials, she told him she was hopelessly bored by him. Of course, by that time, she'd learned that the bulk of his assets had been transferred to his kids' names for tax purposes and that his life's fortune would never be hers. When he returned from a Saturday golf outing, he found his condo emptied of all of her belongings, and all that remained of their marriage was a set of wedding proofs and a note that said, "Sorry. You're too old and we're too different." That was that. Milt vowed never to make a mistake like that again.

He'd never find another woman like Alice, so true, trustworthy, and loyal. Never.

Ruby was no Alice, but Ruby would have liked Alice and Alice would have liked Ruby. And Alice definitely would have approved of Ruby over the likes of Samantha. She'd have wanted him to pick up his life again and get over the embarrassment of being dumped like that. He knew that Alice was up there rooting for him somewhere, and it made him feel more confident moving forward with someone else.

"I've been thinking about our post-Weeki Wachee plan," he said to Ruby.

"I don't have a post-Weeki Wachee plan," Ruby said. That was the truth. She hadn't given it a single thought.

"I was thinking you'd continue on the road with me so we could spend some time at the beach before we head back and pick up your things. I love you, Ruby. I want you in my life."

He waited for that Ruby smile, the one he told himself was only for him. The one that says, "I love you, y'old coot." But if he were looking for approval, he sure didn't get it. She stared at him, bewildered.

"We could move you out of the city and then just look at the map and decide where to go to next. I like the idea of doing the Pacific Northwest. You'll love it. The terrain of coastline changes every hour of the drive. It's spectacular. The water's too cold for swimming, but it is really something to see."

"Milt, what the heck are you talking about? Picking up my things? Moving me out of the city? I never said anything about picking up and moving."

"Ruby, I enjoy your company so much…"

"But who came up with that plan? I certainly didn't."

"Well, I was thinking…"

"Because you are a wonderful man, but I don't want you thinking for me."

"I didn't mean…"

"I have been on my own for twenty-five years and I make my own decisions. You don't make decisions for me. You don't tell me what you envision for my life because it is my job to envision what I want for my life. You don't tell me what to do. Nobody does that."

She was firm—and cold. She didn't wear resentment well. The couple at the next table noticed and leaned closer toward Milt and Ruby so they could hear the old lady tell her old boyfriend off.

"I'm serious," she said. "Who are you to be telling me how I am going to lead my life? It's my business, my decision—not yours. I am offended by this. You've really stepped over the line. That took a lot of nerve, Milt, and I resent it," she said.

She wouldn't back off, and she sounded shrill.

"Ruby, I didn't mean to offend you but…"

"You did offend me. I may be overreacting, but if you know anything about me it should be that I decide how I am going to live. Not you, not my girls—not anybody. I decide. I realize you are of a generation of men that thinks you can push women around and make us do whatever you want, but we don't have to take that kind of chauvinist garbage anymore."

"Uh, excuse me. I was being nice."

"Don't do me any favors."

"I wasn't doing you any favors. What is your problem?"

Milt was not about to sit there and let her emasculate him any longer, especially since he felt certain he'd done nothing wrong except try to be kind to a woman he liked and thought he loved. He would not grovel or try to explain himself either, because she obviously didn't want what he wanted, and he couldn't stand another rejection. Besides, was what he was offering so lousy? Was this the *real* Ruby? How could she be so warm and loving one minute and turn it off the next?

"You insulted me."

"You have insulted me," he shot back.

Milt signaled to the server to bring the check, which she did in a flash. He paid cash, not wanting to slow things down by waiting for his credit card to be processed.

"Ready?" he said to Ruby.

"I'm not finished with my dessert," she said.

"Eat your damned pie. I'll be outside."

"Milt…" she tried, but he kept walking.

He didn't want to talk on the ride home and she didn't know what to say, so that big RV was mighty empty. Milt didn't even ask if she was spending the night with him, because he didn't want her in his space. He drove her straight to the Day's Inn to her room with the girls. His mind raced. Maybe he would split in the morning. Maybe this was it. He wondered how he could have been so wrong about a woman—again.

"Milt, I'm sorry. I didn't react well," Ruby said.

"I'm sorry too. There was nothing sinister in what I was suggesting."

"I know it. It's just, you've got to *ask* the other person if they like the plan before you act like the plan is a done deal. You've got to find out if the person is even open to making a plan. You don't just announce something like that. Dictate somebody else's life. You don't do it. Especially not with me."

"I *was* asking."

"No, you were telling."

"You think I was telling and I know I was asking. You don't understand me very well. I respect you."

"Well, you have to show it a little better."

"And you shouldn't automatically jump all over me without considering my intent. I did not intend to hurt your feelings. You had to know that. Don't overreact and completely rip me apart when I trip up. You aren't perfect and I'm not perfect. We've got to work with each other."

"Point taken," she said.

They sat there in the RV for a long, silent minute.

"We don't have unlimited years ahead of us," he said.

"Don't I know it."

"This isn't the time to be stubborn. I want to live my life. I want to travel and laugh and get the most out of every day I have left. I figured you would too."

"I do. But I don't want to live your life. I want to live *my* life. It's my decision whether I want to follow your lead—not yours."

"So tell me then. Do you like the plan?"

"I don't like thinking about having a plan. It reminds me that we'll be at Weeki Wachee tomorrow and this trip will be over soon. After that, I can't imagine a single thing for myself. I haven't thought that far into my head. Do I like your plan? How should I know? I just heard about it. Let me sleep on it."

"Okay."

"For awhile."

They kissed goodnight, and Ruby went to go sleep on it.

Chapter Thirty-two

Reality can really destroy fantasy. When Maria pulled the taxi into Weeki Wachee, Ruby wanted to cry. She climbed out of the cab and moved sadly to the edge of the front fountain, realizing the place was as tired and worn out as she.

The once-lush park was now about as appealing as a dish of week-old leftovers. The mermaid fountain out front shot gray-brown water into the air, and the once meticulously detailed landscaping had deteriorated into shrubs and bushes that showed more bark than greenery. The sprawling green lawns now were interrupted by big patches of sand. Weeds invaded the gardens. The once-brightly-painted statues of flamingos, mermaids, and dolphins had faded decades ago, and yet there they stood, monuments to neglect.

Poor Weeki Wachee. She looked so darned worn out.

Park crews had tried to spiff the place up for the anniversary, but that was as effective as brushing especially hard to hide the fact that your three front teeth are missing. Actually, it seemed pretty hopeless.

Ruby just stood there with her hands on her waist, shaking her head, diminished by disappointment.

"Ruuuubeeee!"

　　　　　　　　　　　　　　　　　　　Mermaid Mambo

Ruby cringed, instantly recognizing the grating voice of Iris Jones. How Ruby'd dreaded this inevitable moment, for weeks wondering what Iris and the other mermaids would see when they looked at her aged body. Always the original, Ruby was stylish, but the wrinkles! The weight! The neck! The jowls! The love handles! The belly! Sixty years into this mermaid business and still, the competition continued. Mostly, it is friendly, but it is there—always. At the end of the day, every mermaid takes inventory of the following categories, ranked in order:

1.　　　　Weight
2.　　　　Wrinkles
3.　　　　Marital status and history
4.　　　　Financial security
5.　　　　Number of grandchildren

Ruby had stopped eating once they crossed the Florida state line—no exceptions—like it would matter. Could any human being lose that last ten pounds in one day without surgical or divine intervention? She still hoped. And it was funny how she worried so much more about the other mermaids seeing her flab than all the paying spectators taking pictures and making videos in the underwater theater. Oh, why Iris? She was the cattiest of all of them, and Ruby knew that Iris would say something snarky about her weight and, like usual, Ruby would not have a comeback at her ready.

"Ruuuubeeee!" Iris called again.

Ruby turned slowly. Oh. My. God. Iris was so, so... voluptuous! Yes! Voluptuous and wrinkled!

"Iris!" Ruby called back and warmly embraced the once delicate and diaphanous sea damsel who now looked more like one of the manatees that would swim into the spring. Iris was at least thirty pounds overweight—at least. There is a God.

"You look great!" Ruby said.

"I got fat!" said Iris.

"Well, more for us to love!"

Iris smiled, and whatever competitive jealousies they'd once indulged now dissolved.

"Girls!" Agatha called out as she rushed to join them. "Girls! My God, Ruby, you are all over the news!"

Suddenly, Ruby's old mermaid crew was all right there beside her. Damn, it was so good to see Estelle, Winnie, Bea, Millie, Alma, Myrtle, Edie, Trudy, Martha and Fay! And there came the next decade's crew, all the Lindas and Cindys and Pams and Tinas, and the next crew of Tiffanies and Britneys and the current crews of Nicoles and Allisons. Sixty years of mermaids, all sisters.

The good news was, almost everyone had gained weight. Everyone except Millie, and everyone knew that Millie got what she paid for from that liposucking plastic surgeon. It didn't matter so much anyhow because Barbara, their unofficial leader, took the liberty of ordering everyone flesh-colored tights that would nip and tuck them right fine by showtime. Right fine.

Some of the younger mermaids—the ones who were only in their forties and fifties—started singing and invited the rest to join in (singing their song to the tune of "I Wish I Were an Oscar Mayer Weiner") as they walked through the gates to the faded park.

"Oh I wish I were a Weeki Wachee mermaid, that is what I'd truly like to be-e-e, 'cuz if I were a Weeki Wachee mermaid, everyone would be in love with me!"

The one thing outsiders like Joni or Maria or Milt or the Originals would never grasp was that getting to the reunion wasn't about performing water ballet, although that was an obvious plus. It was about the water. The crystal clear spring, the *real* Weeki Wachee, where they grew from teenagers into young women, the spring where they became mermaids. Real mermaids.

The minute they walked through the turnstiles, they raced to the water's edge for a quick look. Despite the bad cosmetics above ground, their sanctuary was as safe and pristine as it had ever been. Humans may have betrayed the grounds on the surface, but God must have protected the spring. Weeki Wachee, safe and sound, as always. It hadn't changed at all. Just as alive as ever with fish and plants and aquamarine water, clear to the deep, deep bottom.

Milt, Joni, and Maria hung back with the other family members, letting the women have their moment, and the mermaids lived it loud.

"I know that you all are dying to get in the water," said Miranda, the choreographer. "But we want that to be an unforgettable moment for you, so you will have to earn the experience. Land drills start in two hours."

Their collective groan hadn't changed since the old days. Land drills suck.

But the mermaids were back in town.

Chapter Thirty-three

"I've got Ruby live on the line. Ruby girl? How's my lover?"

"I'm not your lover."

"Whatever, Ruby. Quit being such a grouch and admit you'll marry me."

"I'll never marry you."

"I told you, you don't have to sign a prenup."

"I want everything!" she laughed.

"Where are you, girl?"

"Well, Steve, I'm finally here at my destination."

"Where's 'here'? Where's your destination? You've driven two hundred million people crazy trying to figure it out."

"It's like coming home for me."

"Ruby, where are you? Where was the destination? Give it up!"

"Luv, I am in a place called Weeki Wachee."

"Weeki Wachee."

"Yes, Weeki Wachee."

"You were on the road to Weeki Wachee? Is that somewhere by the shores of Gitche Gumee?"

Ruby let out a loud frustrated groan, the kind moms reserve for their annoying sixteen-year-old sons.

"Don't mock me, son."

"I'm not mocking you, baby cakes! What the hell are you doing at Weeki Wachee? Isn't that where they have all the water skiing shows or something? I didn't even know that place was even open anymore!"

"You are so ignorant. That is Cypress Gardens. Weeki Wachee is where the mermaids perform."

"Mermaids?"

"Mermaids."

"And why did you care about seeing these mermaids perform?"

"I have been traveling here and getting ready to squeeze into my old tail and perform in the sixtieth reunion of the Weeki Wachee mermaids."

"So Ruby, what are you telling me? You're an old mermaid?"

"A mermaid, yes. Old, no."

"And you're going to be in a show?" Rosenthal motioned for Sister Liz to get on the Internet and start looking it up. "Liz, look it up. Ruby, how do you spell Weeki Wachee?"

"W-E-E-K-I SPACE W-A-C-H-E-E."

Liz typed Weeki Wachee into a search engine and the park's home page popped up with a big advertisement that promised "Mermaids of Yesteryear! Join us for our sixtieth reunion!"

"You gotta be kidding me. You're gonna wear a tail and swim around in a sexy bathing suit?"

"Something like that."

"Ruby, you're getting me turned on."

"Stop it. Anyhow, I want you to come to the show."

"I'll be there!"

"And I want you to fill this park with a few thousand of your crazy listeners, because Weeki Wachee needs a little help from you folks. The park's looking a little tired. We've got to save it!"

Rosenthal saw a huge opportunity and grabbed it. Imagine the publicity! He didn't even wait to get approval for these expenses because Mermaid Ruby was a publicist's dream.

"Ruby, I just have to go home and pack some clean underwear. I'll be there as soon as I can! Sister Liz, you coming?"

"You bet!"

"Listen throughout the day, people. We're going to be giving away expense-paid trips to see our Ruby don her tail again at Weeki Wachee. Call the media brigades, everybody! The Rosenthal Cavalry is coming!"

"Yes!" Ruby shouted. "Everyone should come to the park."

"Now, where exactly is this Weeki Wachee? I know it's in Florida, but where is it?"

"It's in Hernando County, north of Tampa and Clearwater, close to the Gulf."

"So we fly into Tampa airport?"

"Exactly. Or you can do what I did," Ruby said.

"Which is what?"

"Which is hail a taxi and come on down!"

"Ruby, you're in a pretty good mood."

"I'll be in a much better mood if you come and bring a thousand people."

"Ruby, we're going to bring at least five thousand people. Gimme time and we'll fill the place with fifty thousand."

"There's no room for fifty thousand, ya big goon. Just get me a few thousand!"

By nightfall, two thousand people had descended on little Weeki Wachee, completely filling the long-empty parking lot. By morning, three thousand more people arrived, along with television crews from every network and cable news operation, as well as *Entertainment Tonight, E!* and *Extra!* And there were still twenty-four more hours until showtime.

Weeki Wachee roped off a press area right next to the spring and passed out releases telling the crews to be ready for Rosenthal's arrival at the park at approximately eleven a.m. Ruby would be waiting in the press area so they'd all be able to record their first meeting and ship it out live to her millions of fans.

If anyone thought this was Weeki Wachee's big day, they were wrong.

If they thought it was Ruby's big day, they were also wrong.

Rosenthal made sure that this was *his* big day. A circus of a dozen bikini-clad strippers arrived, carrying him on their shoulders. Upstaging everyone, *he* wore his own sequined mermaid tail and a blonde Goldilocks wig. They gently put him down in the press area with Ruby.

"Kiss me, Ruby," he cooed as the cameras rolled.

She went with it, leaning forward and planting one on that most unattractive hairy media king—square on the lips. He pretended to stick his tongue back in his mouth when she pulled away, and everyone laughed. He wrapped his arms around her, and she let him. Their bond was instant and evident.

"You know, I'm having trouble walking with this tail," he said.

"Try swimming with it," Ruby said. And that's when she got the idea, considering how her loudmouthed disc jockey had so perfectly positioned himself. Ruby leaned forward as though she were going to give Rosenthal another big kiss, and pretended to lose her balance and fall into him. He wobbled and could not right himself because of his complete lack of experience with a mermaid tail. He teetered, he tottered, and Ruby gave him one tiny little push toward the spring, sending him butt first into the seventy-two-degree water. Cameras caught it all, and Rosenthal grooved with it, swimming in the spring as though he were the most graceful synchronized swimming mermaid alive. A front crawl! A backstroke! A sidestroke! He really did have what it took to be a mermaid, but Ruby would never tell him that.

Practice proved rigorous, and Miranda made them earn their place back in the water with hours of land drills and a refresher on breathing techniques. The park looked dilapidated from the surface, but the view of the spring from the underwater theater immediately jacked up everyone's enthusiasm and nerves.

"Just let us swim!" Myrtle snapped.

"Quit whining!" shot back Miranda.

Finally, finally, *finally,* the first ten women (and no doubt Ruby made sure she was in the first group) put on their bathing suits and dropped into the entry tube that led from their dressing room into the spring. Back in the day—in Ruby's day—they didn't enter through a tube. She remembered the old platform above the water where the mermaids used to dive in to start their shows and remembered blue skies, puffy white clouds, and brilliant pink azaleas that bloomed everywhere. She remembered breaking the surface of perfectly still water, diving into that glittering underwater world. Like diving into liquid diamonds. Where did sixty years go?

Ruby held her breath, then dropped down into the cool azure water. Her heart pounded, a little scared, but more excited and alive. The water felt so very, very cold. It felt good to be so alive.

The mermaid is always called back—always, because that spring takes her to the moment when she was her very best, and makes her that way again. In that intoxicating moment, Ruby was again seventeen years old. Fresh, new, free of any aches and pains, free of all of her emotional clutter. It felt like the water wrapped her body in soft, flowing silk.

Ruby and the other mermaids held hands in a circle, those nineteen and thirty and fifty and eighty. There is never a generation gap between mermaids. Freedom makes them all sisters. They high-fived each other in the water. They pulled apart and playfully somersaulted, forward, backward, so many somersaults that lesser mermaids would have gotten dizzy or disoriented—or sick—but these mermaids were alive and in their place.

By sunset, more than ten thousand tourists, rednecks, fruitcakes, and lookie-loos had arrived at Weeki Wachee from as far away as Newfoundland and Baja.

Ten thousand people who adored Ruby in all of her brilliance, and two daughters from the West Coast who didn't know what to do with their now famous seventy-eight-year-old mother.

Nina and Jacqueline crossed their arms, raised their brows in unison, and told Ruby, "Mama, we've got to talk."

Chapter Thirty-four

Ruby leapt into the air and wrapped her girls in a mama's loving hug when they were escorted into the dressing room. Maria watched, and felt a little jealous. Yeah, that was it. The first painful sign that whatever "family" she, Joni, Ruby, and Milt and Buster and Ethan and all the Originals had built on the road was only water, and the blood had arrived. The "get-out-of-the-way" vibes sent most deliberately from Nina and Jacqueline were thick as they embraced their mother and intentionally warded off Maria and Joni by blocking them with their backs. Ruby caught the slight and pulled their huddle apart, introducing her girls to "my temporarily adopted daughters, Maria and Joni." The way the girls looked at Maria and Joni, then at each other, then back at Maria and Joni said most definitely that the outsiders' turn with Ruby was over and it was now theirs.

The *real* daughters assumed position.

"Your mother is amazing," Maria said warmly. Nina just nodded.

"She's a handful," said Jacqueline, who then kissed Ruby on the cheek. "But she's our handful. Gotta love her."

Joni thought for a moment what they must be thinking, then sympathized. Their mother had hailed a $12,000 cab to Weeki Wachee without calling in or saying where she was going. What would she have felt if her own mother had done that? Joni would have been frantic—and angry. And if *her* mom got on the radio and told the whole country how awful it was that Joni wanted to lock her away in assisted living—when Joni was only worrying about her mother's safety and best interests—Joni would have been completely pissed off. Plus, if *her* mom went and traveled to Florida and did all those fun things with a bunch of strangers, Joni would have been envious and resentful. So Joni couldn't really blame them for being cold.

"I have the feeling we may have intruded on some pretty important mother-daughter issues," Joni told Nina. "But we kept her safe and she had a wonderful time. We all did."

Jacqueline gave her an "I'm sure" nod.

"Thanks," said Nina. "I think."

Ruby caught sight of Milt and excused herself for a moment.

"We did have a good time," Maria said.

"That's nice," Nina said. "I'm sure Mom enjoyed it. She's sure paying enough for it."

Maria ignored the attitude.

"Whatever," Maria said. "I just thought the two of you would want to know that she took care of us as much as we took care of her."

"She's not a crazy old lady," Joni said. "She just does some crazy things for the fun of it."

"Mmmm. Well, thanks for the report card," Jacqueline said, bitchy.

Ruby came back and held her arms out in front of her. "I'm so glad you all are getting to be friends!"

Maria and Joni excused themselves to let Ruby spin her own damage control with her daughters. A lecture most certainly was coming. But, as only Ruby could do, she opened her arms and held her babies to her, and she loved her daughters and they knew it, and they loved her and she knew it, and so much of the anger and anxiety melted right there. Nobody can stay mad at Ruby Witherspoon, and that riled Jacqueline because her mother always weaseled out of trouble by just being her sweet, doting self. It's hard to play the disciplinarian to a rabble-rouser you secretly admire, and that made it especially trying for the girls.

"Mom, we need to talk," Jacqueline said.

Ruby pouted.

Jacqueline melted.

"Ma, stop playing us," Nina said. "This is serious."

Ruby nodded, humoring her daughter.

Nina giggled. Jacqueline shot Nina an angry glare.

Ruby used to say, "You have to get up pretty early in the morning to pull one over on ol' Ruby Witherspoon," and those who haven't lived their whole lives as one of her daughters may well think it is a joke. But it is not a joke. You can't pull one over on ol' Ruby Witherspoon. Ever.

Nina shook her head, helpless.

"You're right," Ruby said. "We do need to talk about this. I can't dodge it much longer."

Despite Joni and Maria trying to reassure the girls, the time on the road did prove that Ruby didn't have as tight of a grip on things as she'd thought. There was the whole bit with her stealing and hiding Joni's gambling winnings, the drug rationing, the dehydration, the sprained ankle. Ruby ran her mind through the previous one thousand miles and tried to remember if there were any other misfortunes she'd forgotten. As if those things weren't enough.

Well, on top of that, some people could say she had really lost it because she chose to take a $12,000 cab ride instead of buying a $250 plane ticket, and spent all that money because she thought it was so necessary to swim in a *mermaid reunion* at a decaying old roadside attraction.

Ruby thought for a moment. If you wrote all those things down, some so-called sane person from the Department of Elder Affairs might be able to conclude that she was not exactly "competent." But she wondered, what exactly was "competent" about giving in to old age and beginning the long, downhill slide?

"Ma, you made us out to be these conniving, sinister people," Jacqueline said. "Do you really think we've ever done anything that wasn't because we loved you?"

"No, but we disagree about who is in charge of my life."

"You're in charge," Nina said. "You've made that abundantly clear. You are still the boss."

"Good," said Ruby.

"But you aren't exactly making good decisions," Jacqueline said.

"I'm living a lovely life. I think I am making wonderful decisions, if you ask me. Who are you to say whether I am making good decisions or not?"

"I'm the daughter you brought into this world. I hope you remember that."

"It's not something a mother forgets."

"Okay, good. What I don't get is this: Most of my friends' parents are mad because their kids don't care enough or do enough. Half of them probably had kids so that, when they got old, they'd have someone to watch out for them, but their kids don't do a damned thing. We *want* to be here for you."

"Well, I am glad you want to be good daughters."

"You don't want us to do anything."

"That's not true," Ruby said.

"Ma, it is true," Nina said.

"No, I do want you to do something," Ruby said. "I want you to enjoy this time with me. I want us to make a lot of memories that will survive longer than I will. I want you to come on the road and..."

Nina interrupted, "But Ma, we have jobs and homes and partners and responsibilities. We have lives."

"I have a life too," Ruby said. "I have my life. It is rich and colorful and filled with life. I'm not wasting a minute. If you'd have been with me on this trip you'd have seen..."

"We heard all about it," Jacqueline said. "Then we heard all about it again. Even our friends were rooting for you to get away from the grasp of your evil daughters. Christ, Ma, the way you were going off on the radio, I was even rooting against your evil daughters."

"That's not what I was doing."

"Well, that's how you made it sound. Tell me what we did that was so God-awful."

"Not God-awful. But you've treated me like a child, like I have no say about my life."

"What did you think we were going to do?" Nina asked. "Come and arrest you and stick you in an assisted living facility where you would have been locked in your room with bread and water? Mom, we just wanted to work with you. We wanted to make it easier for you."

Ruby glanced off for a moment.

"You are perfect daughters," Ruby said. "You want what is best for me, and somehow I gave others the impression you are selfish, controlling, and mean. I am truly sorry for that."

Shoe about to drop! Shoe about to drop! Alarms sounded in Nina's and Jacqueline's head because that much contrition would never come from their mother without some sort of a catch.

But there was no but. Ruby let the words stand for themselves.

"Ooookay," Nina finally said suspiciously.

"It's not that you want to stick me away in some stupid assisted living facility that makes me mad," Ruby said. "Maybe it *is* that time. Maybe I'm supposed to go there now. But maybe I don't want that time to be here."

Both girls nodded. Ruby teared up.

"I can't help that I am seventy-eight or a little dotty. I can't help that I am physically weaker than I used to be or that I get lost or that I do things that may seem a little eccentric. But this is all the time I've got here on this earth. I'm doing the best I can to keep living and laughing."

"But you can keep doing that while you live in a safe environment," Jacqueline said, very adult-like. "Assisted living doesn't mean 'Last stop before the grave.' It means you don't have to worry about things like cooking meals or hailing cabs or lying on the floor for days before anyone notices that you've fallen and can't get up. It isn't a nursing home. It's an apartment with people who check in on you to make sure you are all right."

The sales job again. Oh, how Ruby hated hearing it.

"Let me turn on my record player," Ruby said. "I've got the recording of your last sales job for that stupid place. What is it called? 'Sunny Shores'?" She turned her voice into a sing-song rendition of the pitch she'd heard way too many times. "La-la-la-la, you'll be happy at Sunny Shores, Mom, so happy as can be, you'll see so much more of Nina, and so much more of me. You'll have good friends until the end and when you're feeling down, you need just look outside your door and friendly faces will abound!"

She rolled her eyes before the girls had the chance to do it themselves.

"Girls," Ruby said. "It doesn't matter if that is the less stressful option. I am not going there. Yet. The time has not come. I am still my boss and that is still what I think."

Jacqueline bristled.

"Mother, we are on the same team here. You're hurting us."

"You're hurting me," Ruby said. "You're not my boss."

"I never said I was your boss," Jacqueline said. "I just want to be a good daughter."

"You are a good daughter. I love you. I love you even when you annoy the hell out of me."

"Mom, you really can't be alone anymore," Nina said.

"You're right about that," Ruby acknowledged, almost amused that Nina thought she was alone, even though Ruby was surrounded by people. "I'm not up to being alone."

Shoe about to drop! Shoe about to drop!

"I'm getting married."

Chapter Thirty-five

Ruby rapped forcefully on Milt's RV door in the Weeki Wachee parking lot, and didn't stop until her boxer-clad boyfriend opened it and pulled her in. He kissed her cheek.

"Nice surprise," he said, pulling her close. "You want to let me tear off your clothes and give you some toe-curling he-man to mermaid sex? I hear it is quite excellent."

"Sounds good, but I'm here on other business."

"Business?"

"I just told the girls we're getting married," Ruby blurted.

Milt blinked. Before saying anything he went into the bedroom to throw on a pair of shorts. She'd told the girls they were getting married? Had he even asked her to marry him? Even though the mind is the first to go, he certainly didn't remember that. And what happened to that whole belittling lecture about how presumptuous *he* was to have assumed she'd want to continue traveling on with him? Now she was doing all the assuming and he was supposed to just fall over with gratitude?

"How did all of this come about?" he asked.

"Oh, don't get your knickers all in a twist," she said, plopping onto the couch. "You aren't going to marry me, I'm not going to marry you. Just tell the girls we are going to do it so they will stop bossing me around. They'll think I'm your problem instead of theirs. It's a great plan."

"What did they say?"

"They shut up about the assisted living and started asking me if I was getting you to sign a prenup."

Milt chuckled.

"Neither of them offered me any congratulations, so I started acting real hurt. I was perfectly passive-aggressive about it," she smirked. "They couldn't wait to get away from me so they could conspire behind my back."

If Ruby wanted to change the subject with the girls, she sure found the way to change it. You couldn't have two more loyal and loving daughters, but don't even begin to threaten that golden inheritance that Walter had built. They had to be motivated by greed on some level—who wouldn't be?—but they also wanted to protect their father's legacy and keep it from passing on to a stranger or his children.

"So, woman, what exactly is your plan?" Milt asked.

"Um, that's still in the drafting stages," she said.

Her first objective was to get the girls to back off on moving her into some old folks home. Her second objective was to outsmart her osteoporosis, arthritis, bad hip, and high blood pressure and do whatever it took to prolong "the inevitable" as long as possible. And, finally, to keep on doing what she was doing. Ruby wanted to leave this earth in real style, which meant continuing the big adventure.

"The big thing is to get the girls to stop obsessing about my life," she said. "I'm not some helpless old bag."

"Ruby, we're old," Milt said, dropping onto the couch next to her. "Anyone who wants to can make a case that we are too frail of person or frail of mind or frail of something to be on our own."

"You're so negative."

"It's a fact. You have your moments and so do I."

"And?"

"So far our moments have not coincided."

"That's a good thing."

"A very good thing."

"We're a great couple," he said. "You could do worse than me."

Ruby thought for a moment. Sure she could do worse than him, but as far as being a "great" couple? She and Walter were a "great" couple. Ruby and Milt were, well, two old farts fighting not to give up on their way out. It felt good to have a boy "friend" and to be attractive to someone else, and it even felt good to rediscover her body (actually, it felt fantastic), but as far as being a "great" couple, they were not Ronnie and Nancy or Hepburn and Tracy, or Walter and Ruby.

"We have a good time," Ruby said.

"Is that all this is?" he asked.

"No, of course not," she said, getting up to fetch a Diet Coke from the fridge. "I enjoy being with you."

"Do you love me?"

She popped the top of her soda can and did her best to speak with great affection because she could never imagine saying those words to any man other than Walter.

"Milt," she said, "I adore you."

Milt's expression told her that that stung. As if he knew he'd be nothing more than a consolation prize.

"You take in a busload of misfits on this trip and worry that every single one of them feels at home, is having fun, and has a full belly, but you push me away. I don't get it."

"Milt, I'm not pushing you away," she said, patting his knee. "I'm just trying not to rush this."

"We don't have time to move in slow motion anymore," he said. "Maybe you do, but I don't. Don't you get it? Our combined age is pushing one sixty."

"Well, don't combine them then. I'm not going to be rushed or pushed by you or anyone. Let's just have some fun," she said.

He nodded silently, then stood up and walked to the door.

"I'm goin' for a walk."

He walked out, just like that, and Ruby sat there on his RV's couch, feeling a little goofy and knowing she'd have to make some sort of amends when he returned. Okay, she acted a little insensitive. She knew that. And the thing she'd never be able to get across to Milt was that, in some cases, insensitivity is the simple byproduct of oversensitivity. And Ruby wasn't exactly the type to admit to going deep with self-analysis, but she had noticed in the past that she could simply mask her hurt by pretending she didn't hurt at all. Like with Nina and Jacqueline. Every time they'd start the assisted living conversation with her, she puffed up and acted all miffed and insulted because it kept her from looking at how she felt betrayed and emotionally dismissed by the two people she loved the most. She'd deliver her cold rebuffs, and then *they* felt betrayed and emotionally dismissed by the person *they* loved the most. But she seldom noticed their feelings because she was so busy trying to protect her own. Right now, she felt conflicted. She'd played the one trump card that would work, and it didn't feel good.

Ain't it a bitch that the only way we women can call off the wolfpack of our offspring is to hand ourselves over to a man? Ruby thought society would have gotten beyond all of that. Regardless, the decision to pledge herself to Milt had far more to do with Milt himself than quieting her meddling daughters.

Did she love Milt? Why should she have to answer that? At this point in life, it seemed silly to even have to say one way or another. Of course she loved him. Not like Walter, but different. Good. What would be the next step? Would he claim her with his fraternity pin and ask her to go steady with him? Take her to the prom? Ask her to meet his ma and pa? No! And why should she have to state her intentions emotionally or otherwise? Why couldn't they just keep on having a good time until they stopped having a good time? When a woman is pushing eighty, the drill changes dramatically. In Ruby's case, the goal was to keep on keeping on. It wasn't that she couldn't consider a commitment; it was that she wondered why she had to bother. It'd mess up her rhythm, and everyone would have to admit, she had a pretty good rhythm for a woman her age. She knew how things would change the minute she slipped into a "real" relationship. Milt would start wondering, "What are *we* doing today?" She'd have to start worrying that she might be taking too long or that Milt might be waiting or that someone was hungry or whatever. She'd lived alone too long to have to worry about someone else, and, face it, she was enough to worry about on her own.

She considered taking off before he got back because she only had another half-hour before the next rehearsal, but Ruby decided against it because she didn't want his feelings to get even more hurt. So she waited. And he made her wait, boy did he, so long that Ruby fell asleep on the RV couch and missed the rehearsal. Two and a half hours, he was gone.

When he came back, she lay spread out on the couch, snoring, and it was quite an attractive site: mouth wide open, nostrils flaring, pig snorts in rapid succession, drool dribbling out of the side of her mouth. Milt looked at her and knew he couldn't save himself from loving her. Absolutely unpredictable. Completely uncontrollable. Magnificent woman.

He watched her for a minute, then gently shook her arm until she slowly woke up.

"You still mad?" she asked innocently.

He shook his head, letting her off this time. "Wasn't mad."

She made room for him to sit beside her. Ruby leaned into Milt's chest and he wrapped his arms around her. She listened to the sound of his heart beating and felt the warmth of his skin. He felt safe. He would love her no matter what, and she could love him too, maybe, if she could think about what she was gaining instead of losing.

"So what you've been trying to say is that we could take care of each other?" she asked.

"Exactly."

"But what do we do when it's too much, when we can't do it alone?"

"Then we hire someone to ride in the RV with us and drive the bus and change our diapers," he smiled. "We can get old the way other people tell us to get old, or we can get old on our own terms."

"That sounds good," she said.

"It does," he said, kissing her forehead. "I love you, Ruby. And you don't even have to say it back because I know you love me too."

She didn't say the words out loud, but she said them inside and knew it was true.

"I'll marry you," she whispered, then couldn't believe she'd said it.

He looked at her, rather bemused.

"Uh, did anybody ask?" Milt inquired.

Ruby stood up from the couch, then slowly dropped to her arthritic knees, reaching for his hand.

"Will you marry me?" she asked.

That is how Ruby won her man and how he won her.

Chapter Thirty-six

"We're screwed," Milt said to Buster.

Buster nodded somberly. Screwed. He and Milt watched from the parking lot as gorgeous, shirtless, rippled Ethan knocked on the door to Ruby's second-story motel room and presented Maria with two dozen long-stemmed red roses and a kiss on the cheek.

The guys groaned. Ethan beamed at Maria, and you could see Maria getting all gooey about it. Really. She hugged Ethan, gave him a kiss on the cheek, whispered something in his ear, and then Mr. Fab Abs turned to leave, nodding politely toward the guys downstairs.

"Jerk," said Milt.

"Show-off," said Buster.

What normal-looking man could compete with that? Ethan came off as studly and handsome and romantic and chivalrous and generous and thoughtful and...

"'Mornin', guys," said Ethan, passing them in the parking lot. "Gorgeous day, isn't it?"

"Hey," Buster and Milt sighed in unison.

"Want some breakfast?"

"We already ate," said Milt, grumpy.

"Oh, that's too bad. The girls told me to ask you to meet them down at the Riverside Café in twenty minutes. I'll pass on your regrets."

He shrugged and headed off, but Buster and Milt would be damned if they'd let Mr. Fab Abs Hollywood Movie Star hone in on their time or place with the women. In fact, they'd be damned if he'd show them up on anything. So they were at the café, all right. The guys, and a huge crew of the Originals, who by now had infiltrated all of Hernando County.

Milt kissed Ruby on the lips. Someone yelled, "Woo-hoo!" Milt ignored him. By this point in the trip, there was no privacy when it came to all things Ruby. Milt persevered, regardless. He reached in his pocket and passed her a tiny jewelry box—one he'd personally wrapped in tin foil.

"Sorry about the wrapping," he said. "I didn't have anything else."

She opened it and inside was a perfect, fresh four-leaf clover.

"For luck, sweetheart. I know you won't need it, but it's for luck."

Not two dozen roses, but in her book, he'd come through with something much, much better.

"I love you, Milt Flynt. I can't help it. I just do."

Buster saw Milt's coup and couldn't help but admire the old guy for pulling that four-leaf clover out of his drawers. But then Joni sent Buster an expectant look, hopeful he'd brought her something too, and Buster hadn't brought her anything. He was the nerdy high school senior picking up his prom date without a corsage. It wasn't anybody's birthday, it wasn't a holiday, it wasn't anything. Buster needed prep time for gift-giving. His hands were empty, so he quacked.

"I sure do think you're pretty, lady," Buster said in his very best Donald Duck voice.

Joni burst out laughing at her precious man, but then Ethan chimed in with his own Donald Duck impersonation, and it was far better than Buster's.

"You call that Donald Duck?" he asked. "I'm the duck! I'm the duck!"

Maria loved it.

Buster shot Milt a look. Milt rolled his eyes. Ruby noticed and suppressed a laugh.

Ethan quacked on. "I'm the duck! Please, Miss Maria. Wanna go for a ride?" He cleared his throat.

She got up and off they went.

"Good riddance," Buster muttered, but Joni overheard.

"Jealous?" she asked playfully.

"Hell no," said Milt.

"What an ass," grumbled Buster.

When Ethan opened the passenger door to his car, Maria noticed his keychain, a puzzle piece keychain where he'd kept half and someone got the other. His half said, "ALWAYS." She reached for his hand with the keychain. He thought she was trying to caress his hand, but she wanted a closer look at that keychain. She thought of the "LOVE YOU" puzzle necklace she'd been sent by her stalker, but dismissed it because hers was gold and it was a necklace and his "ALWAYS" piece was silver and a keychain. But the two could have fit together, for sure.

He hugged her. "Sorry," he said, completely unruffled. "It's left over from an old girlfriend. I'll get a new one."

She stared straight into his eyes, looking hard for some sort of revelation, but she saw nothing. Nothing. Maria ordered herself to stop being so hypersensitive, always looking for something wrong, some way to distance herself between herself and anyone who dared to venture close. It was just a stupid keychain, not even a real match. *Drop it,* she told herself.

"It doesn't bother me," she finally said. And when she said it, she realized it didn't. That made her feel better. Like maybe she might be able function without being so damned paranoid.   "I can't believe I joined this crazy hootenanny and found a woman like you." Ethan smiled. "Incredible."

"Well, I am sure glad you came."

Ethan was a good guy. She loved his humor, his ways, and the fact that he could discuss anything with her, from the World Wrestling Federation to great books.

He leaned over her across the seat and wrapped his arms around her shoulders, hugging her gently. The sensation was jarring.

She felt safe. Protected.

While Ruby spent the day in land and water drills, and Joni and Buster played at the water park, Maria and Ethan got to know each other. He told her everything—how his father died in a car crash when he was twelve, but his mother was a college professor and raised him well. How he raced through college and had his MBA from Wharton by the time he was twenty-five, and spent ten years in New York as a premier investment broker.

"I made enough to retire," he said. "So I thought I'd at least take a little time out."

He moved to an oceanfront home in Hilton Head, South Carolina, and spent most of his time working on his paintings. He still dabbled with his investments, but for now he was just living his dream, doing what he wanted to do, chasing whatever adventures he wanted to chase. He'd just been on a two-month safari in Africa, he said.

"It's a great life."

"Sounds like it."

"You'll have to come to Hilton Head sometime," he said.

"Or on a safari."

Maria thought about that for a minute. Just leaving for Africa with that gorgeous man. Maria Muñoz was letting go and letting herself fall.

Ethan sure held his own with women, but of course he did. He was hot. The guys were threatened by it because, of course, he was hot. With Ethan around, they looked like rejects.

Buster ran into Ethan at the Weeki Wachee ice cream concession and said, "Looks like you're taking a shining to Maria."

"That is one fine and delicious woman."

"Yeah. All three of them are."

Then the conversation stalled out.

"Why made you come and join the posse?" Buster tried again.

Ethan didn't answer. He just gazed off. "I'm going to marry Maria," he said after a long pause, then cleared his throat.

Buster figured Ethan wanted him to say something like, "Really? You want to marry Maria and you've known her all of, what, *three days?*" But instead, Buster didn't say anything. Ethan got on his nerves.

Chapter Thirty-seven

Maria rummaged through the once-empty trunk of the big yellow taxi the night before show day, shoving aside piles of tourist brochures, the "See Rock City" birdhouse, snow globes (three from every single state visited so they'd each have a complete set), a South of the Border beach towel, the remote-controlled fart machine purchased at the redneck games, and piles and piles of mementos before pouncing on the t-shirt she and Joni purchased at a truck stop in Maryland.

"Whacha got there, lady?" Ethan asked as he approached.

Maria extended the shirt, then smiled at him warmly.

"We bought it for Ruby back when we were in Maryland," she said. "I'm trying to figure out if that happened two weeks ago or two months or two years. So much has happened since then."

He held up the shirt and read it aloud: "'At My Age, I've Seen It All, Done It All, Heard It All...I Just Can't Remember It All,'" he read. "I'm not Ruby's age, but that applies to me too," he said, edging closer to Maria and pulling her to him—so close that their lips were just a breath apart.

"I've loved every minute of this crazy trip with you," Ethan said.

"Me too."

"Fate did right by me this time, bringing us together."

"Ruby, Joni, and I hit the trifecta," Maria said. "Screw the online dating thing, just hail a cab and head south."

"Well, I guess you all are three gosh-lucky gals!"

She teasingly popped him in the gut. She couldn't believe any man would still use the word "gal," much less with the words "gosh-lucky."

"Don't call us gals," she said.

"All right, all right," he said. "Lucky women."

"The luck is all yours."

"Exactly." He leaned forward and grabbed a quick kiss from off of her lips, then two slower ones, then went in for a very long, deep, and passionate kiss.

"Mmmmm," she said, and it was just too dreamy. Almost embarrassing. If she were watching someone else swoon like that, she'd have rolled her eyes, but this was her moment and she would swoon in it if she wanted. She could feel Ethan's muscles beneath his shirt pressed up against her.

"I've been wanting to kiss you like that for a very long time," he said.

"Why didn't you?"

He cleared his throat, then started clucking like a chicken.

"No kidding," said Maria. She kissed him again, drawing him so close that he could barely breathe. Maria took the lead, kissing him deep inside his mouth. She could feel his heart beating hard against her chest.

"You're not going to just drive off in that cab tomorrow, are you?"

"Gal's got to make a living," she said.

"But you don't have to run off so fast, right?" he said, sounding a little desperate. "Can't we spend some time together? Run over to the beach and spend a few days baking in the sun?"

She kissed him again, pushing his back up against the back door of the cab. "We've got lots of time to get to know each other. I can't drop everything to travel with someone I barely know, even if it's a guy as cool as you."

"So you're leaving tomorrow? Just like that?"

"Just like what? I have to get this cab back up to the city."

"Stick it on the auto train. Please. Stay. I'll pay to ship it back."

She gave him a quick kiss.

"I don't know you," she said, pulling back flirtatiously.

"You know me," he answered, and kissed her sweetly.

"Mama told me never to talk to strangers, much less kiss them," she said.

"But you and I have traveled a lot of miles together," he said. "I'm no stranger."

"No, you are no stranger. You are a temptation. A huge temptation," she said.

"Surrender to it."

"Come visit me in New York."

Ethan stepped back, staring at her lips for a long, pensive moment before he shook his head, a little angry. He roughly pushed his lips to her, forcing his tongue inside her mouth, probing her in a dominating, manful way that assumed he knew she wanted exactly what he needed.

Maria pulled away to catch her breath. It was too much. Way too much. She felt vulnerable.

"Wait…" she said, trying to get it together.

Wait? "What are you talking about?" he muttered, pulling her face back to his, as he kissed her lips even more insistently. His hands grabbed at her—urgently, desperately.

"No, don't…"

"Go with it," he whispered hotly into her ear. "You know what to do, baby. C'mon. You know what to do."

Her body craved the attention. She felt that, and felt like giving in to it.

You know what to do, baby.

Maria stiffened as she reran the words in her mind. Ethan kissed her neck. Her mind raced, trying to calculate what was going on. It couldn't be a coincidence, it couldn't be, she told herself at least five times in rapid succession. *You know what to do, baby.* She looked at his face, and it seemed different. Menacing. She felt frantic, and tried desperately to think, think of her plan, the plan she always had just in case, but Maria couldn't think at all. What to do? What to do? Fuck! *Him? Ethan?* Fuck!

"Down, boy," she told Ethan sweetly. She looked around the empty parking lot, but there was nobody else there. Nobody. She was alone with Ethan.

The first time I laid eyes on you, I knew we would be together…"

She hoped he was cooling off, but he wasn't. He kept pushing himself against her and it felt scary and threatening.

"This doesn't feel right," she said. *Think!* She tried to figure out an instant plan.

He cleared his throat.

That throat clearing. Those words. The keychain. His story about Wharton and New York and retiring to Hilton Head—all bullshit. Such obvious bullshit! She knew it, every word was a lie. She looked into his eyes and realized that she now knew everything about him that she needed to know.

He was *him. He* was the *stalker.*

Time moved into a soundless, slow-motion haze. This man, this movie star perfect man, was her nightmare, and she'd snuggled right up to him! STUPID!

Ethan turned her around and forced her against the taxi, and pressed himself up against her.

"It's right," Ethan said. "It's right. I love you." He licked her neck, but she visibly recoiled. He noticed, but kept at it. There was nothing sensuous or romantic about it.

"Ethan, slow down."

"No, baby," he breathed into her. "Speed it up."

"No…"

"Speed it up. You know what to do…" He leaned into her and spread her lips with his, forcing his tongue inside her mouth. She didn't reciprocate. He pushed into her mouth again, and she bit his tongue, an unplanned but natural defense.

"You're a fucking tease!"

She pushed him off, but he was right against her again.

"Don't do this!" she said. "Respect me, Ethan!"

"Respect this," he said, pushing her head against the taxi and again shoving his tongue in her mouth as he used his free right hand to rip her shirt open. He shoved himself against her even more insistently—proud of his arousal.

"Stop it!" she exclaimed.

"Stop ruining this!"

She pushed herself away, but he pulled her right back, clamping her hands with his left hand as he took her right hand and put it on his crotch and tried to massage himself with it.

"NO!" she screamed to the parking lot which was so full of cars but sadly devoid of people. Every person on earth was celebrating inside Weeki Wachi, and Maria was about to be raped.

"Shut up! You want this!" he yelled, then opened the cab and threw her onto the back seat. As Ethan unzipped himself, Maria reached for her gun from its hidden pocket. She swung it straight toward his face in a fluid, sweeping, emboldened motion.

"You wouldn't!" he yelled, then threw himself toward her, grabbing for the gun.

Oh yes I would. Yes, I fucking would, you motherfucking motherfucker.

She pulled the trigger.

It clicked, a hollow, dead sound.

Helpless.

The bullets.

Ruby.

"You fucking bitch!" Ethan growled angrily as he grabbed at the gun and then knocked it from her hand. "Jesus," he said. He restrained both of her arms with one hand as he pulled her shorts and panties down and tried to put himself inside of her.

"Come on! Just take it in!"

As he lunged his body forward, he was suddenly pulled back by the hair as Joni shouted, "WHAT THE FUCK ARE YOU DOING!" Joni yanked him backwards and Maria kicked him in the chest until Ethan was outside the cab, on the ground. Joni kicked hard at his balls.

Twice.

He buckled over, tried rolling onto his stomach so he could push himself up, but that's when Maria took her turn kicking him in the balls hard, with precise aim to level the blow that would render him useless for some time.

"Like that? Want some more?" Maria yelled. She kicked him again. "You know what to do, baby!" She cleared her throat a couple of times. "You know what to do, baby! LOVE YOU ALWAYS!" She kicked again. "Call the cops!" she yelled to Joni.

Powered by his anger, Ethan rolled upwards, trying to just stand up. He looked utterly stunned. What the hell was going on? Maria knocked him back down with ease. In the moment of crisis, she and Joni both found superhero strength. Thank God Joni'd come out looking for her camera. Thank God.

"Maria, don't do this!" he yelled. "Don't ruin us!"

Maria pushed him right over again, then sat on top of him as Joni dialed 911 and told the dispatcher to rush a car to the only yellow taxi in the Weeki Wachee parking lot. Ethan tried to rock Maria off of him, but she wouldn't have it.

"Look, you son of a bitch, you move once and those sore little balls of yours are coming right off. I'm not kidding. I'm going to twist them right off of you."

He then tried to push her off, but she'd put so much weight on both of his arms that he couldn't move her one bit.

"You totally misunderstood this! I wasn't hurting you!"

"Shut up," Joni said, bracing his feet. "Just shut the fuck up!"

Two squad cars from the Hernando County Sheriff's Office pulled in at the same time, lights flashing. Female officers get out of both cars—one was five-two, the other was at least a six-footer.

"Freeze!" shouted the short one as she approached, gun drawn. "Everybody!"

Ethan stopped resisting.

"We got a report of a sexual assault in progress," said the tall officer. "This the perpetrator?" she asked, pointing to Ethan.

"Yes," Maria said.

"I'm going to switch positions with you, ma'am," she said to Joni as she then straddled Ethan, rolled him over, and handcuffed him behind his back. She then lifted him and started walking him toward the squad car.

As he was being walked, he overheard Maria say the word "stalker" to the other officer and then reach for a pile of his letters that were in a zippered case in the taxi's trunk.

"I wasn't stalking anybody, and if I were, I wouldn't be stalking these bitches," he snarled. "She's fantasizing!"

"The detective will get your story at the station," said the cop. "Right now, just have a seat in our nice squad car."

The other officer began reciting his Miranda rights. "You have the right to remain silent…"

"Just get me out of here," he said, then yelled toward Joni and Maria. "This is ridiculous. My lawyer will get me out of this in two minutes!"

Twenty minutes later, as the cops finished taking the initial statements from Maria and Joni, Ethan was hauled off by the cops.

"Maria, I've called for a victim's advocate. She'll be here in a few minutes," the officer said. "I'm sorry you had to go through this."

She patted Maria on the shoulder, then waved as she walked off.

"You okay?" Joni asked.

Maria clenched her fists. "I'm not going to cry. I'm not going to cry. He. Is. Not. Going. To. Make. Me. Fucking. Cry. Again. He is not…" The first tear dropped down her cheek, and almost immediately, her mascara smeared badly around both eyes as the tears turned to sobs—loud, pained sobs. "Fuck him! I am not giving him this power!" she cried. Joni sat Maria down on the pavement and wrapped an arm around Maria's shoulder.

"Let it out, honey," Joni said. "Just let it out. You don't have to be the tough one anymore. He's gone."

"He'll never be gone," Maria said. "I wish I *had* killed him. My life is like some sort of cheap TV movie. Just another helpless female in peril," Maria said.

"Helpless? Hardly."

"I *invited* that man into my life," Maria said. "I *invited* the man I was running from to join us, to get close to me! I'm so stupid!"

"Yeah, but he looked like Peter Callahan. And I don't think you or any of us can be blamed for getting caught up in the absurdity of what has been going on around us. For God's sake, we got on the nightly news because we were traveling all the way to Weeki Wachi in a flippin' taxi cab."

"I should have figured it out," Maria said.

"Look at how you protected yourself," Joni said. "You're not the victim, you're the warrior. Don't you get it?"

"Get what?"

"You protected yourself," Joni said.

"I victimized myself."

"No. You took care of business."

Maria nodded.

"What if you hadn't come by?"

"I somehow have the feeling that he wouldn't have left with his balls intact."

The festivities in the park ended for the evening and suddenly, the parking lot filled with people. Ruby finally made her way to the taxi and saw Maria looking a mess and Joni holding her. "What's up with you two?"

"Oooooh Ruby," Maria said. "You missed it all."

"What'd I miss?"

"Let's say that the moment came when I needed the bullets," Maria said.

"You needed the bullets?" Ruby looked stricken. "Were they in the gun? They were, right?"

Maria shook her head no.

"Uh-oh. What happened?"

Joni looked at Maria and shook her head "no." Ruby did not need the details, especially not the night before the show.

"We did okay, Mermaid Ruby," Maria said. "My girl Joni was better'n any gun."

"But what happened?"

"That guy Ethan? He was no good," Maria said.

"Ohhhhh." Ruby nodded.

"And I feel incredibly stupid about it. I haven't wanted to tell you too much about my life, about why I am in the cab, and why I am so nervous. But I've been running from a stalker for more than a year now. It was Ethan."

"What?" Ruby asked, incredulous.

"He'd broken into my home in Atlanta and sent very, very threatening letters. The cops couldn't find him, and I had to give up everything just to be free of him. I guess he saw the photos on Rosenthal's website and tracked down our little caravan," Maria said.

A pall fell over Ruby, sadness that she'd been so insulated from them for so long.

"Oh Maria, I'm so sorry," Ruby said. "But I'm no wuss. You could have told me, and you should have told me."

"Ruby…"

"I know you aren't up for one of my lectures right now, but it'll come, young lady. You should have told me."

"I didn't want to ruin one minute of your big adventure," Maria said.

"We're family," Ruby said. "And I'd have kicked that man's tail, if given the chance. I would have, and you know it."

Maria and Joni smiled, because they did know it.

"Well, maybe now I can stop looking over my shoulder."

"But you needed the bullets? What happened?" Ruby asked.

Joni shook her head no to Maria again.

"No more secrets," Ruby said.

And Maria told her everything, about the near rape, about Joni coming to the rescue, about the ball kicks and the cops. Ruby took it all in, very stoic.

A heavyset, middle-aged woman approached them and extended her hand.

"I'm Katie Baldridge from the Victim's Advocate's office," she said. "Which one of you is Maria?"

"I am," Maria said.

Kate handed her a business card. "You doing okay? Can we go talk for awhile?" she asked.

"That'd be good," Maria said. "But gimme a second."

Maria turned toward Ruby and took her hands.

"Ruby, I have to go. I'll be fine."

She wrapped her arms around Ruby.

"I don't want you treating me like some crazy old lady who can't handle whatever it is that you are hiding from me," Ruby said. "And I am going to worry about you. You are a daughter to me. Both of you are."

Joni closed in to complete the hug.

"I'll be back," Maria said. "Meantime, go be a mermaid. We've come way too far for you to let me down on this."

"You ain't kidding," Joni said.

"But I should be with you," Ruby said.

"You aren't using me as an excuse to get out of squeezing into that tail," Maria said. "Go be a mermaid."

Across the parking lot, Estelle and Trudy—all plump but lively with fire red hair—called out for Ruby to "hurry up, gal! You're going to miss the square dance!" Ruby waved them off, but Maria elbowed her and commanded, "Go. Get outta here. I'm not kidding. Go be a mermaid or I'm gonna have to kick your tail."

Ruby skipped off to meet her friends, ever the teenager again. But she stopped halfway and turned to Maria, who waved for Ruby to keep moving.

"I'm not sure what to do about tomorrow," Maria said to Joni.

Joni shrugged, not sure what Maria meant.

"The show."

Joni nodded. "Don't worry about tomorrow. Ruby will understand if you aren't there. For you, tomorrow isn't about Ruby anymore. It's about Maria. Do what you need to do."

Maria hugged Joni, then kissed her warm cheek. She held the hug longer than normal because, somewhere between the stuck elevator and the worst moment of her life in that parking lot, Maria discovered the heart of another sister.

Chapter Thirty-eight

Rosenthal? The boy did his job. More than ten thousand people flowed through the gates on show day—so many that Weeki Wachee asked the mermaids if they could perform four shows instead of two, and then asked if they minded staying the next day to do *another* four shows, which of course, they could and would. They'd do it a hundred times, as long as they could still swim in the spring.

Rosenthal? He was everywhere, holding press conferences, charging ten bucks for a photo with him as a fund-raiser for Weeki Wachee, dancing with the mermaids at the family dinner and even trying to sneak in the locker room for a peek at the naked mermaids when he was live, on the air. That damned bastard milked the moment and met with so much unconditional love from the mermaids and the masses that Ruby had to admit he was as much a part of her new family as Joni and Maria.

"Ladies and gentlemen." He stood on a stage in front of the underwater theater, talking with his deepest announcer voice. "Now for the moment we have all been waiting for. Let's welcome our mermaids!"

Three lines of mermaids covered in satin and sequins paraded into the Weeki Wachee theater, a glittering chorus line of women ranging from seventeen to eighty-two.

"We have many mermaids in this park—hundreds of them—but just forty will perform for you this weekend. Let's take a moment to welcome everyone here who has come back home to Weeki Wachee!

"First, the current Weeki Wachee mermaids!" Up walked ten women with perfect long hair, no cellulite, no wrinkles or age spots, and no worries. They waved to the clapping crowd.

"Mermaids from the nineteen nineties!" Again, a beautiful bevy of mermaids came forward. "From the eighties!" Mmmmm, not bad for women in their forties. "From the seventies!" Still not bad, although the cellulite and wrinkles were starting to show. "From the sixties!...Fifties!...Late forties!" The senior mermaids walked out with great dignity to the most fanfare. The older they were and the more visible the flaws, the louder the applause. Ruby tried to blend within her group so she didn't steal everybody's attention, but the crowd chanted, "Ruuuu-bee! Ruuuu-bee! Ruuuu-bee!" Finally, Nell pushed her forward and Ruby took a bow.

Rosenthal handed her the microphone. "Thank you all for being here," Ruby said. "This is a magical moment."

"So can you still swim, old lady?" Rosenthal asked.

Maria rushed in from the back of the theater and squeezed in between Buster and Joni, who were sitting with Jacqueline and Nina in the third row. Ruby glanced toward Maria, winked a proud, grateful wink, then snapped back to attention and pointed at obnoxious Rosenthal. "Love him like a son," she said. "But thank God he's not. Enjoy the show everybody!"

The curtain lifted with a recording of Nat King Cole singing "Unforgettable" as the youngest mermaids performed their routines. The senior mermaids raced backstage to the locker room to don their bathing suits and tails.

Ruby hurriedly grabbed for her panty hose, but some smart-aleck had tied them in knots to slow her down, a practical joke some mermaid had invented many decades earlier.

"Who did this?" she yelled as she desperately tried to unknot the knots. "This isn't funny anymore! My fingers are arthritic!"

Myrtle started cracking up, then tossed Ruby a fresh pair of hose, which Ruby caught in mid-air.

"You'll pay for this!"

But that was nothing. Ruby squeezed into her tail, and really, *squeezed* was the operative word because that tail wasn't happening at all for Ruby, no way, not under any circumstances.

Tillie jabbed Doris in the ribs and they both started cracking up. Both wore feline outfits, complete with yellow striped, long-sleeved leotards and tights, and kitty ears.

"Where's my tail!" Ruby yelled. "C'mon! I'm gonna miss my cue!"

"Gain a few pounds?" Barbara asked. "That tail sure looks snug!"

"This is not funny!" But everyone was laughing, and so Ruby tried to suppress her own laughter. This kind of thing was, after all, the theme of the re-occurring nightmares she'd suffered since graduating Weeki Wachee into the real world. It was always the same dream. Late for the show, wrong costume or it just wouldn't fit, she'd miss her timing, and everything would be ruined. "C'mon!" Ruby yelled. "Maybe it is a little funny, but give me my damned tail!"

Barbara pulled a larger mermaid tail from her locker and presented it to Ruby.

"You sure are a grouch," Barbara said. "But you're our grouch."

"Hurry up, Ruby! You're making us late!" Tillie yelled as she scooted over to the drop-down hole that let them go straight from the locker room down to twenty feet in the spring. The others followed as the opening strains of "What's New, Pussycat" came on and the felines grabbed their air hoses and went straight into their routines.

Ruby was finally ready, and she and six others shimmied down the drop hole, then swam to the spring's air pocket, built directly below the underwater theater. In that large air pocket, they could all put down their air hoses and breathe freely as they waited to go on or changed their costumes.

"You all are nuts!" Ruby said to the girls. "But I love ya!"

"Can you believe we're here again?" Iris was absolutely giddy.

"Thanks for the Memories" began playing the call for the oldest mermaids to swim their first number, and Ruby looked skyward with her gratitude, humbled by her surroundings and how special she felt. Adored. Alive. She and Estelle and Edie hugged each other, then swam out and then up with the others, taking a look at the first audience they'd seen in so many decades. Ruby held her hand to her heart, then blew kisses to Milt and Maria and the others. She and the girls moved seamlessly through their routine, remembering which direction to kick, not by thinking "kick left" or "kick right," but thinking instead, "Theater. Castle. Giftshop. River." A kick to the theater meant forward. To the castle meant behind. To the giftshop was to the left. And the river was to the right. They'd use those directions for all of their moves, the dolphins, the pikes, the pinwheels, the leaps. Ruby's heart beat wildly from the adrenaline, and she knew it would for the rest of her life.

They swam back down to the airlock, unzipped their tails and hung them up, then put on grass skirts and different bathing suits. Ruby grabbed her prop, a ukulele, as a traditional Hawaiian hula song broadcast through the speakers. The underwater speakers were so powerful that the sound of the music was as good in the water as in the theater.

"Hurry up!" Winnie shouted to Ruby.

They swam out and did the hula to an uproarious welcome.

Giftshop leap, forward river leap, kneeback dolphin, pinwheel…

Bea and Estelle's kicks were way off. Half the time, they were going in the wrong direction, but the others remembered not to look because, when one mermaid watches another mermaid screw up, she'll follow the lead and screw up too.

"Waaaaaahooo!" Winnie shouted when they swam back down to the airlock.

The middle-aged mermaids went out for a couple of numbers, then there were a few performances by the current mermaids. The show hit its crescendo when the opening notes to Swan Lake began to play.

"Please help me celebrate the return of Weeki Wachee's most beautiful swan, Ruby Witherspoon," Rosenthal told the crowd as it erupted into applause.

A hydraulic lift raised Alma, Fay, and Ruby—all in white tutus—to the level of the audience. Alma and Fay stretched out their arms, creating a ballet bar for Ruby, who moved to the middle of their outstretched arms and ran through a ballet routine. She brushed her left foot forward, then stretched it up to the sky, then swept it back again, using Fay and Alma's arms for support. Alma gave Ruby a little shove as she tucked into the kneeback dolphin position and thrust upward, and Fay grabbed for Ruby and brought her back down and around.

When she landed, she felt the tears fill her eyes.

Everything was perfect, and beautiful.

After the final performance, Ruby joined Steve Rosenthal and about 150 of The Originals for a tailgate party in the Weeki Wachee parking lot. Curly got out his fiddle for a bluegrass marathon, and everyone danced and hugged and exchanged information and swore they'd all see each other again—even though they all knew they wouldn't.

The memories were worth a lot—everything, actually. You could take videos and tell all your friends about it, but outsiders would never quite "get" what happened on the road to Weeki Wachee. There aren't many moments in life when you find yourself accepted, loved, and embraced because of your eccentricities, but this was one of them. In that parking lot, people who never really felt at ease in the real world created their own little world together—and it was a good one.

"I don't know how to say good-bye to all of you good people," Ruby told them. "So I won't. I'll just say, 'Happy trails to you, until we meet again...' "

She was the most original of all her Originals, and she felt so loved. She waved once more and slipped off with Milt.

Chapter Thirty-nine

The real world. It hovered over everyone the whole time they were gone, because you can pretend you have left it behind, but you just can't. The real world is filled with obligations and duties and bills and paperwork and voice mail and e-mail and newspapers and lunches with people you are supposed to meet with and days that get lost to chores and errands and… The only thing real about the real world is that it is a real bitch when compared to Ruby's World.

The idea of going back to an empty apartment and empty life did nothing for Joni. How could the new and improved her go back to the same old stuff? She imagined what it would be like, sitting at the computer, satisfying her old Internet addiction, watching *The View* at eleven and Oprah at four and writing about some stupid knight in shining armor sweeping his maiden into his arms and taking her to a blissful happily ever after. In her time on the road, Joni being Joni was enough. She didn't have to search for someone else to complete her because she felt complete. Not being needy was a good thing. Apparently, not needing love is the one thing you need in order to find it, because something kicked on those pheromones and suddenly made her attractive to men, and if only she'd known that little secret, she could have stopped clinging to bad relationships and just let the good ones find her. She vowed to stop forcing things that can't be forced.

So, Buster. Buster the redneck. What to do about him? He would be miserable fitting into her life back in the real world, and he still had to define his own real world. Like the man said, he was "in transition." Sounded uncertain and unstable, but being "in transition" appealed to

Joni, and she decided right then that she too would be "in transition." But not with Buster. She vowed to honor the one sacred relationship she had yet to define—the one with herself.

She wondered if she could last a year without needing a relationship or a fix-up or a date or some sort of male/female contact to validate her as living and breathing. Could she actually take a time out? If Buster showed up, that'd be great. But if not, it would also have to be great. Forty-two years old had seemed so old to her before, but it now occurred to her that she would never be so young again. She imagined what it would be like, at eighty-two years old, looking back at forty-two. She knew forty-two would seem like a kid by that point. She vowed to be a kid for awhile.

She wondered if she could ever do what Ruby did. Meet a stranger in the park and then just hail a cab and go south. Go wherever. Leave a boring reality to create a bold one. She vowed to start to talk to strangers.

She'd known Ruby for sixteen and a half days, the same amount of time she'd spent locked in self-loathing in her apartment after Doug left. In the one case, sixteen and a half days added up to 396 hours of nothing. In the other, it added up to the best 396 hours of her life, not just because of Ruby or Maria or Milt or Rosenthal or Raylene or Dwayne or Buster. They were the best because of Joni Herrschwitz. The on-the-road-to-Weeki-Wachee version of Joni was the best version of Joni.

Could that woman return home to New York? New and improved Joni goes back to the same old shit?

She sat on a Weeki Wachee bench next to the water and stared into that crystal clear spring that had called Ruby home, and the sight was so peaceful and calm—so unlike the raucous journey that brought them there.

"Missy, when am I going to see you?" Buster sneaked up behind her, putting his hands on her and massaging her shoulders. He leaned over and kissed her forehead.

"Oh, mister. I surely don't know," she said quietly. And she didn't. For the first time in twenty years, she was not desperate for a man—not even this very cool, arm-farting, handsome man in transition. She felt no need to make an appointment or get him to commit to something in the future, because she knew she had a good future—regardless.

"Whenever our paths cross? That's it? No Hollywood ending?" he asked, disappointed.

She stood up on the bench and turned to him, now much taller than he, and leaned over him and kissed him hard, like she were Rhett and he were Scarlett. Ooh la la!

"Good 'nuf?" she asked.

"No ma'am," he said. He scooped her up by the waist and began slowly twirling her in a circle as he sang like one of the old Ronettes…

> *"The night we met I knew I needed you so,*
> *and if I had the chance I'd never let you go.*
> *So won't you say you love me,*
> *I'll make you so proud of me.*
> *We'll make 'em turn their heads every place we go.*
> *So won't you, please, BE MY BE MY BABY*
> *be my little baby MY ONE AND ONLY BABY*
> *Say you'll be my darlin', BE MY BE MY BABY*
> *be my baby now. MY ONE AND ONLY BABY*
> *Wha-oh-oh-oh…"*

He lowered her until her face was even to his, then he kissed her. "Come on the road with me," he said.

"Not yet," she said. "But maybe someday."

And he got it because he got her. She'd be there for him if he were there for her.

"I'm the least patient man on earth!" he spoke up to the sky.

"This will not kill you."

"And if I come for you in a month or two?"

"My laundry will be clean by then. I may just be ready for another road trip."

"You won't forget me?"

She looked at him, rolled her eyes, then cupped her left hand in her right armpit, and swung down her right arm, creating a magnificent arm fart. He'd taught her well.

Love would be grand, for a change.

"You think I'm scared of assisted living, but I can't be. It's staring me in the face." Ruby looked beyond Joni, off into the distance. "In assisted living, you've got to make the best of it. If that's where I'm going, then I'm going there with style. I'll go there and get everyone in shape. Am I going to go in all negative? I won't say, 'It's awful.' I am just going to organize and say, 'C'mon, girls!'"

"I can see it now," Joni said.

"But until that moment when I know it is best for me and I know it is time, I am going to do what I've got to do. I'm not going to be here forever. I want to kick a little more tail and see a few more sunsets and drink a few more margaritas."

Joni couldn't help but think of how much time she'd wasted or days she'd left unlived, but there wasn't anything she could do to get them back. And why did she sacrifice all of that living? Because she felt fat or gross or inadequate or unworthy? Chronologically, Ruby was almost twice as old as she, but lived twice as young. If only Joni could bottle some of Ruby's moxie and take a swig on those mornings when she couldn't get herself moving. Joni thought about how Ruby lived compared to her and she realized that she, not Ruby, was the one who needed assistance living. Why did she always choose to sit still instead of move? To hold back instead of leap? To regret what she'd lost rather than count what she'd learned. And to think, Joni *made* those choices. She chose to hide from life, rather than embrace it. Why? Because she hadn't found a husband? Big deal! Because she should lose a bunch of pounds? Big deal! Joni's body worked beautifully. It was healthy. Why had she spent so many days/weeks/months/years flogging herself? Perhaps she should get on with the business of getting on with her business.

Maria pulled up in the cab and honked the horn.

"Ready?" she shouted to Joni as she jumped out of the car.

"No," said Joni and Ruby in sad unison.

"Me either," said Maria.

"You forgetting something?" Ruby asked.

"Nope. Hand it over, lady. I'm re-opening my studio, and I need to redecorate."

Ruby handed Maria an envelope with a check for the $12,000 cab fare, plus a $3,000 tip.

"Best money I ever spent," Ruby said.

Maria teared up. "I feel guilty even taking this. You changed my world."

"You changed mine," Ruby said, hugging her.

"Do we really have to go back?" asked Joni.

They'd known each other sixteen and a half days, the same amount of time Joni'd locked herself in her apartment. Sixteen and a half days were enough to learn to gamble, dance the polka, and arm fart. To become best friends with people you never would have noticed. To fall in love, to heal, to find strength, and to travel all the way from Central Park to Weeki Wachee. Enough time to find yourself, or enough time to sit home and not do a damned thing. Time to realize you don't need a plastic surgeon to bring out the beauty that is already inside of you. Like Ruby says—you either live life or you waste it.

They quite naturally closed in on a group hug—never mind the cliché. There were tears and they felt a deep sadness because maybe they'd see each other again, maybe not, but if they did it wouldn't be the same. It would never be the same, they would never feel what they felt in that very moment, and it was beautiful or it was sad, depending on how you looked at it. So they had to just remember what Ruby said. If you stop and think about it, you'll get depressed. So you don't stop and think about it.

Nina and Jacqueline actually accepted the invitation to go to the Keys with Milt and Ruby, and Ruby was already taunting them, telling them in all seriousness that she planned to get good and drunk on Rum Runners before getting her naval pierced. She was even going to get a tattoo of a mermaid on her butt, and she would definitely not tell her daughters that the tattoo was only temporary until after they made fools of themselves giving her another one of their dumb "stop acting on impulse" lectures.

She'd given them a hard time while heading to the reunion, but hell, they deserved it. And to think it brought them together like this! She couldn't have been more thrilled that she'd finally gotten the girls to join her on a family vacation. Once they saw that the rest of the world thought their mom was so darned cool, it occurred to them that maybe she really was.

Joni and Maria and Ruby could all promise to do it again in a year, maybe go to the see the double-decker outhouse in Dover, Arkansas, at the Booger Hollow Trading Post, or see the World's Largest Twine Ball in Cawker City, Kansas. They could go to the museum in Chicago where they say there is an exact replica of an electric chair that gives a real, live electrical shock with the price of admission. And definitely, they could make a visit to the International UFO Museum in Roswell, New Mexico.

But all of them knew the next time out would be a trip, not a passage.

The last night belonged to the mermaids, and Barbara organized a barbecue and told everyone to be there at five—mermaids only, no family. Ruby, running late, rushed to the edge of the spring to find nearly fifty of her sisters already frolicking in the water.

"Ruuuu-bee! Ruuuu-bee! Ruuuu-bee!" they called.

She hid behind a bush and threw on her bathing suit, then jumped in the water as Nell shouted, "COWABUNGA!" Ruby landed with a huge splash, then immediately started doing dolphins, one after another. Adelle followed her moves, and then all the mermaids spun into dolphins at once.

It was actually the best show yet, and it was about to get even better.

Barbara swam over to Ruby.

"We ready?" she asked quietly so the others wouldn't hear. Ruby nodded, then winked over at Nell, who gave Tillie the signal.

As the other mermaids continued in their reverie the foursome free dove down to the airlock and stripped down—naked—like they used to in the old days when they were young and their bodies perfect.

"I'd like to see the look on my kids' faces now!" Nell said, as the bare-skinned mermaids all high-fived each other in the airlock. "They think I am too prude to be nude!"

"Time to do the mermaid mambo?" asked Ruby.

"It sure has been awhile," said Barbara.

"We look damned good," said Tillie. "Considering."

"Once a mermaid…" said Nell.

"Always a mermaid!" they all answered together.

"Let's mambo," said Ruby. "C'mon, girls!"

The mermaids grabbed air hoses, swam out, then down toward the ancient boulders in the "deep hole" of the spring where they would skinny dip for twenty blissful minutes, as though they were seventeen again, so free and alive.

No masks, no fins, no bathing suits.

Just mermaids, home.

ABOUT WEEKI WACHEE

It's kitschy. It's old Florida. If you haven't been to Weeki Wachee, go.

Just enter the gates and drift back a few decades to when it didn't take so many gimmicks to impress us. Weeki Wachee takes us to the days of Ozzie and Harriet or Lucy and Ricky or, well, Uncle Milty. The park was the vision of Newton Perry, a former Navy SEAL who found the site in 1946 in the backwoods of Florida. When he bought it, the Weeki Wachee spring was littered with abandoned refrigerators and cars. Perry cleaned it out and the again-pristine 72-degree spring became the focal point of the roadside attraction that was a mainstay of Florida tourism in the pre-Disney era. Generations have watched the mermaids perform underwater ballet or drink RC Colas while submerged. Mermaids have acted out everything from *Alice in Wonderland* to *The Wizard of Oz*.

Perry devised a breathing system where air compressors pumped oxygen through hoses that allowed the mermaids to swim and frolic without being hindered by bulky scuba tanks.

When the American Broadcasting Co. (ABC) bought the park in 1959, it upgraded the facility and built a new underwater theater. Soon, women came from other countries to try for the prized jobs as mermaids. Celebrities, including Elvis, visited the park.

These days, Weeki Wachee struggles to stay alive. It sits an hour north of Tampa, along the clear-to-the-bottom Weeki Wachee River – a secret treasure to the Floridians who go there for kayaking or canoeing.

The "Save Our Tails" campaign has attracted national media attention as young and old mermaids fight to keep the park alive. But, what Weeki Wachee really needs is for you to stop by and drink in the magic. It's still there.

Mermaid Barbara Wynns, a major inspiration for Mermaid Mambo.

The "Mermaids of Yesteryear" as they are today. From left: Susie Pennoyer, Crystal Robson, Marianne "Miri" Bennett, Bev Sutton, Dottie Meares, Becky Young, Vicki Smith, Billie Fuller, Lynn Colombo, and "The Merqueen" Barbara Wynns.

ABOUT AUTHOR FAWN GERMER

The truth of it is, if you are a professional speaker and author, and Oprah loved your book, you are going to use her quote. Over and over and over again, because Oprah doesn't feature many books and if she has told the world how "very inspiring" you are, you'd better milk it.

Maybe that is why Fawn uses it. Or maybe it is because she once had a boss tell her she wasn't going anywhere with her career. In the decade since, Fawn has written two best-selling books and become one of the nation's most sought-after speakers. Fawn has experienced the same self-doubt and fear that the rest of us have, but she's dared to stand up in front of thousands of people and talk about it.

Her first book, *Hard Won Wisdom*, came out a day before Sept. 11 and she had to promote her book — and herself — at the most difficult moment in U.S. history. The experience taught her everything about obstacles, risk-taking and success. The book was buoyed by this four-time Pulitzer nominee's ability to connect with audiences, and soon, thousands of people had connected to her message of possibility. Once Oprah chimed in, Fawn's speaking career rocketed.

Her second best-selling book, *Mustang Sallies*, features interviews with trailblazers including Hillary Clinton, Susan Sarandon, Ann Richards, Janet Reno, Martina Navratilova, Arianna Huffington, Carly Fiorina, Erin Brockovich and others. It looks at how we can succeed by being ourselves in a world where there is so much pressure to be like everybody else. Audiences love Fawn because she's been there. Up, down, winning and losing. Fawn shares stories of creating triumph out of defeat, inspiring others to believe in themselves and take the risks involved in living a bold life. She is also a book consultant, helping authors to stop procrastinating and write their books.

This acclaimed investigative reporter has worked as a Florida correspondent for both *The Washington Post and U.S. News and World Report.* Her distinguished reporting career earned her numerous state and national awards. She has worked as a staff writer for *The Miami Herald* and Denver's *Rocky Mountain News* and was an editor for *The Tampa Tribune.*

Fawn now dives head-first into fiction with *Mermaid Mambo*. She'd love to hear what you think of it.

**Fawn Germer loves to hear from readers. E-mail her at
fawn@fawngermer.com**

Visit www.fawngermer.com for the latest.

To book Fawn for speaking, call (727) 467-0202.